What to Bring to Your Ex-Girlfriend's Wedding
A Cornwall Lesbian Romance
By Sabrina Kane

Prologue

Darcie watched her girlfriend pack her bags, preparing to leave. Currently, Jeannette was focusing on her "shoecase," as she called it: a suitcase full of nothing but shoes. It was one of three suitcases opened on Jeannette's bed, and she had just put into it yet another pair of high heels.

"Seriously, Jeannette?" Darcie said, laughing. "That's five pairs of heels you're bringing!"

Jeannette looked over at her, smiling.

"New York City, my love," she said. "A woman can never have too many high heels in that town."

"Even on vacation?"

"Even on vacation, Darce," Jeannette answered. "Besides, I plan on enjoying some meals in a few of my favourite restaurants, and I plan on looking fabulous while doing so."

Darcie could only shrug. She'd never been to New York, and she wasn't going on this trip with Jeannette. Her girlfriend—an American expat—was flying there to visit her parents, particularly her father, who had recently suffered a stroke. New York was where Jeannette grew up, went to uni, and started her career as an attorney for one of America's largest aerospace companies. That corporation had transferred Jeannette here to Cornwall six years ago, to oversee the legal department at their British headquarters in the nearby town of Newquay.

"How much time do I have?" Jeannette asked, standing at her shoe rack now, evidently trying to find even *more* shoes to take with her.

Darcie checked her watch.

"Barry should be here in less than twenty minutes," she said.

"Aargh!" Jeannette exclaimed, walking back to the shoecase with two more high heels. "Why do I always do this?"

Darcie laughed.

For an incredibly accomplished and amazingly smart woman, Jeannette was terrible at prepping for a trip. She was always packing at the last minute, often to the chagrin of Darcie, who always made sure her bags were packed and—when necessary—airport-ready the night before. But, as she technically wasn't affected by Jeannette's piss-poor planning this time, she was able to sit back and be amused at her girlfriend's struggles.

Under different circumstances, Darcie would have gladly accompanied Jeannette to New York. But because this trip came up suddenly, Darcie knew she would have no way of finding someone to run her bookshop for her in her absence. Her parents—her usual go-to people for taking over the shop in her absence—were on a biking holiday through Cornwall.

Darcie's Plan B—Mrs. Rosewarne—had just suffered a nasty fall and broken her hip, putting her out of commission for anything for at least six weeks.

There was no Plan C.

Her ten-year-old niece, Cleo, whom she was guardian of, was not only far too young to look after the shop on her own, but probably wouldn't even want to once she became an adult. Naturally, it was a little too early to tell, but with a great big world out there, what were the chances Cleo would want to stay in sleepy Tremont selling books? If such things as books even still existed by time Cleo grew up.

In addition to the bookshop, however, there was another factor preventing Darcie from being able to just pack up and get on the plane with Jeannette.

She had Beavers to take care of.

Darcie was a Beaver Scout leader, and as such required more notice than what Jeannette had given her in order to abandon her duties.

Her shoecase full now, Jeannette approached Darcie.

"I wish you were coming with me!" Jeannette whined, wrapping her arms around Darcie's waist. She pulled Darcie's pelvis against her own, and Darcie's clit began pulsing rapidly. Jeannette still had the effect on her.

Her girlfriend was stunning. As tall as she was at five-seven, Jeannette was a shapely blonde who reminded people of Marilyn Monroe, with that perfect combination of girl-next-door wholesome looks and scorching sex appeal.

And she's all mine!

They had been dating for over a year now and were deeply in love. The only reason they weren't now living together was because Darcie had wanted to take that bit slowly, out of consideration for

Cleo. But over the past few months, she had been integrating Jeannette into her life with Cleo, and it had worked out well. Cleo and Jeannette got along quite well, with Jeannette even stating that she adored the child.

Because of this, once Jeannette returned from the States, the plan was for them all to finally live together. Jeannette would move into the cottage Darcie owned near the centre of their small village.

"As soon as you get back, you need to start packing for the move, my love," Darcie said. Jeannette had yet to put so much as a sock in one of the boxes Darcie's dad had brought over for her to use.

"I know," Jeannette said. "And I will, I promise. We'll have a packing party, how does that sound?"

"That sounds like fun," Darcie told her. "Anyway, I wish I was coming with you too," she added before claiming Jeannette's lips in a kiss. While they kissed, she felt Jeannette's hands move down to cup her arse over the midi skirt she was wearing.

Darcie pushed her tongue into Jeannette's mouth. This apparently triggered even more aggressiveness in her girlfriend, because now Darcie felt Jeannette pushing her skirt down.

"Excuse me," Darcie murmured against Jeannette's lips. "What are you doing?"

"Isn't it obvious?" Jeannette murmured back.

By now the waistband of the skirt had gotten past Darcie's hips. Gravity was able to take over from there, and the fabric dropped to the floor at her feet.

Darcie chuckled.

"You are starting something you cannot finish!" she exclaimed.

"Oh ye of little faith!" Jeannette said, pushing Darcie backwards until she bumped into the wall beside the wardrobe.

Darcie gasped when Jeannette yanked down her underwear.

"Jeannette!" Darcie exclaimed. "Barry will be here in—*Oh fuck...bloody hell!*"

Jeannette's hand was on her sex now, her fingers rubbing her folds while her palm was pressed firmly against her clit, which was swelling, ready for attention.

"Oh my god," she murmured, nuzzling Jeannette's neck and entangling her fingers in her hair, not caring about mussing it before her girlfriend left for the airport. Jeannette started this, after all. She could pull it back into a ponytail if she needed to.

She gasped when fingers entered her. Only the tips though, and very shallowly. So, she then wrapped her right leg around Jeannette's hip, opening herself up more. Jeannette took advantage of this and thrust those fingers in more deeply, giving Darcie what she wanted.

With her arms resting on Jeannette's shoulders, and her leg snaking around her midsection, Darcie surrendered herself to being fucked up against the wall. With each thrust of Jeannette's fingers, Darcie's passage got wetter until she began feeling her arousal on her upper thighs.

This wasn't going to take long. She was always fast at reaching climax when there was time pressure, or when she and Jeannette went at it somewhere public—like the night when they fucked on the Old Bridge which crosses Lewisham Creek in the middle of the village. Tremont being such a small and sleepy hamlet, two women can get away with having sex on the Old Bridge at half past one in the morning, and Darcie probably could have taken her time reaching climax. But that night she had rocketed to orgasm so fast she had even surprised herself.

And right now, she was already practically there. The pleasure beneath her mound was roiling, getting ready to burst.

"God, Jeannette..." she muttered. "*Mmph!*...God, Jeannette!"

"Tell me when, baby," Jeannette whispered.

"Trust me...*Mmmmph!*...You'll...know!"

A few seconds later, euphoria.

Her pussy trembled as she came undone, and she had to tighten her grip on Jeannette to keep from falling. Inside her vagina, her walls squeezed the invading fingers while simultaneously bathing them with her come.

"Ooh, there it is!" Jeannette said.

"*Fuck! JEANNETTE!...Oh my gahhhhhhhd!*"

As the orgasm wracked her core, her entire body began trembling, and her cheeks started going numb.

Jeannette curled and uncurled her fingers a few times inside Darcie's quaking passage before withdrawing them and immediately dropping to her knees, forcing Darcie to lower her right leg. Darcie, knowing what Jeannette wanted, thrust her pelvis forward, giving Jeannette's mouth easier access to her still convulsing pussy.

Jeannette's tongue gave her clit a few quick swipes, sending thrillingly electric jolts through Darcie's lower half, giving the orgasm a little more fuel to continue. Then, Jeannette started licking her folds and opening, moaning in delight as she did so. Darcie tilted her head back against the wall, whimpering with pleasure as her girlfriend tasted her. Her hands were on her breasts over her fitted black tee. Fortunately, today she had chosen to wear a floral lace bralette under her shirt, rather than a padded bra, and so she was able to easily find her stone-hard nipples over her clothing and squeeze them while Jeannette's mouth finished off the climax for her.

Finally, the orgasm subsided. Just in time too.

Two quick honks from a car horn sounded from outside.

Darcie felt Jeannette give her clit a quick kiss, which caused her spine to spasm.

"That was so nice," Darcie breathed out. A bit of an understatement, perhaps, but it was all her mind could come with at the moment.

Jeannette rose to her feet again, and Darcie grabbed her for a kiss. The lower half of Jeannette's face was slick and shiny with her arousal, which she tasted as their mouths worked together.

"Now your taste will be in my mouth during my flight," Jeannette said with a laugh. "At least until I have my first cup of coffee! I have to leave, though! Can you do me a favour, babe?" She started heading to the en suite.

"Of course," Darcie said. She was still breathing a bit hard.

"Can you run out and tell Barry I'll be right out? I just need to clean up."

"Absolutely," Darcie replied. She left her knickers where they were on the floor, and just pulled on her skirt. She figured she might as well change into clean underwear from the supply she kept here at Jeannette's after she completed her mission to Barry.

She decided to make herself useful and take two of Jeannette's suitcases with her, wheeling them behind her. She left the "shoecase" on the bed. With all those shoes, it was probably the heaviest anyway. Let Jeannette deal with it.

As she walked through the house and then outside, she realised her choice to leave her knickers off might have been a mistake.

She was *wet!* The evidence of her orgasm was still streaming out of her and was coating her thighs. She even felt a little trickle of it running down her left leg. Fortunately, the length of her skirt would hide this from Barry.

Quite frankly, the sloppiness between her legs—and the fact that she was now outside on Priory Lane—turned her on. It was like she had a sexy little secret known only to her.

Barry, the cabdriver, seeing Darcie approach, got out of his dented, old, but still reliable Renault.

"Here, let me take those, luv," he said.

Barry was an avuncular middle-aged bloke who was heavyset, yet still quite nimble.

"Jeannette will be out in a sec," Darcie told him, relinquishing the suitcases to him.

"Tell her to take her time, luv," Barry said, opening the Renault's boot. "Slow day for me."

Barry's was the only taxi service in Tremont. And Barry's was the only car, and Barry was the only driver. There was nothing sinister behind this apparent monopoly. Tremont simply didn't *need* a fleet of taxis—or even two. For one, the village was small enough that anyone could typically walk anywhere they needed to be, and for those too lazy to walk, they could bike.

But Barry nonetheless provided an essential service: Giving rides home to those who'd had a little too much to drink at the pub, getting senior citizens to their medical appointments or even just to what passed for a high street here to meet their friends for tea, or providing rides into Newquay to catch a plane.

"Sorry to keep you waiting," Jeannette said, coming out of her house, the shoecase trailing behind her. Barry took the bag from her and dropped it in the boot with the others.

"Whoa, that one was heavy!" he said. "Airline's gonna hit you with a fee for sure!"

Jeannette shrugged in the way Americans tend to do, as if such minutiae was not worth them even thinking about. She hugged Darcie tightly and then gave her a lingering kiss. Whereas the visible evidence of what she had done recently with her mouth was gone, Darcie still tasted herself on Jeannette's lips.

"I'll miss you so much!" Jeannette said.

"Me too," Darcie told her. "Call me when you arrive."

"I will," Jeannette promised. She stepped over to the Renault and got in the backseat. A moment or two later, Barry was pulling away from the kerb and driving east on Priory Lane. Darcie watched them until they disappeared from view after turning left on Keeley Street.

She sighed.

She'd miss Jeannette terribly, but she'd only be gone a fortnight. Then, when she returned, this house on Priory Lane would be emptied, and Jeannette would be moving in with her and Cleo. The anticipation of that—of the three of them starting a life *together*—would make this separation somewhat bearable.

Chapter 1
(Five months later)

Darcie nodded at the woman in front of her.

"I'll consider it, Mrs. Beckley-Hopworth," she said.

The elderly woman nodded.

"I think it is a good idea and would do the children of this village some good," she said.

Again, Darcie nodded.

"I agree," she said, though that wasn't entirely true. But Darcie really wanted to close shop for the day, and Mrs. Beckley-Hopworth was the lone obstacle to her doing so.

The lady was a regular customer at Shelf Life Books, and had just cornered Darcie, suggesting that Darcie hold a regular reading hour during which the classics of British literature would be read aloud to children.

The problem with that idea, as Darcie saw it, were twofold: One, kids today couldn't give a shite about the works of Byron, Thackeray and Dickens—just three of the authors Mrs. Beckley-Hopworth suggested.

Two, many of the so-called "classics" were problematic based on today's sensibilities and should not just be thrust upon children as Darcie was sure they had been back in Mrs. Beckley-Hopworth's youthful days. Many of those writers had some horrible ideas when it came to depicting characters of different races or religions. They also had some awful ideas when it came to depicting women and their role in society.

Here in the twenty-first century, such material needed to be presented to children in such a manner as to provide the proper contexts of the stories that were written, and to engender discussions about how society has changed with regards to race and religion differences, as well as gender roles. And here in Tremont especially, children were sure to ask why there were no gays or lesbians in any of these classics. Such efforts required an educator—which Darcie was not; or someone who was trained to speak to children about such things—which Darcie also was not.

Apparently satisfied for now, Mrs. Beckley-Hopworth nodded and said a curt goodbye, carrying her canvas tote bag which was full of several new mystery releases that had just come in.

Darcie sighed, glad that conversation was over. But then she reminded herself to be charitable in her thoughts. Mrs. Beckley-Hopworth may be the Queen of Wasting Someone's Time, but she bought a lot of books, and in the age of Kindles and iPads, that was not something to take lightly.

It was just after four p.m., and though Shelf Life Books was usually open until five on a Tuesday, it had been a slow day. Besides, Darcie wanted to shut early. It would give her some extra time at home with Cleo. So, after clearing out the till and locking the money and the receipts in the safe, she took a look around to make sure the store looked nice and tidy. With all that done, Darcie put on her jacket, grabbed her handbag, and left the shop.

Shelf Life had been owned and run by her parents all of her life until recently, when they both decided to retire, giving the shop to their only daughter. Darcie had never imagined another career for herself growing up. She had always known that she would remain in the little village of Tremont for all of her days, and that she would one day be sole proprietor of the village's only bookshop. She had inherited her parents' love for books and had been such an avid reader as a child that her mother had to bribe her with sweets to go outside to play.

She often wondered what would happen to this shop whenever she decided to pack it in and retire. Her niece—though a lover of books herself—seemed to be more inclined towards all things scientific, and often spoke about one day becoming an astronaut, a worrying prospect which caused Darcie no end of advance unease. After all, she was effectively Cleo's mum since obtaining legal guardianship over her, due to her brother Patrick's incarceration at HMP Whitemoor. And how on earth was the mum of an astronaut expected to get any sleep at night worrying about her child's safety on bloody Mars?

Darcie reached home in less than ten minutes. Her small cottage, built in the 1850s, but updated generations ago with all the mod-cons, was only a few streets away from the bookshop.

"It's me!" Darcie called out upon walking in the front door. She immediately noticed the post littering the floor just inside the door. Sighing, she crouched and picked up all the envelopes, without noticing if any of them were important. She'd sort through it all later.

"Kitchen, luv!" her mother's voice rang out.

Sure enough, her mother Irene, and Cleo, were both in the kitchen, sitting at the small island and working on a jigsaw puzzle together.

"Her schoolwork is done," Irene said. She was nearing sixty-five, but was still slim and wiry, much like Darcie's father still was. That was a result of them being quite active physically, as they always had been. Now that they were retired, they spent even more time running in 5K charity races or biking ever further distances into the Cornish countryside. Darcie was certain that one day she'd receive a phone call from them saying they'd biked all the way to Plymouth and would she mind driving over to bring them back home.

"Thanks, mum," Darcie said. "Cleo, why didn't you pick up the post when it was delivered?" She held up the small bundle of envelopes in her hand.

"Oh, sorry!" Cleo said. "I forgot!"

Her niece had black wavy hair, like her real mum, whom Cleo hadn't seen since she was three years old. Her brown eyes also favoured her mother, at least, that's what Darcie seemed to remember. She had only met the woman once. The rest of her face was courtesy of Patrick.

"Auntie?" Cleo asked.

"Yes, luv?"

"Do you think cockroaches worry?"

Darcie blinked.

"Erm…How do you mean?"

"Well," Cleo began, "you know how cockroaches have families?"

"I suppose you can call them families…"

"Well, do you suppose that when the Daddy cockroach goes out to look for food, that the Mummy cockroach worries if he'll ever come back, that he might get squished by someone stepping on him?"

Irene looked at Darcie.

"It's been silly questions like this all afternoon!" she said. "Thank goodness you weren't a curious kid when you were this age."

Darcie gasped in indignation.

"I was too a curious—"

"Auntie, the cockroaches," Cleo interrupted.

"Erm...well, first of all," Darcie said, "we shouldn't assume that it's the Mummy cockroach who has to stay home, right? Remember our talk about gender roles? It applies to the insect world as well. In fact, there are some insect species in which the female does the work."

"Oh, right," Cleo said, fitting a puzzle piece into its proper spot. "Auntie? Do you think there are gay cockroaches?"

"Alright, that's my cue," Irene said, getting off the stool she was sitting on. "I don't care if it's the Mummy cockroach stuck at home washing the dishes, nor do I care if there are gay cockroaches, all I know is that if I see one of the little buggers, I'm going to step on it." She looked at Darcie. "By the way, you're home early!"

"Slow day," Darcie explained. "I closed early."

Irene tsked, shaking her head.

"I won't tell your father," she said. "Otherwise, he'll be ringing you up tonight talking about the bloody American Tour Group."

Darcie rolled her eyes.

Her dad, Frederick, had *never* closed Shelf Life Books early back when he and Irene were still running it. Each day, he kept the shop open until the very minute of the posted closing time. His rationale for this had nothing to do with viewing the posted hours of operation as a kind of promise to the village. Rather, it had to do with his fear of being closed when the American Tour Group came by.

The American Tour Group was a fictional entity he invented to impress upon a young Darcie that she should never take anything for granted once she took over the business—such as closing shop early because it was a "slow" day.

"Suppose you close the shop even thirty minutes early one day," Frederick used to tell her, "and while you're home watching telly, an American tour group makes a stop here in town, all of them wanting to buy books to enjoy on their trip. you'll miss out on quite a big payday then, won't you?"

The tour group was always American, by the way. Never Dutch, French or German. Always American, because her dad had a firm belief that it's the Americans who have all the money.

Over the years, the American Tour Group became something of a bogeyman Frederick used to try to scare Darcie into making sure she never turned her back on a potential opportunity.

Needless to say, the mythological American Tour Group never appeared. Or any tour group, for that matter. Sleepy little Tremont was not exactly a destination that travel agents flogged while selling Cornish itineraries to foreigners.

Irene gave Cleo a kiss on top of her head.

"See you tomorrow, luv," she told her granddaughter.

"Yeah, bye!" Cleo said, fitting yet another puzzle piece into place.

Darcie saw her mother out, thanking her—as always—for watching Cleo. She was lucky, she knew, not having the worries about childcare that other women have. Her parents made themselves available to watch Cleo as much as their athletic lives allowed them to.

Returning to the kitchen, she was greeted with, "Auntie, the cockroaches."

She sighed.

"I don't think cockroaches worry, Cleo. They're too busy being disgusting. I also doubt there are any gay cockroaches, otherwise they'd be much more fabulous somehow. Now, forget about the cockroaches, luv. How about we make our own pizzas for dinner?"

"Yay!" Cleo exclaimed.

"Excellent," Darcie said. "We'll get started after I take a shower."

Taking the day's post with her, she headed to the stairs. There was probably nothing but bills delivered today, anyway, and upstairs in her bedroom was her bill-paying desk.

In the room, she toed off her trainers and started looking at the envelopes delivered.

Bill…

Bill…

Promotional offer from Vodafone...

Bill…

And finally, something that wasn't a bill.

Frowning with curiosity, Darcie opened the rather nice cream-colored envelope and withdrew what was inside.

Her heart stopped momentarily, and she felt as if she had just gotten punched in the gut.

A mixture of anger, hurt and betrayal coursed through her body as she stared at what she was holding. She noticed that her hand was trembling.

It was an invitation.

An invitation to Jeannette's wedding.

Darcie closed her bedroom door and then sat on the edge of the bed, unable to stop staring at the invite. Her eyes were stinging, but she was proud of herself that not a single tear had fallen yet.

Katelynn Jefferson.

That's who Jeannette was marrying. Darcie didn't know her, nor had she ever heard Jeannette mention that name. But, of course, that had to be her: the American woman Jeannette had told Darcie she met in New York when she had gone back to visit her parents.

Darcie had never seen Jeannette again after watching her get into Barry's taxi, which was still so unsettling. It was as if her girlfriend had simply vanished, one of those *Missing, Presumed Dead, Body Never Recovered* kind of scenarios. All she had gotten was a phone call full of *sorrys* and repeated assurances that Jeannette had *never meant for this to happen,* and tearful pleas to *forgive me, Darce.* It had all been so formulaic, so...American romcom, that part of Darcie's anger had been because Jeannette had reduced the love they had shared down to platitudes and cliches.

Somehow, Jeannette had cleared out her house on Priory Lane without Darcie—or anyone else—ever catching sight of her. And in a nosy town like Tremont, that was quite an accomplishment. It was still talked about. Then one day, a box arrived at Darcie's home containing all of the things she had left at Jeannette's. Clothes, mainly, but also some cosmetics and bath items, including— ridiculously—a mostly-empty bottle of Pantene shampoo.

And now she was getting an invitation to Jeannette's wedding?

The fucking cheek!

And the wedding was in Newquay!

Newquay Royal Arms
N Quay Hill
Newquay TR7 1HF

Posh.

The Newquay Royal Arms was one of *those* hotels, where even the bloke who cleaned your toilet was a toffee-nosed prat.

So this meant, what exactly? That Jeannette had been in Cornwall these past five months? Darcie had always assumed that she had moved back to America to be with…

Katelynn.

…that cow who had stolen Jeannette away from her.

And did the wedding being in Newquay also mean that the cow had agreed to leave the States to come live here with Jeannette? So, there was *another* American in the country, talking too loud like Americans do, and putting ketchup on everything?

Hang on…what's this?

Her fingers had detected something stuck to the back of the invitation. It was one of those sticky notes, and when Darcie saw Jeannette's careful handwriting on it, she had to swallow a sob.

Darce, I know it is unlikely you've forgiven me, but I do hope you'll consider coming. It will give us both some closure. P.S. Sorry for the short notice.

Turning the invitation back around, Darcie noticed for the first time the date of the wedding.

"The bloody fifteenth!" she exclaimed out loud. That was a week from this coming Saturday!

And closure?

Jeannette could take her bloody closure and shove it up her bloody twat!

"Fucking cow!" Darcie seethed. "Like hell I'm going to your wedding!"

Standing up, she marched over to the rubbish bin under the bill-paying desk and dropped the invitation into it. She wiped her hands together as if cleansing them after they had touched something foul. Remembering her promise to Cleo that they could make pizza, she then started undressing so she could take her shower.

Chapter 2

"Two caramel lattes, please, Bridge, yeah?" Rylea called out to Bridget.

"Got it," Bridget acknowledged.

Rylea took the payment from one of the young women the lattes were for: Jemma, who was here on a lunchtime date with her wife Liz. Jemma and Liz operated the vintage clothing shop two doors down from Rylea's café, Bean There/Done That—known locally just as The Bean.

"Fancy a blind date?" Jemma asked Rylea. "One of my mates from uni just moved to Newquay, and she's single!"

Rylea smiled. Jemma was apparently never going to be happy until she was matched up and married off.

"Yeah, but is she *fabulous?*" Rylea asked jokingly.

"*So* fabulous!" Liz added hurriedly. Jemma had apparently recruited her wife to the cause. "And so beautiful!"

Jemma was nodding enthusiastically.

"Stunning!" she said, evidently feeling a stronger adjective was in order.

Rylea looked past Jemma and Liz. There was no one else queued up waiting, so she said, "Tell me more."

Jemma looked as if she were about to burst with excitement at having made some headway. Rylea couldn't blame her. So far, she had resisted all of Jemma's previous matchmaking attempts. But now—though she wouldn't in a million years admit this to Jemma—she was getting a little tired of being single. Not that she was looking to rush to the altar and become a Mrs. Somebody. Rather, she was simply feeling a yearning to not be so...alone.

"She's our age," Jemma told Rylea, meaning this mystery woman was twenty-four, "and she's just been made manager of one of those American hotels in Newquay."

Beautiful—no...stunning—and employed.

Rylea had to admit that so far…

"What's her name?" she asked.

"Lauren," Jemma provided.

...that so far Lauren sounded pretty good. But a blind date? Never once had that method worked for her. Straight women seem to think they have a monopoly on horrible blind date stories involving men. Well, Rylea could inform all straight women that lesbians can encounter some pretty wonky women on blind dates also. However, Jemma seemed like a good judge of character—she had married Liz, after all.

"Tell you what," she said, "why don't you let Lauren get sorted in Newquay, and then, if she's interested, give her my number."

"Excellent!" Jemma enthused. "You are going to *love* her!"

Rylea laughed.

"Why don't we start with seeing if I sort of *like* her first?"

Once her matchmakers had gone, Rylea started second-guessing her decision. She was only twenty-four-years-old, and by all accounts, good-looking—lithe figure, auburn hair, and pretty features. So then why did she need to rely on others fixing her up with women in order to find dates?

Part of it, she knew, was her natural introversion. Oh, she was fine chatting up her customers, but that was part of her job, wasn't it? When she had bought this coffee shop using the insurance money following her mum's death, she knew she would have to be two Ryleas: Outgoing coffee shop owner by day, hermit-like woman by night.

Despite her youth, she wasn't one for hitting the pubs in Newquay every weekend, like many of her friends. She wasn't even one for hitting the Ladle & Spoon—Tremont's local—very often, other than Saturdays, which was trivia night. So, Rylea knew her lack of a dating life was most likely caused by the fact that she wasn't really putting herself out there much.

I ought to change that.

Rylea nodded. Yes, that seemed like a good idea. She could start by agreeing to meet with Lauren, Jemma's friend, but she could also be a little more receptive to some of the local lesbians whom Rylea detected interest from, when they came in to order their coffees. After all, Tremont was practically Lesbian Central in the UK now, or at least in Cornwall. And a lot of them were single and rather gorgeous too.

Speaking of single and rather gorgeous…

Darcie, the owner of the bookshop directly across Tretherras Road from Bean There/Done That walked in as she always did right around this time, for her afternoon cup of herbal tea to go. Watching her approach the counter, Rylea tried to keep her face neutral as she admired the way the maroon maxi dress Darcie was wearing showed off her figure.

She considered this would be the perfect time to make herself more receptive to a local lesbian.

The only problem was, she had never detected a smidgen of interest from Darcie. Nothing. Zip.

Maybe if I…

When Darcie reached the counter, Rylea turned on her most *I-am-deffo-receptive-to-you* smile, and even thrust out her chest a little more.

But…

"Hiya Rylea," Darcie said, pleasantly—as always—but not in a *I-am-receiving-your-receptiveness-and-would-like-to-invite-you-out-for-white-wine* kind of way. "My afternoon usual, please," Darcie continued. This time, Rylea detected a hint of either melancholy or tiredness in her voice. But nothing suggesting a discussion about white wine was coming up.

Rylea sighed.

"Of course," she said, withdrawing her chest. "Right away."

***

"Bloody California!" Rylea's best friend Tamsin exclaimed, sitting down opposite her at a table in the Ladle & Spoon that evening.

The pub—which dated back to the early nineteenth century—was not overly crowded this evening, and the patrons were the usual mix of old men sitting together telling stories, old women sitting together complaining about the old men, and others like herself who fell somewhere between old enough to drink and pensioner, out with friends or out on dates.

One couple in particular caught her eye: Robin and Sheila, two middle-aged women, both of whom had been married to men, but who were now openly dating.

Though it was Wednesday, and usually Rylea preferred staying in and catching up on her reading on Wednesday, she had allowed Tamsin to convince to meet for a pint. Well, Tamsin would be having the pint; Rylea had never developed a taste for beer, and though that meant a possible loss of her British citizenship, would stick with white wine.

"And what did California do to you?" Rylea asked, sliding the pint she had already bought for Tamsin over to her. "To the best of my knowledge, you've never even been."

"Ta," Tamsin said, lifting the pint and taking a sip. She was a striking green-eyed ginger with large breasts that she had no problem calling attention to by wearing tops which not only fit snugly around them, but which also highlighted the fact that beneath them, her abdominals were perfectly flat.

"They took the number one spot," she continued. "We're number two! Bloody number two!"

If anyone was eavesdropping, Rylea was certain they would have no idea what Tamsin was referring to. But Rylea did, and nodded in commiseration, even though she couldn't possibly care any less.

Over the past decade or so—back when Rylea and Tamsin were still teenagers—for some reason, the small village of Tremont had become a place where gay women started settling. It had just sort of happened.

Of course, there were always a handful of lesbians in town— lifelong residents like Rylea (who had known she was gay since the age of twelve), Tamsin, Darcie, Darcie's ex Jeannette (who was now gone), as well as several older women who made no secret about their sexuality. But ten years ago was when the Lesbian Wave of new residents started. It began with professionals from Newquay who wanted to live outside of the larger town. Then, once those women started posting on social media about lesbian life in beautiful Tremont, Cornwall, other lesbians from elsewhere in England, Scotland or even Wales began arriving. Jemma was among that lot— she came from Liverpool. Her eventual wife Liz came from Cardiff.

Seemingly overnight, Tremont had gone from a sleepy little village outside of Newquay that had nothing remarkable about it, to a sleepy little village outside of Newquay that many gay women loved to call home.

Tamsin—a travel agent for an agency in Newquay—had wanted Tremont to capitalise on this.

To that end, several months ago, she had contacted the largest LGBTQ travel website and proposed they make a list of the top ten lesbian-friendly towns in the world. Not just *gay*-friendly, Tamsin was sure to point out to Rylea when explaining her idea. After all, there was no way Tremont would be able to compete with inclusively *gay*-friendly destinations like New York or Berlin. But *lesbian*-friendly was a whole other matter. She was certain Tremont would top that list.

But apparently not.

"Where in California?" Rylea asked.

Tamsin waved her hand dismissively.

"Some place near San Diego I've never heard of!" she exclaimed. "Bloody California lesbians!" She took a big swig of her beer. "You know why they won out, don't you?"

"Educate me," Rylea said, amused at her friend's ire. Tamsin—usually as pale as Dover chalk—was now red-faced.

"It's because of the bloody weather!" Tamsin said. "Bloody California lesbians *have* to stay in shape because it's always bloody sunny there and they get to prance around in their bloody bikinis and active wear! And I looked at the pictures of this place! All those women are bloody Amazons!"

Rylea laughed and wondered if she should book a trip to this town in California for her next holiday. She'd invite Tamsin, of course. Tamsin might be rather upset with California and its lesbians right now, but once she arrived and found herself surrounded by gay Amazons in bikinis and active wear, she'd forgive them.

"Meanwhile, look at us," Tamsin said. "Bloody month of May and we're in sweaters and jeans!"

"Excuse me," Rylea protested. "I happen to think I look rather cute this evening." Yes, she too was in a sweater and jeans, but the jeans were skinny, practically painted on her long legs, and her sweater was soft pink in colour and adorable, and it flattered her figure up top. "Anyway, forget California—"

"Bloody California," Tamsin interrupted.

"Cheers," Rylea said. "Bloody California. Forget that and tell me how you're making do with that ginger from the city."

Tamsin rolled her eyes.

"She's unstoppable!" Tamsin said, a bit of a whine to her voice. "She wants to have sex all night long! I'm, like, 'Luv, we're British, we don't do that.'"

"Speak for yourself, Tams," Rylea said, and then took a sip of her wine. She herself had a strong sexual appetite and preferred partners who could match it. After all, if two women had all day or all night together, with no obligations or appointments, and nothing better to do, why not spend hours exhausting each other sexually?

Her best friend, however, had never made a secret about being a one-and-done gal. Maybe a two-and-done gal, if the right woman was with her.

Again, Tamsin rolled her eyes.

"You have sex," she began, "you come, you get on with the rest of the day. Boom!"

Rylea laughed.

"I love you, Tams," she said.

"I love you too, Rye Bread," Tamsin told her.

"But I am so glad we never tried getting together," Rylea added.

Tamsin made a face.

"Ugh!" she exclaimed. "You'd probably try keeping me up all night having seven orgasms!"

"Only seven?" Rylea asked. "If I had the flu, perhaps."

"Whatever!" Tamsin said. Then her eyes widened, and she slapped the tabletop with the palm of her hand. "I bet that's another reason bloody California beat us!" she said. "Those bloody Baywatch babes probably go all night long!"

Rylea laughed.

"You're not making California sound horrible," she said, "Book me a ticket there, please."

Chapter 3

On Friday evening, Darcie locked the door to Shelf Life Books and then stood outside her shop, wondering what to do now.

She didn't want to go home just yet. What's more, she didn't *need* to go home. Cleo was spending the weekend with her grandparents because they had bought a new puppy two days ago, finally replacing Chester, their English bulldog who had succumbed to old age three months ago. In fact, with a new puppy at their house, Darcie figured Cleo would want to live there until she went off to uni.

In any case, she didn't want to go home to her empty house just yet. It was inevitable, of course, but not just yet.

Because, really, what was there for her at home? Her lovely old cottage would just seem barren and lifeless, the silence within its ancient walls reminding her over and over that with Cleo absent, it was just herself—and no one else.

Like Jeannette.

This kind of child-free weekend was *supposed* to be the type of weekend she and Jeannette were meant to enjoy together, bereft of all parental responsibilities. They were supposed to be able to drink wine or G-and-Ts any time of the day or night—not only after Cleo went to bed. They were supposed to be able to have sex anywhere in the house and be as loud as they wanted doing it. They were supposed to be able to sleep in and even spend the entire day in their pyjamas if they liked.

Instead, there was no Jeannette to enjoy this child-free weekend with. Instead, Jeannette was probably in Newquay going over seating arrangements with Katelynn.

Of course, Darcie knew she could do all the child-free weekend privileges on her own. Drink alcohol whenever she wanted, sleep in, stay in her pyjamas…everything. Well, except the have-sex-in-every-room bit. Unless she managed to pull sometime between now and when Cleo returned Sunday night. Quite frankly, though, she wasn't in a pulling mood, which meant that instead of having sex anywhere in the house this weekend, she could masturbate anywhere she wanted, and at any time. And if she used one of the vibrators she rarely bothered with anymore, she would certainly be loud.

Still standing outside her closed shop, Darcie sighed.

"Great," she muttered. "A Cleo-free weekend and the most I can look forward to is getting myself off in the dining room. Oh, hello Mrs. Chenoweth!" she greeted the pensioner who had just walked by and quite possibly overheard her masturbating plans. "Lovely evening isn't it?"

Darcie blushed scarlet.

Sighing yet again, her eyes alighted on The Bean directly across the street. Remembering that Rylea stayed open one hour later than Shelf Life on Fridays, Darcie decided to stop in for a cuppa. She liked the herbal tea blend Rylea served, and it might very well lift her spirits a bit.

Inside the coffee shop, there were several customers seated throughout, mostly youngsters, some of whom were probably on dates. But there were also some older ladies, the type who preferred a place like The Bean on a Friday evening over the Ladle & Spoon.

"Hi Darce!" Rylea greeted her from behind the counter. Rylea's assistant, Bridget, also turned to give her a wave.

Darcie smiled.

"Hiya, ladies," she greeted.

Despite her overall glumness, Darcie couldn't help but appreciate Rylea's beauty, as she always did when she came into this establishment.

The auburn-haired young woman had on a black turtleneck today and her usual skinny jeans, so the entirety of her slender shape was on display, and Darcie mentally patted herself on the back for not ogling.

At the counter now, her heart raced a little faster at the smile Rylea gave her. A smile from the barista was not unusual—Rylea was always friendly with her customers. But lately, Darcie had noticed that Rylea's smile seemed to be more…

She couldn't decide on the right word to use. *Flirtatious* couldn't be it. Why on earth would Rylea be flirting with her? Rylea was a gorgeous single woman in her early twenties who could have her pick. Thus, why would her pick be a thirty-one-year-old woman with custody of her niece?

Nevertheless, Darcie's breath almost hitched when she also noticed that Rylea seemed to be pushing her chest out more. It was as if Rylea had pressed a hidden button and her boobs had just…inflated a bit.

"Where's our little astronaut, then?" Rylea asked.

Darcie blinked, her mind still fixated on the notion of Rylea having inflatable boobs.

"Huh?" she asked.

"Our little astronaut?" Rylea said. "Cleo?"

"Oh, Cleo!" Darcie said. "Right! She's with my parents this weekend. Probably driving them batty with silly questions or space trivia."

Rylea laughed.

"I think her questions are kind of cute," she said.

Darcie smiled. That was sweet of Rylea to say.

"Yes, well," she began, "she asked me the other day if cockroaches worry."

"They bloody well better worry," Rylea said. "Every time I see one of the little buggers, I crush it. So, the usual?"

Darcie considered. Her afternoon usual—as opposed to her morning usual—was tea, but she didn't particularly feel like tea right now. However, an Americano—her morning usual—at this time of the evening would keep her up all night. Although, if she wanted to do all that wild masturbating later, it wouldn't hurt to have a jolt of caffeine.

She considered it, but in the end, shrugged.

"Herbal tea, please," she said.

"Herbal, please, Bridge," Rylea said, tapping the screen of the till. Unlike the machine Darcie used at Shelf Life, Rylea's was more space-age, with a touchscreen that had an integrated card reader.

"But I'll have it here, if you don't mind," Darcie said, fishing out the two pounds fifty needed.

Rylea took the payment.

"No plans tonight, then?" she asked.

Darcie shrugged.

"Nope," she answered, immediately feeling old. Rylea probably had plans, she figured. Certainly more plans than just sipping herbal tea in a coffee shop and then going home to possibly have an orgasm in the dining room.

Or maybe I should have one in the dining room and then another in the living room since I have so much freedom…

She sighed.

She wasn't just feeling old, she realised. She was missing bloody Jeannette.

***

Sitting at a table in the coffee shop that was set apart from others, Darcie realised for what felt like the umpteenth time that she had been staring blankly down into her cup of tea.

She kept trying to tell herself to snap out of it, but so far that wasn't working.

God damn her!

After five months, Darcie had finally started to feel as if she was getting over Jeannette; that she could possibly move on past the betrayal and maybe even start dating again. Then, that bloody invitation showed up!

Closure? Jeannette suddenly wanted closure? As if meeting another woman in America, obviously shagging her, and then deciding to marry her wasn't closure enough? Darcie couldn't help but feel that it was less about Jeannette wanting closure, as much as it was about Jeannette wanting to rub it in.

I found somebody better than you.

I found somebody who makes me happier than you.

And here she is…Ms. Katelynn Jefferson.

A thought came to Darcie. Wasn't Jefferson the name of one of the founding fathers of America? She wondered if Katelynn was descended from that bloke. That would make her American royalty, wouldn't it? After all, the Americans made a big deal about those founding fathers—they're the ones who featured on all their money. Little wonder then that Jeannette would get her head turned by meeting someone from such a prominent family.

Darcie rolled her eyes.

Jefferson, she was sure, was a popular surname in the States, and Katelynn (the cow) Jefferson probably had as much relation to *the* Jefferson as she herself did to Princess Di—whose surname was also Spencer.

Suddenly, she was interrupted in this pathetic reverie by the appearance on her table of a plate bearing a blueberry scone.

She blinked rapidly a couple of times and looked up. Rylea was standing beside the table.

"On the house," Rylea said. "You looked like you could use it."

Darcie gave her a wan smile, a little annoyed with herself for being so obvious. So un-British.

"Cheers," she said.

"Is everything alright?" Rylea asked. Then, to Darcie's surprise—and a bit of delight—Rylea sat down opposite her at the table. Darcie was about to insist that, really, everything was fine; that Rylea shouldn't trouble herself. But when her eyes locked with Rylea's, she saw genuine concern in them. She then realised that she hadn't told anybody about the wedding invitation, and about how—if she was being honest with herself—it had gutted her receiving it. Not her mum, not her best friend Emma…no one. She was realising now that Rylea's obvious interest in listening was welcome to her heart.

Darcie gave a dry smile.

"Am I alright?" she asked. "Compared to people who are starving in Africa, or compared to oppressed women in Afghanistan, I'm dandy."

Rylea laughed.

"Well, at least you're keeping things in the proper perspective," she said.

"Just thought I'd lead with that," Darcie explained, "so that you don't think I'm a right tosser."

Rylea held up her hands.

"No promises, Darce," she said.

Now Darcie laughed. It felt good.

She waved her hand, indicating the rest of the coffee shop.

"I'm not keeping you from…?"

Rylea took a look around.

"Nah," she said. "It's half an hour to closing. I doubt anyone else will be coming in, and if they do, Bridge can handle it. I'm all yours."

If only…

"So, here it is," Darcie began, quietly. "Do you remember Jeannette?"

Rylea nodded.

"I do," she said. "Sorry you two aren't together anymore."

Fortunately, Rylea left it at that.

In a small village like Tremont, it was inevitable that the truth of her and Jeannette's demise as a couple would get out. For a while, it had made Darcie a minor celebrity in town. Also, for a while, it had meant an uptick in business at Shelf Life Books when all of the town's gossips descended on her shop, hoping to pry more details out of Darcie, and buying books in the process.

"Yes, well…" Darcie began. "In any case, just the other day, I received an invitation to Jeannette's wedding."

Rylea's demeanour suddenly changed. Sitting back in her chair, she crossed her legs and her arms, while her brow darkened.

"Cow!" she exclaimed. "Why do people do that? Invite their exes to their weddings, I mean? Like, what bloody purpose can that possibly serve?"

Darcie nodded. Her thoughts exactly!

"She says she wants closure," she added.

Rylea rolled her eyes.

"Closure?" she asked, sarcasm dripping from her voice. "No offence, Darce, but that just seems *so* Jeannette. Do you know what I mean?"

Darcie nodded vigorously.

"I mean, I understand I didn't know her very well," Rylea continued. "Or, really, like *at all*. But she just seemed so…American! And a little full of herself if that makes sense?"

"It completely makes sense!" Darcie agreed. "Well, she's a lawyer. An *American* lawyer, at that."

"Well, now I'm mad at her for sending you that invitation," Rylea said. "If it makes you feel any better, you're well rid of her."

Surprisingly, it did make Darcie feel better.

"Thank you," she said.

Rylea leaned forward, resting her arms on the table.

"So, what did you do with the invitation?" she asked.

"Binned it," Darcie answered.

"That was good," Rylea said. "Exactly what I would have done." She paused, her eyes full of thought. "Actually, what I would have done was burn it."

Darcie laughed.

"Still an option, actually," she said. "I chucked it in my upstairs bin and have yet to empty it."

This was true. Her so-called "bills bin" under her desk in the bedroom wasn't emptied nearly as often as the kitchen bin, as it usually only contained paper items. Thus, Jeannette's wedding invite was still in there. Darcie wondered now if that was to blame for how poorly she had been sleeping lately; if perhaps, like in Poe's *The Tell-Tale Heart*, her subconscious could somehow detect the presence of the invitation in her room, not beating like a heart, but nonetheless…*there*.

Rylea's eyes widened with delight.

"Totally burn it!" she instructed. "It will make you feel so much better!"

Darcie couldn't believe this. A few minutes ago, she was sitting here with her spirits low, and now she was actually…happy!

She reached out to place her hand on Rylea's arm.

"You're magical," she told the younger woman. "You've made me feel so much better!" Then, she removed her hand, not wanting Rylea to think this old woman was hitting on her.

Oddly, Darcie had never before considered herself old. She had never been one to panic about her age, probably because the reflection in the mirror still showed a beautiful woman staring back at her year after year. However, sitting now across from someone as young as Rylea—whom Darcie could recall still being in Year 6 at school when she herself was taking her A-levels—she *did* feel old. Well, old enough to *not* be leaving her hand on Rylea's arm.

"I'm glad I made you feel better," Rylea responded. "And since the little astronaut is off at her grands, you can burn that cow's invitation tonight!"

"I will," Darcie told her. "I'll light a match to it and be done with it as soon as I get home."

But Rylea was shaking her head.

"What's wrong?" Darcie asked.

"This kind of evil requires more than just lighting a match to it, Darce!" Rylea replied. "You have to turn this into a ritual!"

"A ritual?"

"Yes!" Rylea exclaimed. "An eradication ritual!"

"Good word usage," Darcie complimented.

"Thanks," Rylea said. "I read a lot. Anyway, that American cow first made you miserable by running away with another American cow, and then she rubbed it in your face by inviting you to their wedding! You can't just burn the invitation. This calls for a relationship exorcism."

Darcie blinked.

Like that film?

"Um…"

"What are you doing tonight?" Rylea asked.

Masturbating in the dining room and possibly the living room—I still haven't decided yet. A cup of tea. A good book. Bed.

"Nothing, really," Darcie answered.

"Then we shall have the exorcism tonight," Rylea stated.

"Um…I don't know how to do a relationship exorcism," Darcie said.

And… "we?"

Rylea sat back again and gave her an unconcerned look.

"Trust me," she said. "I know just the person."

Chapter 4

"Bloody Americans!" Tamsin said as she and Rylea walked to Darcie's house that night.

The weather was lovely, though a bit of a breeze was blowing, the scent of rain to come lingering in the air.

Rylea rolled her eyes. Normally, her friend did not have a particular prejudice against Americans. The Belgians were another matter, but not the Americans. However, Rylea figured that Tamsin would be holding onto this resentment of women from the States for quite some time, due to Tremont losing out to California on that ranked list.

In any case, the way Rylea saw it, Tamsin's current ire against Americans meant that tonight's exorcism would be that much more potent.

Rylea didn't hold to any particular religious beliefs. What she did believe was that the Church—in all its different flavours—did not offer to her anything she felt comfortable grasping onto, especially when many in the Church still had a problem with the LGBTQ community. As such, she considered herself *open* to alternative spiritual concepts.

Such as relationship exorcisms.

The Church would just tell someone to pray away the hurt and sadness. What a load of bollocks! On your knees, hands clasped, praying to an unseen God who may or may not actually be there, was *not* the way to get over a broken heart. Action was required. Action and burning stuff.

She and Tamsin had been performing this ritual since Year 11, and had it down to an art form, especially with Tamsin's track record. Her best friend had experienced her share of broken hearts, sure; but she had also had her share of shitty relationships with women that she was well rid of.

They turned off Corwin Lane and onto the footpath which led to Darcie's front door.

Darcie's cottage was very typical of many found in this part of Cornwall, including Rylea's own, which she inherited after her mother's death. Two-storey, made of stone, looking like something out of a fairy-tale—at least that's what foreign visitors often stated.

Darcie's had a lovely front garden, with a bench and several flowering bushes that were in bloom. Rylea couldn't help wondering if Darcie and Jeannette had spent much time sitting on the bench on warm days, enjoying the garden and each other's company.

Rylea had never been in Darcie's home, though when she was a teenager, she had often imagined herself coming over here quite a lot. She'd had a mad crush on Darcie then. It hadn't even bothered her that Darcie had a kid to take care of. Her teenage self—with the silly romantic notions all teenagers have—imagined that Cleo could be like a little sister to her. Darcie, of course, would most definitely be like a wife to her—with all the benefits that her active teenage mind was able to come up with.

And although Rylea never really got over her crush on Darcie, once Jeannette had entered the picture, she and the other lesbians in town had pretty much known Darcie was off the market. Of course, she was now back on the market. However, Rylea very seriously doubted Darcie would be interested in the kid she used to babysit back when she was fifteen and Rylea was eight.

"Hiya!" Darcie greeted Rylea and Tamsin after they knocked on the door. She stepped aside to let them in.

"The exorcists are here!" Tamsin exclaimed as she entered, holding up a large tote bag, which contained the essential exorcism gear.

Rylea smiled at Darcie.

Darcie's hair looked a little damp, and there was a clean, floral scent enveloping her. Rylea guessed she had just gotten out of the shower recently. Rylea loved the fact that Darcie hadn't put on anything special for them. Instead, Darcie was dressed in pink pyjama pants which looked very comfortable, and a white t-shirt, the fabric of which was thin enough to reveal there was a black sports bra beneath it. On her feet were thick white socks and fuzzy slippers.

Overall, it gave Rylea the impression that this was how Darcie chilled at her house every night. Well, except perhaps for the bra. Rylea was certain *that* bit had been added due to company coming over. This, of course, made her imagine Darcie in that shirt *without* a bra, and how Darcie's nipples would be undoubtedly visible through the fabric.

Now her heart was beating a little faster.

What kind of nipples did Darcie have? It was her favourite game when eyeing a beautiful woman. Well, that and wondering how much of a bump-up the woman's bra added to her breasts.

When she was a teenager, Rylea always imagined Darcie with dark little nipples, probably much like her own. But lately— over the past year or so—she had been imagining Darcie with larger areolas that were a soft, almost-not-there pink. She had no explanation for that shift in her thinking. Just that, one day Darcie had dark little nipples, the next she had large pink ones.

Christ!

Rylea realised now that she probably shouldn't be standing here in the entryway of Darcie's home thinking about her host's nipples.

"Tamsin is super-excited to get this exorcism going," Rylea said, feeling herself blushing, wishing she wasn't because she was certain it was only telling Darcie that images of her breasts had been flitting through her mind.

"Well, come on in, and let's get started," Darcie said, leading the way further into her home. "You know, when Rylea first mentioned this, I thought it was a really out-there idea," Darcie said as she walked. "But as I had nothing better to do tonight, I figured, why not? And now I'm looking forward to it!"

"Trust me, Darce," Tamsin said, "you will thank us."

Darcie laughed.

"Well, I could certainly use some out-there thinking," she replied.

She led them through the house, Rylea trying to take in as much as she could.

It was cosy and homey, with lots of pictures on the walls and soft furnishings. There was hardly anything with a sharp corner or hard edge anywhere, and it took a moment for Rylea to realise that was obviously for Cleo's benefit—proof of a guardian protecting the child in her care from accidental bumps.

As for Cleo, there was evidence of her throughout. Her backpack and purple wellies were waiting neatly by the staircase; some of her artwork was hung on the walls; and there was a *Thomas and Friends* blanket draped over one end of the sofa in the living room. Certainly Cleo was too old for *Thomas and Friends* by now, but Rylea guessed that the blanket was her favourite from when she was a wee one, and that she probably still enjoyed snuggling under it on the couch while watching TV with her auntie.

The three women eventually ended up outside, on the well-lit back patio. A set of outdoor furniture was there, featuring a round table.

"Bugger," Darcie said, wrapping her arms around herself. "I should have brought my jacket."

Without hesitating, Rylea took her light jacket off and draped it over Darcie's shoulders. She was dressed warmly enough anyway in the yellow cable knit sweater she had chosen for tonight.

Darcie looked at her, the most beautiful smile on her face.

"Thank you!" she said. "Of course, I could just run back inside and grab one of my own. I mean, I don't want you to be—"

Rylea, blushing yet again, waved her off.

"I'm fine," she said. "The walk over here warmed me up."

And the smile Darcie was still giving her was warming her up even more.

"Do you have the offending object?" Tamsin asked without preamble, holding out her hand.

"I'm sorry?" Darcie asked.

"The invitation," Rylea whispered.

"Oh!" Darcie said. "Yes! Right here!" She reached into the pocket of her pj bottoms and withdrew the invitation.

Both Rylea and Tamsin gasped. Tamsin even put her hands to her mouth.

Darcie, looking from one to the other, asked, "What? What's wrong?"

Tamsin quickly took the invitation from Darcie.

"You had it near your womanhood!" she exclaimed.

Darcie looked at Rylea, and Rylea nodded, knowing a further explanation would be necessary.

"The offending object should not have been carried so close to your vagina," she stated. "Bad ju-ju."

"Oh!" Darcie said. "I didn't know. Um…is that going to be a problem?"

"Only if you ever want to have sex again!" Tamsin explained, digging in the tote bag. "But I'm on it!" In a moment, she withdrew a sage bundle and a lighter.

Rylea leaned closer to Darcie.

"Don't panic," she whispered.

"Panic?" Darcie whispered back. "Panic about what?"

"The fact that there's about to be some smoke near your lady parts," Rylea answered.

Darcie snapped her head to look at Rylea. But Rylea could tell by the humour evident in Darcie's eyes that although she might be finding this a tad weird, she was nonetheless amused.

Tamsin had the sage bundle lit now. She let the flame burn for about twenty seconds and then blew it out. Now a fragrant smoke was curling up from the bundle. She then stepped forward and waved the smoking sage in front of Darcie's crotch for several seconds.

Rylea's heart and clit thudded when Darcie suddenly grabbed her hand. They shared another look, and Rylea could see that Darcie was trying her hardest not to burst out laughing. Seeing this made Rylea want to burst out laughing herself, but she managed to contain it. While Tamsin continued "cleansing" Darcie's womanhood—chanting something under her breath, Rylea noticed, which was new—she and Darcie stared at each other, both of them turning red-faced from holding in their laughter.

Finally, Tamsin was done, stepping away from Darcie and placing the still smoking sage bundle on the metal table.

"Now your vagina is cleansed," Rylea whispered.

"Funny, that," Darcie whispered back, "I thought I took care of cleansing it during my shower."

Rylea snickered, glad that Tamsin was too busy once more digging in the tote bag to have noticed. Tamsin took the relationship exorcism very seriously, and there was no laughing allowed.

"Bugger!" Darcie exclaimed. "Where are my manners? Would you two like something to drink?"

"I'd love a Carling," Tamsin said.

"And I actually have some," Darcie told her.

"But we can only drink red wine tonight," Tamsin continued.

"Oh," Darcie said, and Rylea loved how she immediately looked at her for an explanation.

"Red wine," Rylea began, "symbolizes the blood of a dead relationship."

"Got it," Darcie said. "Red wine coming up!"

When Darcie had disappeared into the house, Tamsin approached Rylea.

"Wow," she whispered. "She's looking nice! I'd forgotten how cute she is! For an older woman, I mean."

Rylea smacked her arm, also wondering how on earth anyone could forget how cute Darcie is.

"She's not even ten years older than us!" she pointed out.

"But you do admit she's older?" Tamsin asked.

"For fuck's sake!"

Darcie returned with a bottle of wine and three glasses. She quickly had the wine poured.

"Don't drink it yet," Rylea told her. "We must wait until after the ceremonial stabbing."

Rylea almost laughed at the expression Darcie's face took on just then. She decided to have some fun and *not* explain what the ceremonial stabbing was.

"All set," Tamsin announced.

In addition to the offending object—the invitation—Darcie's patio table now bore two pillar candles (both lit), a large metal bowl, a small block of wood, a bottle of lighter fluid, and a dagger. The dagger was from Tamsin's father's collection. She had "borrowed" it for the first few relationship exorcisms she and Rylea had done, back when they were teenagers, and never bothered returning it.

"Darce," Tamsin began, "if you would step up to the table, please."

Rylea thought she would die when Darcie took her hand as she approached the table.

Doesn't mean anything! Doesn't mean anything! Doesn't mean anything!

But that did nothing to quell the increased heart rate in her chest.

Tamsin stood in front of Darcie, a solemn look on her face. Rylea knew she was about to recite the exorcism litany.

"Darcie Spencer," Tamsin said, "you have suffered great heartbreak and anguish at the hands of an American cow."

Rylea rolled her eyes. The nationality of the cow was *not* part of the litany. Tamsin really needed to get over this anti-American kick she was on.

Tamsin continued.

"We are here to purge those demons from your soul so that you may suffer no longer and start afresh." Tamsin gestured to the table. "The two candles represent what once was—you and Jeannette together as a couple. Please blow out only one of the candles."

Leaning forward and using one of her hands to keep her ponytail from the flame, Darcie huffed out a short breath, snuffing out a candle.

"That candle represents Jeannette in your life," Tamsin went on. "And you have now extinguished her from it."

"That actually felt rather good!" Darcie said, smiling at them both.

"The next part feels even better," Rylea told her.

Tamsin took hold of the offending object in both hands, raised it above her head as if offering it to the gods, and then placed the invitation on the wooden block. She then picked up the dagger and presented it to Darcie, handle first.

"That invitation was sent to you by the American cow. No matter her true intentions, the invitation has caused you anguish; therefore you must slay it by stabbing it."

"Just once?" Darcie asked.

Tamsin shrugged.

"However many bloody times you'd like," she said.

Darcie squared herself in front of the table, and plunged the dagger forcefully down, piercing the invitation with a solid-sounding *thonk!*

She looked up at Rylea, smiling.

"Oh my days, that was fun!"

"Go on, then," Rylea encouraged. "Keep at it!"

Darcie waggled her eyebrows impishly at her.

Thonk-thonk-thonk-thonk-thonk-thonk-thonk-thonk!

Rylea watched as Darcie really went to town on the offending object.

"Whoooo!" Tamsin yelled.

By the time Darcie was done, the invitation looked as if someone had used a cheese grater on it.

"I'm going to start calling you the Terminator," Tamsin said. "Time for the wine!"

Rylea leaned close to Darcie.

"Symbolizes the blood of the now slayed relationship," she explained.

They all lifted their glasses and took sips.

"Wow!" Rylea exclaimed, examining the red liquid in her glass. "This is the best blood we've ever had, right Tams?"

"Damn right!" her best friend agreed. "Much better than the shite we normally buy."

"I have standards when it comes to wine," Darcie said.

"Blood," Tamsin corrected.

"Right, blood," Darcie said.

"Now, pick up the offending object and place it in the bowl, please," Tamsin instructed.

Once Darcie had placed the shredded invite into the bowl, Tamsin doused it liberally with lighter fluid.

"Bloody hell, Tams," Rylea said. "Does a *paper* invitation really need that much help catching on fire?"

"Hey," Tamsin began, "if we're going to make a fire, we're going to do it right, yeah?"

She handed a book of matches to Darcie.

Darcie peeked inside the bowl, and then up at the portion of the roof which overhung the patio. Lifting the bowl off the table, she said, "I'm just going to carry this out here," she said, heading onto the lawn, under the wide open sky.

Rylea smacked Tamsin's arm again.

"Are you trying to burn her house down?" she hissed.

"I'm trying to exorcise the demons!" Tamsin retorted.

They joined Darcie, who had placed the bowl on the grass.

"Here goes nothing!" Darcie said, striking a match and then dropping it in.

Fwhooooooooooooooooooooooosh!

A spout of flame geyersed up from the bowl.

"Whoa!" Rylea exclaimed, stepping back.

"Now, that's a fire!" Darcie said, laughing. She then crossed her arms and stared down at the burning invitation, an introspective look on her face.

Rylea noticed Tamsin check her watch.

"Well, my work here is done," Tamsin said. "Darcie, I hereby pronounce you officially exorcised. Now, I must be off, I have a date tonight."

Darcie laughed.

"The irony is inescapable," she said. She turned to Rylea. "I assume you also have to leave?"

Shaking her head, Rylea said, "Nope. Nowhere to be."

"Good," Darcie replied. "Then you can stay and help me finish off that bottle of wine."

Rylea felt her heart rate kick up again.

"Absolutely," she said.

"Will you…? Tamsin asked Rylea, leadingly, indicating the exorcism accoutrement.

"I'll take care of it," Rylea assured her.

"Right, then, I'm off!" Tamsin said.

Darcie gave her a hug.

"Thank you so much," Darcie said. "This…actually helped me feel better."

"The relationship exorcism never fails," Tamsin told her. She then gave Rylea a brief hug. "Wish me luck," she said. "Let's hope she doesn't want to have sex all night."

Rylea shrugged.

"Just be yourself," she said. "I'm sure that will dissuade her."

"Oh, fuck you!" Tamsin said.

Chapter 5

Darcie couldn't remember when she'd had so much fun!

Okay, at the most recent Beavers meeting this past Monday, she had gotten to dance with all the little ones, and then had let all the little girls braid her hair. That had been amazingly fun.

But fun with adults? It had been a while.

And as silly as the relationship exorcism had been, it had truly made her feel better! Particularly the stabbing bit. That had been fun. There was something cathartic about the whole ritual and its symbolism: blowing out Jeannette's candle, stabbing the invitation…

No, the offending object!

…drinking the symbolic blood (in this case a very nice 2017 pinot noir), then burning the offending object.

She saw Rylea packing up the exorcism items in the large tote bag.

"Oh, leave that for now," Darcie said. "Let's go inside. Don't forget your wine glass."

She was glad Rylea had agreed to stay. It would be nice to have some company, even if just for a little longer. Even though Rylea didn't have any plans tonight—which was hard to believe—Darcie was certain the younger woman would rather be doing anything else. Certainly anything other than staying in with a woman who had been unceremoniously dumped by her girlfriend, and whose idea of a wild Friday night was getting comfortable in pjs and then giving that new *Sex and the City* sequel a try.

Besides, it had been quite a while since Darcie had a beautiful woman with her in the house. Even if Rylea spared her only half an hour, Darcie would appreciate it. The yellow sweater Rylea was wearing was very flattering on her, and its colour made Darcie think of spending a spring day with her, out in the garden.

Inside, she took off Rylea's jacket, and they made themselves comfortable in the living room, sitting on the opposite ends of the large, distressed leather sofa, the bottle of wine on the coffee table.

Darcie was thankful that her home looked neat. One of the advantages of having a ten-year-old now was that it was (somewhat) easy to prevent the house from looking as if she lived in a preschool playroom. Fortunately, Cleo was a good kid and didn't put up too much of a fuss when it came to straightening up.

"So, does Tamsin really not like having sex all night?" she asked, tucking one leg under the other and facing Rylea.

Rylea laughed. She also blushed, which Darcie thought was totes adorable.

"Yeah, afraid not," Rylea said. "I believe she has a two orgasm limit before she says 'Enough, let's move on.'"

Now, Darcie laughed.

"Almost defeats the purpose of being a woman," she said.

"My point exactly," Rylea said. "Us women have a gift. Seems a shame to waste it."

Sounded to Darcie like Rylea was the type of woman who could be persuaded to have sex until they both practically passed out from exhaustion.

Of course, now her mind was wondering what Rylea was like in bed, and such a thought was making heat bloom between her legs.

She took a hurried sip of wine to divert her thoughts, drained her glass and then poured herself some more, topping off Rylea's glass as well. Granted, she hadn't had sex since Jeannette left, but that was no reason to let her mind wander down that path.

Or down the path of what Rylea was wearing under her sweater…

Stop!

She almost wanted to laugh at herself for being so silly. But then, Rylea would ask what was so funny, and then she'd have to come up with something that was so funny other than, *Just thinking about shagging you, is all.*

"That was quite a ritual you and Tamsin put together," she said. "Very inventive."

"Gah!" Rylea exclaimed. "We've been doing that since we were kids, haven't we? The funny thing is it helps."

"It really does!" Darcie agreed. "My favourite part was the stabbing. God, I just felt like more and more weight was lifted off my shoulders with each thrust of the knife."

"You did seem to enjoy it," Rylea said, cocking her eyebrow at Darcie.

"I did, didn't I?" Darcie replied. "I hope this doesn't mean I've a hidden psychopath in me. So, come on, tell me…what sorts of things have you stabbed during past relationship exorcisms?"

"Oh, Tams and I have stabbed all sorts of stuff," Rylea said. She toed off her shoes and then mimicked Darcie's posture on the sofa—with one leg tucked under herself. "Let's see…love letters, photographs, bras, knickers, you name it. Oh! I once dated a girl—Catherine—who had given me this *enormous* stuffed elephant for my birthday one year. This bloody thing was almost as big as I am! Anyway, after I found out she was cheating on me, Horton the elephant played a key role in that relationship's exorcism."

"You stabbed poor Horton?"

"Bloody butchered him, I did!" Rylea said. "And there was stuffing all over the flat—I was still at uni at the time—and months later I was still finding it."

Darcie laughed, downed another sip of wine, and then shook her head.

"Christ, who would cheat on you?"

Bugger!

She really did say that out loud! For fuck's sake! Bloody wine! She ought to write a letter to Washington, tell the CIA that instead of waterboarding, just use bloody pinot noir to get the Al Qaeda operatives talking.

"I just meant," she began, "that you're so nice and…"

"No, that was a super sweet thing to say, thank you!" Rylea said.

Darcie was certain Rylea would make her excuses and leave now.

Instead…

"And for what it's worth," Rylea began, "why Jeannette would leave you is beyond me."

Darcie smiled. She had often wondered the same thing and had never gotten anything close to a satisfactory answer. The best Jeannette offered up, during that last phone call with her, was, "I just found someone I feel more connected to."

More connected to! After *a year* of being with her, Jeannette had found someone she was more connected to!

Even now, it made bile rise in her throat to recall that conversation. But, interestingly enough, she wasn't feeling any of the attendant sadness that went along with it! That had been the pattern these past five months, after all, whenever she thought of that last phone call with Jeannette: anger, followed by sadness.

But now…no sadness.

The relationship exorcism worked!

***

They were on their second bottle of wine now. This one Darcie had described to Rylea as being "an impudent yet bold California cabernet sauvignon, with hints of raspberry, thistle and honeycomb."

Rylea, upon hearing this description, had started laughing.

"Good thing Tams is not here," she had said, her words a bit slurred. "About the only thing she hates more than Americans right now, is *Californian* Americans!"

They had both burst into laughter at that. They were definitely tipsy, Darcie realised, and she had already decided to insist on calling Barry to drive Rylea home. She would even pay for it. She knew that her young friend only lived two streets and a left turn away, but it would make her feel better if Rylea wasn't walking those streets on unsteady legs.

Darcie had wanted to ask why Tamsin hated California Americans, but she'd had to go pee really badly by that point. Mentioning that to Rylea, she learned that Rylea also had to pee really badly. So, after pointing Rylea to the downstairs loo, she went upstairs to use the one attached to her bedroom. Now, returning to the living room, she sat back down on the sofa, having forgotten the question she wanted to ask.

Rylea appeared just a moment later. However, instead of resuming her seat on the opposite end of the sofa, she sat right to Darcie, which made Darcie feel a little flushed with happiness.

"So," Darcie began, after clinking her glass with Rylea's, "I can't believe you have nothing better to do tonight than drink wine with me."

Rylea smiled.

"It's true, though!" she exclaimed. "You know what I would be doing right now if I were home? Drinking wine and reading."

Darcie thought that sounded lovely. And she knew Rylea read a lot because she was one of her best customers at Shelf Life Books. Nonetheless, she was surprised.

"But it's Friday!" she said. "You're supposed to be out doing Friday night things!"

Rylea shrugged.

"I've been known to do some Friday night things," she said, laughing. "But I'm not much of a party girl; never really have been. And I typically only enjoy going out if I'm dating someone, or if Tams is with me." She took a sip of her wine. "By the way," she said, "this had better be my last glass of wine. I need to open shop tomorrow, after all."

Darcie nodded. Rylea made a good point. Though it was tempting to take full advantage of this Cleo-free night and spend it drinking, enjoying Rylea's company and continuing to imagine what was under her sweater, she did have to open Shelf Life tomorrow.

"Yeah, me too," she agreed.

"What about you?" Rylea asked.

"What about me?"

"The little astronaut is away at her grands'," Rylea began. "So, why are you here with me instead of living it up in Newquay or something?"

Darcie hadn't flirted in so long that she was certain she had forgotten how. So, it was with some relief when her mind immediately came up with *Because nothing in Newquay could top spending an evening with you.*

But, of course, she couldn't possibly say that.

"I don't really 'live it up' anymore," she explained. "Sometimes, my mate Emma and I will go mad and have a girls' weekend in Newquay, away from the kids. Sometimes, we'll even take the train to London and stay a few days there. But to be honest, me having two women over for a relationship exorcism and wine is pretty much the definition of 'living it up' for me nowadays." She raised her half-finished wine glass. "To living it up."

"To living it up," Rylea repeated. They clinked glasses. "So, do you think it worked? The exorcism? I would like to know that my customer is completely satisfied."

Darcie had to take an emergency sip of wine to cover the intake of breath she was forced to take when, inside her core, things started fluttering at the notion of Rylea completely satisfying her.

"Um…yeah, I do think it worked," she said, readjusting her posture on the sofa. "It made me feel like I had actually done *something* other than faffing about feeling sorry for myself. And, I repeat…stabbing things is really bloody fun! In fact, I think I'll go through my house one more time and try to find anything else of Jeannette's that I might take a knife to."

Rylea laughed.

"It only works with the official relationship exorcism dagger, so I'll be sure to leave that with you when I go home." She paused. "Still though, I kind of wish we could do something more…*revenge-like*, you know? Like, I don't know…we could egg her house, or we could put a banana in her tailpipe."

Darcie smiled. She liked all the uses of "we" in Rylea's rant.

"The egging idea sounds fun," she said. "I'd have to find out where she lives first, though."

Rylea waved that off.

"Tamsin has evil supervillain skills like that," she said. "That'll be easy for her."

"Well," Darcie replied, "I appreciate you taking such an interest in helping my catharsis."

Rylea shrugged. Suddenly, she seemed a bit shy.

"I just think that was a rotten thing for her to do," she said softly, looking down at her glass of wine. "That's not how you call it off with somebody. Especially someone you claim to love." She looked back up at Darcie. "Thus, my desire to avenge you!"

Darcie burst out in laughter.

"I love it!" she said. "I've always wanted my own personal avenger. Wonder Woman if I could swing it."

"Oh my god! I have a Wonder Woman costume!"

Darcie's nipples turned to granite.

"No way!" she exclaimed.

Rylea nodded.

"Three Halloweens ago!" she explained. "Went as Wonder Woman to a costume party with my girlfriend at the time." She chuckled. "She couldn't even wait until we got back home to jump all over me. Ended up shagging in our host's loo."

Darcie, amazed that Rylea's then-girlfriend had even made it out of the house without shagging her, felt her clit swell a bit. She herself, upon seeing Rylea made up as Wonder Woman probably would have called their hosts, made their excuses, and ended up fucking the superheroine until they both passed out.

Rylea drained the remaining wine from her glass.

"And on that note," she said, putting the wine glass on the coffee table, "I will say my goodbyes."

Darcie felt a potent wave of disappointment wash over her. But she had no legitimate reason to convince Rylea to stay. Wanting to shag her couldn't be called legitimate.

"Wait just a moment," she said, stopping Rylea from rising by placing a hand on her shoulder. She picked up her phone from the coffee table. "I'm going to call Barry to give you a lift. I'll pay for it."

"I'm fine, Darce," Rylea said. "You know how close I live."

But Darcie shook her head. Her phone was already dialling Barry's number.

"Yes, Barry? Hi, it's Darcie. I have a pick-up for you at my place, if you have time…Great…It's Rylea Morgan, and it's to her place…That's right…Ta, Barry. See you then." The call ended and she looked at Rylea. "Slow night. He'll be here in a few minutes."

"You really didn't have to," Rylea said.

"I'd drive you myself," Darcie replied, "but I think I've had a little too much as well."

They both rose from the sofa. Rylea went back outside to finish gathering up all the exorcism items, but afterwards she handed the dagger to Darcie before shouldering the tote bag.

"In case you find other things to stab," she said, winking.

True to his word, Barry arrived quickly.

Darcie and Rylea hugged.

Darcie couldn't help herself.

"This was so much fun," she said. "We should do it again."

To her relief, Rylea smiled enthusiastically.

"I would like that," she said, and Darcie actually believed her. "I'll provide the wine next time."

"Deal."

Outside, Darcie handed Barry seven quid—more than enough for the short trip he'd had to make from his home to hers, and then his next trip to Rylea's.

"See you for my morning coffee tomorrow," Darcie said to Rylea, and then she headed back into her house.

When she shut the door behind her, she leaned against it, smiling. This had been a good night. And even though she knew it couldn't happen with Rylea, she was thinking that perhaps she was ready to begin dating again.

A relationship exorcism. Who knew?

Chapter 6

The next morning, Rylea had to take two ibuprofen in order to combat the wine headache she woke up with. It wasn't as bad as a hangover, but she nonetheless preferred it to be gone before she got to The Bean.

Thankfully, by the time she finished making and eating breakfast, her head felt completely better, and she was able to get herself dressed for the day while bopping along to the new one by her favourite K-pop group.

Today, she decided on wearing a dress. It just felt like a dress kind of day, though she couldn't explain why. She suspected it had something to do with Darcie. Darcie was always wearing dresses, she considered, as she pulled on a simple A-line number in blue; the memory of her night with her still fresh in Rylea's mind.

Examining herself in the mirror, she frowned. She enjoyed the way the dress, combined with the bra she had chosen, flattered her chest, but she wasn't satisfied with how her bum looked.

Easy enough to fix…

Reaching under the dress, she pulled the bikini-style briefs she was wearing off and tossed them in her laundry bin. She then fished around in her underwear drawer until she found what she was looking for: a pair of high-waisted knickers that would provide some additional lift to her arse. Pulling them on, she re-examined herself.

Much better.

She chose black hi-top trainers for her feet, and then decided she wanted to wear a red chunky bracelet also but couldn't remember where she had put it. It wasn't in with the rest of her jewellery, which was all sort of jumbled together in a plastic storage container she kept in her wardrobe.

Somehow recalling that the last time she had worn it she was at her mother's old secretary desk, here in the bedroom, she stepped over to that piece of furniture. Perhaps she had taken the bracelet off and stuck it in one of the drawers. Sure enough, in the first drawer she opened, there it was. She then had a vague recollection of intending to repurpose this desk into a place to keep her jewellery and hair thingamabobs, and stuff like that, but had yet to get around to doing it. Thus her jewellery was still in the plastic container, and her hair thingamabobs could be found, well, all over the house.

She was about to shut the drawer when a rattling in the back of it caught her attention. Reaching in, she pulled out a pair of her mother's reading glasses.

Suddenly, Rylea's breath hitched, and her eyes began stinging.

Her mum had been dead now for a little over eighteen months, cancer taking her at the young age of sixty-two. Even though Rylea had slowly gotten used to the fact that this cottage—where she had grown up—was now *hers* and hers alone, and even though she had spent time making it *hers* by redecorating it to her tastes, it was, of course, impossible to eradicate the fact that Celia Morgan had once lived here. Nor did she want to eradicate that fact.

However, when artifacts of her mum's life suddenly appeared—like these reading glasses—they were like a gut punch to Rylea's heart. Two months ago, she had been reduced to a blubbering mess when one night, she had discovered one of Celia's old cardis that had somehow fallen behind some boxes in the hall cupboard.

Well, she couldn't afford to become reduced to a blubbering mess now. She needed to leave and get to The Bean.

Placing the reading glasses almost reverently down on the desk, she decided she'd figure out what to do with them later. Perhaps she'd keep them. The frames were actually quite stylish after all, and one future day, when age started affecting her own eyesight, she may have a need for them. She smiled at the notion of a fifty-something version of herself reading a book, using her mother's glasses.

After putting on the bracelet, she went downstairs, grabbed her handbag, and left the house.

***

"Ooh, you're looking posh today!" Bridget stated once Rylea arrived at the coffee shop.

Rylea stopped and looked down at her outfit.

"What?" she asked. "No, I'm not."

"You never wear a dress," Bridget went on.

Rylea blinked.

"I wear dresses all the time, Bridge!" she exclaimed. "You've *seen* me in dresses!"

Bridget cocked an eyebrow. She was busy prepping one of the brewing machines.

"Not in the shop, you don't," she pointed out.

Rylea had to concede this was true. Usually, her uniform—as it were—at The Bean was skinny jeans and a top of some kind, but never a dress.

She shrugged, reaching for her apron that was hanging on a hook outside the storage room.

"I wanted a change today, that's all," she said. She then set about surveying what needed to be done prior to opening.

Bridget had been with her at The Bean since the beginning. She was in her mid-forties, married, with twin daughters that were off at uni. With an empty nest, she gladly took the job Rylea offered, as a way to have something to do. Her husband, Jack, worked as a land surveyor and supported the household, which was a good thing considering the crap wages Rylea was able to pay her.

Despite the difference in their ages, and the fact that the much younger Rylea was her boss, the two of them had become close friends and worked well together.

"Plans tonight?" Bridget asked as they both did their tasks.

"Trivia night at the pub," Rylea answered. It was about the only local activity that she was willing to leave her house for, regardless of whether any of her friends could meet her, or if she had a date to join her. She loved trivia night, and was even on a team of pensioners, all of whom called her Taylor Swift—obviously having no idea who Taylor Swift was, but only doing so because she was young and pretty.

Thinking about it now, she seemed to recall that on occasion, she had seen Darcie there as well, with Jeannette.

It still upset her at how all of that went down. When she had first heard, she remembered feeling betrayed as a woman, as if Jeannette, by her actions, had betrayed all womankind because what she had done seemed like something a man would do.

That was silly, she knew. Women were just as capable of fucking other women over just as well as blokes did. Yet, she had nonetheless started equating Jeannette with all the blokes in the world.

And she had wished she could do something for Darcie back then, comfort her in some way, but they had never developed a close friendship like that—the kind wherein Woman A heads over to Woman B's house to let Woman B cry on her shoulder because Woman B's girlfriend treated her like shite. Rylea supposed that was Emma's role.

Instead, Rylea had implemented what she had called her "Super-Secret Make Darcie Feel Better Plan."

Darcie's morning usual at The Bean was a large Americano with one shot of vanilla syrup added. When Jeannette did her bloke-like move of running out on Darcie, Rylea—having no other way of trying to make her feel better—secretly added *three* shots of vanilla to her Americano, with no extra charge. She even filled Bridget in on her scheme in case it was her making Darcie's drink.

Naturally, after the first few times she did this, Darcie started complimenting her on how much more she was enjoying her Americanos lately—proof that the Super-Secret Make Darcie Feel Better Plan was having an effect. However, it also made Rylea realise that she needed to keep adding those two extra shots of vanilla to Darcie's coffee, otherwise the jig would be up. So, even nowadays, when Darcie came in, Rylea made sure to shield the flavour pump with her body so that Darcie wouldn't see the two extra shots she added, and she informed Bridget to just keep doing the same.

"Hey, Bridge?" Rylea asked now, wiping down the ordering counter after spraying it with disinfectant. "What's the best revenge for when someone breaks your heart? And, no, it has nothing to do with me. I'm asking for a friend."

Bridget scoffed.

"That's easy, innit?" she said. "Shag their brother."

Rylea blinked. She stopped wiping and turned to stare at her employee.

"Shag their brother?" she asked. "That's your default answer?"

Bridget shrugged.

"It's how Jack and I ended up together," she said.

For a moment, Rylea was incapable of speech.

"Okay, right," she eventually began. "But supposing shagging the brother isn't a viable option."

Bridget gave her a wise look.

"Shagging the brother is *always* an option," she said. "Brothers love shagging their brother's birds."

"Well, I would imagine that if a bloke doesn't have a brother, then there's no brother to shag!" Rylea pointed out.

"Yes, well, there's that!" Bridget agreed. "But in that case, you shag the father."

Rylea took a deep breath.

"Okay, can you possibly answer my question in a way which doesn't involve shagging male members of someone's family?"

Bridget looked off to the side, evidently considering the question. Eventually, she shrugged.

"What's that thing they say?" she asked. "The best revenge is a life well-lived? Something like that?"

Well, that was a better answer than *Shag their brother*, Rylea conceded.

Stepping out from behind the counter, she headed towards the customers' loo to make sure it was clean.

A life well-lived...A life well-lived...

Now, how can that be used to help Darcie?

Chapter 7

Busy day!

Darcie wondered what was going on in town that was making seemingly everyone need books today. It couldn't be the weather. Fine, May in Cornwall wasn't ever exactly like the Bahamas, but it was a hell of a lot nicer than November or February. During the colder months of the year, Darcie expected people to buy a lot of books because they were more apt to just stay in. But the weather lately had been rather pleasant. It was gardening weather; beach weather; long strolls weather…yet, people had been coming in all day, buying books as if preparing to hunker down for a siege.

Of course, no complaints would ever come from Darcie about this. Whatever was making the denizens of Tremont want to read so much was good for Shelf Life's bottom line.

"Ta!" she said, thanking Cora Simpson, who had just bought two new novels for herself, as well as a YA book for her twelve-year-old daughter.

"Have a great day, Darce," Cora replied, her purchases loaded in the canvas tote bag Cora always shopped with.

"You as well," Darcie said.

She blew out a breath and checked her watch.

Goodness! That late already?

The whirlwind day had made her lose all track of time! It was after four p.m., already. She had a vague recollection of eating lunch hours earlier—a tuna with sweet corn sarnie she had brought with her from home. She had an even vaguer recollection of dashing across the street to The Bean for her coffee hours before lunch.

She remembered now that she had been disappointed that she couldn't spend any time chatting with Rylea. She'd had such a lovely time with her last night! She was hoping that perhaps they could become friends. And why not? She may not have the unfettered freedom Rylea did, due to her responsibilities to Cleo, but she could imagine occasionally meeting Rylea at the pub for some wine, or maybe even having lunch with her at one of the local restaurants. If she suggested such an outing, however, she needed to be sure to specify it was for lunch. One woman asking another out for lunch…no big deal. One gay woman asking another gay woman out for dinner…well, she didn't want Rylea getting the wrong end of the stick, by imagining she was coming onto her, and asking for a date. It would most likely make Rylea uncomfortable, and Darcie didn't want that.

No…friends with Rylea, she would be satisfied with that, and be happy for it. Friends who have lunch and maybe the occasional drink. That's all it would be, and Darcie knew she would be happy for even that much.

As it was after four o'clock, she set about tidying up in preparation for closing. The shop would be closed tomorrow, and so she could look forward to not caring about what time she went to bed tonight. Which meant, she could also look forward to having a movie marathon with some wine, and then have a bit of a lie-in tomorrow before Cleo was returned to her.

A thought occurred to her as she was straightening a shelf of military history. Perhaps she should take further advantage of her childless night and open her box of toys. She was thinking now that a couple of vibrator-induced orgasms on the sofa would certainly add a little more spice to an otherwise pedestrian Saturday night in.

The bell over her shop's door tinkled. Looking over her shoulder, Darcie smiled when she saw who it was.

"Hey," Rylea said, giving a small wave.

"Hiya," Darcie replied, picking up her feather duster. She frowned and checked her watch. "Closed already?" Today, she knew, The Bean closed at the same time as Shelf Life.

Rylea shook her head.

"Bridge is handling it," she answered.

"I tell you…sometimes I wish I had an assistant," Darcie said, flicking the feather duster over the table of fantasy novels she had recently set up. It was a genre she herself had no interest in, but they sold rather well. That teens bought them was no surprise, but she *was* surprised to learn that seventy-seven-year-old Mr. Rainford was also a big fan. While dusting, she noticed that someone had left a copy of *Jane Eyre* on this table. She picked it up and brought it back to the Classics table.

"Well, maybe Cleo will become your assistant one day," Rylea said. She picked up a children's picture book from another display table and started flipping through it.

Darcie scoffed.

"Unlikely!" she stated. "I'm sure as soon as Cleo is able, she'll catch the first flight to bloody NASA, and then the next flight after that to bloody Jupiter."

And Darcie knew she wouldn't stop her niece from doing so. Of course, she still felt there was very little chance that Cleo would actually become an astronaut. Not that Cleo didn't have the brains or the ability. Rather, it was because Cleo was only ten years old, and ten-year-olds change their minds about future careers as often as they change their socks. Today, Cleo wanted to be an astronaut. Three weeks from now, she'll probably announce she's going to be an archaeologist. Then Darcie could start worrying about her niece growing up to be bloody Indiana Jones and falling into pits full of snakes.

"So, listen…" Rylea began. "I actually stopped by now for a reason, because I didn't want to chance missing you after you left for the day."

"Book question?" Darcie asked jokingly. She paused her dusting to give Rylea her full attention. She then felt her breath hitch.

Rylea looked amazing today! Of course, Darcie thought the pretty, young coffee shop owner always looked…yummy, but today her yumminess was cranked up a notch. Somehow, during her dash across the street to get coffee earlier, Darcie hadn't noticed the dress Rylea had on. Perhaps the apron Rylea always wore had somehow disguised it.

But now, the apron was off, and Darcie was able to see how nicely the dress Rylea was wearing looked on her.

"Wow!" she couldn't help saying. "You look really nice today! Sorry I didn't notice earlier, but I was…frazzled."

Rylea smiled, and Darcie noticed her blushing.

"Thanks," Rylea said.

"I mean, you *always* look nice," Darcie hurriedly added, feeling like a git. "It's just that I usually see you in jeans and not a dress, and so I just meant…" She stopped her babbling, rolled her eyes, and laughed. "Whoo! See? This is what happens when you spend a year dating the same woman. You completely lose the ability to properly compliment someone else! They ought to mention that in personal development classes! Anyway, what can I help you with?"

Rylea was laughing, and Darcie loved how it brightened her face.

"Well, nothing, per se," Rylea said. "I was actually stopping by to find out if, now that you've had a relationship exorcism, you'd want to celebrate by meeting up for trivia night at the pub later. I'm part of a team, you see, and we can always use an extra mind. And since Cleo is still with her grands…"

Darcie blinked.

She hadn't been to trivia night since the Jeannette Era. They used to go frequently—not every week, but frequently enough for it to be one of their favourite pastimes in the village. She and Jeannette were both good at trivia. She, of course, could handle any questions involving literature, but she was also great at world history, geography and science. Jeannette, on the other hand, always seemed to have the right answer for anything involving politics, art, and contemporary music.

She did a quick emotional self-diagnosis. Was Rylea's suggestion of doing an activity she used to enjoy with the woman who had recently broken her heart triggering anything?

She *had* felt a little pang of sadness when Rylea first mentioned it if she was honest with herself. Very quickly, flashes of happier times had flitted through her mind's eye—including a little sex game she and Jeannette used to play related to their nights playing trivia. (Whoever had gotten the fewest answers correct had to eat out the other one for at least thirty minutes once they returned home.)

Those flashes of happier times had been quickly followed by sadness at what she had lost when Jeannette abandoned her, though, and like a wet blanket, it threatened to dampen the high spirits she was in today, enough to make her consider coming up with an excuse for not meeting Rylea at the pub.

But then…

"I would love to go!" she told Rylea. She had started feeling angry—angry at Jeannette for making her feel as if she couldn't enjoy certain activities anymore.

Rylea smiled.

"Fantastic!" she exclaimed. "To be frank, our team could use a little help. I'm guessing you'll be our literature maven."

"Nice word choice again!" Darcie complimented her, remembering that she paid her similar accolades just yesterday. Rylea's vocabulary was increasing her appeal, Darcie realised. She had always had a thing for well-read women who could casually drop words like "maven" into conversations.

"Thank you," Rylea replied. "I pretty much rock the vocabulary questions when they come up."

Darcie laughed.

"You know, it's funny," she began, "I was just thinking earlier how I'd like us to become friends, and do things like meet at the pub. I mean, I know we're kind of friends already, but that seems more like—"

"By default?" Rylea suggested, cutting in. "Because, you know, we live in such a small village."

Darcie smiled.

"Right," she said. "By default. Anyway, it would be nice for us to become friends for real, so, I'm glad you invited me to trivia."

Rylea blushed again, and Darcie noticed how it intensified her beauty somehow.

"I was thinking the same thing," Rylea said. "About the friends thing, I mean. I had fun with you last night and would love the chance to hang out with you some more."

Darcie felt her centre warming but ignored it as the foolishness of a woman who hasn't had sex in a while. Rylea was…unobtainable, and her invitation for pub trivia tonight was just that: an invitation to play pub trivia.

"Well, I should warn you," Darcie began, "being an auntie-slash-mum means I often can't just hang out."

"Oh, I know!" Rylea assured her. "And, by the way, I love that you say 'mum' when referring to Cleo."

Darcie shrugged.

"It's just so much easier than explaining the truth," she said. "Besides, as her guardian, I'm effectively her mum now anyway." Another thought came to her. "Oh, and then there's Beavers," Darcie added. Yet another demand on her time, albeit a pleasant one.

Rylea snickered.

"What?" Darcie asked.

"So, beavers keep you busy, do they?" Rylea inquired.

Darcie could tell that Rylea was trying to keep a straight face.

"Um…well, on Mondays, anyway," she said.

"Hm, I see," Rylea replied, thoughtfully. "So…I shouldn't ever ask to hang out with you on Mondays because you'll be playing with beavers all night, right?"

Darcie was starting to feel a little thick. Clearly, Rylea was having a bit of a laugh at her expense, but she couldn't figure—

Then the penny dropped.

"Oh my god, you are such a child!" She burst out laughing, approaching Rylea and playfully smacking her on the arm.

"Hey!" Rylea exclaimed. "I thought you'd be impressed at my clever double-entendre usage."

Darcie, blushing hotly, kept laughing.

"Yeah, well," she said, "unfortunately, *those* kinds of beavers don't keep me very busy during the week!"

She suddenly felt feverish because even though she didn't think it possible, she was blushing even more.

That sounded a little suggestive! But, hey, she started this!

If Rylea was bothered by her comment, she didn't show it. In fact, she was laughing—a very melodious laugh, which Darcie loved the sound of.

"Well," Rylea said, when she once more had control of herself, "perhaps as your new mate, I can help with that. That's what mates do for each other, after all."

Darcie decided she needed to masturbate this evening before leaving to meet Rylea at the pub. If becoming mates with the coffee shop owner meant this kind of banter, it would help if she had some release beforehand. Otherwise, there was a very good chance her mouth would get her in trouble later…

***

Completely nude, Darcie stood before her wardrobe, debating.

This isn't a date, so…

Jeans, trainers, and a nice-but-not-*too*-nice sweater ought to do the trick.

No, not trainers. Boots…

She nodded. The outfit she just envisioned would ensure she looked presentable, but not like she was *trying* too hard.

She reached out to take one of her favourite pairs of jeans from the pants hanger, when she hesitated.

Granted, not a date, but…

Would it kill her to maybe try at least a *little* harder than jeans, boots and a sweater? After all, how often does she go out nowadays to meet with friends? Sure, it was just trivia night at the Ladle & Spoon, but still…

Dress, tights, cute jacket, and the same boots she was considering earlier could work also.

Now she reached for a dark blue swing dress with a scoop neck, already mentally choosing the bra she would wear—one that would give her girls a little extra lift, to enhance the cleavage shown.

No, no, no…

She dropped her arm to her side and huffed a breath in frustration.

What was she thinking?

Okay, fine, it's been a while since she's been out with friends, especially a new friend, like Rylea, but she could tell she was already overthinking this. Even more alarming, she could tell that this whole *I-haven't-been-out-in-a-while* thing was bollocks. *That* wasn't the reason she wanted to try a little harder with her choice of outfit tonight.

Rylea was.

Which meant that she wanted to impress Rylea, which meant that she was hoping that somehow, Rylea would begin looking at her as more than just the bookshop owner with the cute kid who seemingly knew everything there was to know about the cosmos.

Sighing, she reached for those jeans again.

In twenty minutes, she was dressed and made up. In the end—examining herself in the full length mirror—she decided that she still looked cute. The burgundy sweater she had chosen complemented her skin tone, her legs looked great in the skinny jeans, and her chosen eye make-up picked up the colour of the sweater a bit.

As a sort of penance for wanting to impress Rylea earlier, under her sweater was a sports bra—one which imprisoned her breasts in material that was designed more for keeping them under control rather than showing them off. Thus, once the sweater was on, it looked as if she had actually lost a cup size.

She was ready to go and was heading out of the bedroom when…

"Bugger!" she exclaimed, stopping in her tracks.

She had forgotten to masturbate!

It wasn't that she was ragingly horny and desperately in need of an orgasm, but she felt that if she did come, she'd be less likely to play along with Rylea should she decide to start making double-entendres about beavers again.

She checked her watch. Still plenty of time to walk to the Ladle & Spoon, even if she took a few minutes for some DIY, so to speak. But then she looked down at her outfit, and rolled her eyes, a feeling of apathy coming over her.

Ugh!

The idea of having to unbuckle her belt, then unsnap and unzip her jeans, then yank them down far enough to get her fingers good and in there, just seemed like so much work! And if, for some reason, the floodgates *really* opened—as her body was wont to do—then she'd have to properly clean up, et cetera, et cetera, et cetera…

"It can wait until I get home," she said aloud, leaving the bedroom and heading downstairs.

Chapter 8

"What's wrong with your leg, dear?" Mrs. Kelly asked Rylea.

Rylea looked down at her leg. She was currently bouncing the right one up and down on the ball of her foot.

She gave the old woman a sheepish grin.

"Nothing, Mrs. Kelly," she said, stopping the bouncing. "Just excited for the game to start, I suppose."

Total bollocks, of course, and she knew it. She was anxious for Darcie to arrive.

If she arrives…

Admittedly, Rylea *was* worried that her idiotic jokes about beavers earlier might have turned Darcie off to the notion of coming to hang out with her tonight—or ever. Especially since she knew— by the kind of societal osmosis which comes from living in a village such as Tremont—that volunteering for the Beaver Scouts was important to Darcie, and that she was fantastic at it.

And what an admirable thing to do!

Rylea had been in Beavers also when she was a little kid, and though she hadn't stayed with scouting, she could still remember having fun during the lodge meetings, with all the games and activities. And it was where she and Tamsin had started their lifelong friendship.

"I hope your friend won't be late!" Mr. Trelawny muttered. The old man was a stickler for punctuality, Rylea knew.

"I'm sure she'll be here soon, Mr. Trelawny," Rylea answered.

"And you're certain she's got the goods?" Mr. Trelawny then asked, tapping the side of his head.

Rylea sighed.

"Yes, Mr. Trelawny," she told him. "It's Darcie from Shelf Life! You know her! She's very smart."

Under the bushiest eyebrows God had ever put on a human, Mr. Trelawny narrowed his eyes.

"I hope you're right," he muttered. "Losing last week to Pete Fisher's team was infuriating, and *not* something I'd like to repeat."

Rylea nodded. Mr. Trelawny and Mr. Fisher had an age-old rivalry that stretched all the way back to when they were teens, apparently.

"Ignore him, he's being silly," Mrs. Trelawny said to Rylea. She then turned to her husband. "Be quiet! Darcie Spencer has more brains in her little finger than you have in that big empty head of yours."

Mr. Trelawny, scowling at his wife, made a gesture like he wished she would just blow away.

Oh thank god!

Rylea had just spotted Darcie walking into the pub. She was relieved not only because apparently the beaver jokes hadn't put her off, but because now she'd have someone to share the comical agony of dealing with these pensioners. Rylea thought they were all sweet, but at times it felt like she was babysitting ornery toddlers.

"Darce!" she called out, rising and waving.

Darcie made her way to their table, which was situated right near the fireplace. Of course, it being May, the fireplace wasn't lit, but this table was considered prime real estate, and Mr. Trelawny always made sure to arrive early enough to claim it, making sure it never fell into the hands of Pete Fisher. As Darcie walked, Rylea couldn't help admiring her form. Those jeans were sexy, the sweater was a fabulous colour on her, and those boots were super cute!

"Hey, everyone!" Darcie greeted them all, taking the empty seat next to Rylea. "I'm not late, am I?"

Mr. Trelawny made a point of checking his watch.

"No," he muttered, seeming as if he hated to admit that.

"Oh, good," Darcie said, smiling at Rylea, but widening her eyes slightly, Rylea understanding that she too was well aware of Mr. Trelawny's penchant for punctuality. "It's so lovely to see you all," she then said to the others.

The great thing about a small village, Rylea considered now, was that they didn't have to bother with introductions, and thanks to Darcie's natural charm, soon there was an easy conversation happening at their table.

"So, what's everyone drinking, then?" Darcie asked after a few minutes. "I'll get the next round."

"Don't get so tipsy that you can't think!" Mr. Trelawny warned.

"For heaven's sake!" his wife exclaimed. "Ignore him, dear," she said to Darcie.

Rylea leaned close to Darcie, and immediately wanted to sniff along her neck. The woman just smelled *so* good.

"See what I have to put up with each week?" she whispered.

***

Rylea knew this one.

The next question, displayed on the nearest of the four TV screens in the pub, was, "In China, if you order 'white tea,' what do you get?" Underneath the question, were the four multiple choice options. But Rylea knew it was…

"C," she told Mr. Trelawny, who was in charge of writing the team's answers down on the slip of paper the quiz master would collect. She was careful to keep her voice down so that nearby rival teams would not hear her.

Mr. Trelawny looked at the TV screen, frowning.

"Boiled water?" he whispered to Rylea incredulously. "Are you sure?"

"Keep your voice down, you old fool!" Mrs. Trelawny chided, smacking her husband's arm.

"Why?" Mr. Trelawny shot back. "I've been asking you to bloody well shut up for the past forty-five years and you've never done it!" He turned back to Rylea. "Think, girl, are you sure?"

"Positive," Rylea stated.

"She's right," Darcie added. "I read it in a book somewhere."

"That's the damned silliest thing I've ever heard!" Mr. Trelawny said. But he wrote down the letter C, folded the slip of paper and held it aloft so the quiz master could come collect it.

Rylea smiled. So far, their team—nicknamed "The Geezers and the Girl"—were doing rather well. According to the most recent scoring check, they were in the lead, followed closely by Pete Fisher's team, The Fisher Kings.

Darcie was proving to be an asset, and Rylea could tell that even Mr. Trelawny was respecting her grasp of arcane facts. She wondered if perhaps the team would be renamed to "The Geezers and the Girls." She hoped so because she hoped Darcie would continue coming out to play with them. She could even bring Cleo.

Trivia started early enough in the night, and other parents brought their children. Rylea imagined that Cleo could even participate should any astronomy questions come up.

There was a lull in activity as the quiz master made the rounds, collecting answers.

"I am having such a great time," Darcie told Rylea. "I'd forgotten how much fun this is. Thank you for inviting me."

Rylea smiled.

"Part of the relationship exorcism package," she said. "Consider it a follow-up service. Us exorcists must make sure that recently-exorcised clients get out and do things."

Darcie took a sip of her white wine.

"What else is included in the package, I wonder?" she asked.

Rylea's heart rate picked up. Was Darcie actually…flirting with her?

"I just mean," Darcie went on, "is there any more stabbing of things involved?"

So…no to the flirting…

Yet, Darcie was blushing.

"I'm beginning to worry about you, Darce," Rylea chuckled. "The stabbing seems to fascinate you a little too much."

"Who's stabbing whom?" Mrs. Kelly asked.

"No one, Mrs. Kelly," Darcie said with a laugh.

In a few minutes, the quiz master announced the correct answer to the current question. The Geezer and the Girls (Rylea decided to rename the team now) exulted; however, judging from the groans heard from other teams, most of them had gotten it wrong.

Then, the quiz master stated that the next question was going to be a *Screenshots* one.

The Geezers and the Girls groaned.

Screenshots was when a series of still images were shown on the TV screens, all of them taken from the same film, and each of them only displaying for a few seconds. The challenge was to name the movie the stills were from.

The problem was the images were sadistically chosen to be very ambiguous. Making it even more difficult, they never, ever showed any of the stars of the film, nor did they show any easily recognizable items or landmarks that would give the answer away.

Last week, for example, Rylea had felt a complete fool when it turned out the answer to *Screenshots* was *Imagine Me & You,* a lesbian-themed film she had seen so many times, she had lost count. But the still images shown were so vague, the best Rylea had been able to come up with was that whatever film it was had been shot in the UK.

"Bollocks!" she exclaimed.

"Oh, I remember this category," Darcie said. "I'm terrible at it. Though once I was able to identify *Big*…you know, the Tom Hanks film?"

"Courage, ladies," Mr. Trelawny said, eyeing all the women at the table. "Thanks to Rylea, we are still in the lead, so if we miss this one, we should still be in good form."

"Ooh, so you're our star tonight, huh?" Darcie teased, nudging Rylea, making her feel a warmth spread through her, which initiated at the point of contact. During the course of the night, their chairs had gotten closer together, she noticed. So far, they had used the proximity to whisper snide comments to one another about their teammates. The harmless little comments younger people will make about older folks.

"Oh, they're starting!" Mrs. Trelawny said.

All eyes were turned towards the television closest to them.

As the slideshow of images played, Rylea frowned in concentration. There was something familiar about what she was seeing but bugger it all if the name of the film was coming to her.

Is that a vineyard? Looks like a vineyard...

Another image showed what looked like a shrub or a bush on fire. At night-time, from what Rylea could gather.

Bugger! I've seen this!

When all five stills had been shown, the slideshow repeated itself, yet still nothing but a vague sense of familiarity came to Rylea. Not, unfortunately, the film's title.

She looked at Darcie, and her friend gave her a look which said that she was equally stymied.

Then…

Mrs. Trelawny tapped the table, her eyes bright.

"*A Walk in the Clouds!*" she whispered, gesturing to her husband to write that down. "*A Walk in the Clouds!*"

Mrs. Kelly nodded.

"You're right!" she confirmed, also in a whisper.

Now Rylea made the connection also. She remembered now: She had watched that film several months ago, on Netflix. It had Keanu Reeves in it—one of her favourite actors. She also remembered crushing on the lead actress in the film, whose name she couldn't remember.

"Good job, Mrs. Trelawny," she said.

"Thank you, dear," the older woman said.

"Don't believe I've seen that one," Darcie said to the group at large.

"It's actually kind of cute," Rylea told her. It wasn't the greatest film, by any means, but she had enjoyed it and found it to be a rather sweet romance. She sat there now, remembering the story, about a young salesman who meets a woman who is going home to her family's vineyard, and then somehow…

Rylea looked at Darcie.

Darcie, noticing, turned her head, smiling at Rylea.

"Wow," she began, "you look like you've just figured out Fermat's theorem."

Rylea blinked.

"Fermat's what?"

Darcie laughed.

"Never mind," she said. "I just meant that you look like you've solved a major problem."

"I have an idea!" Rylea said.

Her clit pulsed when Darcie cocked an eyebrow, and she wondered if Darcie's mind had automatically gone *there*.

"An idea about…?" Darcie prompted, and Rylea couldn't help but notice that Darcie was looking at her lips.

But she suddenly once more, became aware of the fact that they weren't alone.

"When's intermission?" she asked her teammates.

"After the next question," Mr. Trelawny answered.

Returning her eyes to Darcie, she said, "I'll tell you at intermission."

That occurred about ten minutes later, after a question about baseball: Which baseball team in America has won the most titles?

The answer was the New York Yankees, which Darcie supplied easily.

When the quiz master then called intermission, Rylea said, "Excuse us, please," to her regular teammates, took Darcie's hand and stood up.

"Don't go far!" Mr. Trelawny chided. "It's only fifteen minutes, you know!"

"We won't, Mr. Trelawny!" Rylea assured him, already walking away from the table, still holding Darcie's hand.

She led Darcie to a quiet corner of the pub.

"What's that thing they always say about revenge?" Rylea asked, releasing Darcie's hand.

"That it's a dish best served cold?" Darcie guessed.

"No, the other thing," Rylea prodded.

"Um…that before seeking it, dig two graves?"

Rylea rolled her eyes.

"Gah!" she exclaimed. "This is what I get for asking a bookshop owner that question! No…they say that the best revenge is a life well-lived."

"I was getting to that one!" Darcie insisted. "George Herbert, sixteenth century. Anyway, what's that got to do with…well, anything?"

"Jeannette's wedding!" Rylea said.

Darcie cocked an eyebrow.

"I love how you say that as if it should explain everything, but it truly doesn't," she pointed out, smirking.

Rylea had to admit her friend was right. She was being too cryptic, which she was prone to do when she had an idea she was excited about.

She took a deep breath.

"What if," she began slowly, "you *do* go to the cow's wedding, but you do so with a date? That way, you can show her that you've moved on. I mean, you don't want her getting married thinking that she's left you broken-hearted and dejected, right? But if you show up with a *girlfriend*…" and here, Rylea made air quotes with her fingers, "…suddenly, you've shown her that you're living an even better life *without* her!"

Darcie stared at her, not saying anything. Rylea wondered if it was a stupid idea, after all. Darcie may not be *that* much older than herself, but she was nonetheless a mature woman with a lot of responsibilities. In other words, not the type of person to play silly games like what she was suggesting.

Rylea chuckled, feeling like a dumb teenager.

"You know what, forget it," she said. "Stupid idea."

But then Darcie said, "Hang on…"

And suddenly, Rylea felt her inner walls fluttering as Darcie's face took on a look of devilish enjoyment as ideas were clearly forming in her mind. It added another layer of sexiness to Darcie's pretty features and made Rylea's own mind immediately start imagining herself tied to Darcie's bed, with a nude Darcie standing nearby, obviously considering where exactly to begin having fun.

No…not completely nude. With high heels on!

She wanted to groan aloud at the perfection of *that* image.

Chapter 9

It was brilliant!

Darcie just *knew* that when Jeannette sent her the invitation to her wedding, she was predicting Darcie would show up solo, or at most, with Cleo. That was *so* Jeannette! And it made sense, Darcie had to concede. After all, during their relationship, Darcie had been the "nice" one. The girl from the tiny Cornish village. The pleasant and friendly bookshop owner. The super nice Beavers volunteer whom the kids called Buttercup.

Of the two of them, it was Jeannette who was always more willing to get into confrontations with anybody, and who was simply the more...*American*...of the two: bold, willing to state what was truly on her mind, not afraid of hurting someone's feelings, if feelings needed to be hurt.

Darcie could imagine the scene with Katelynn, when Jeannette announced she was going to send an invitation to her ex:

KATELYNN: You're not going to get jealous if she shows up with anybody, are you?

JEANNETTE (laughing): Darce? *If* she comes, she'll be by herself. She's British.

"Aargh!" Darcie growled.

"Um, are you okay?" Rylea asked.

"Yes," Darcie said. "Sorry. I was just imagining Jeannette thinking that I would *never* dare to come to her wedding with somebody!"

"Exactly my point!" Rylea exclaimed. "This is why I suggested it! It will show the cow that you've moved on!"

"How did you come up with this idea?" Darcie wanted to know.

"That film, *A Walk in the Clouds*," Rylea answered. "I mean, it's not about a fake wedding date, but Keanu Reeves pretends to be married to...whoever the actress is in it. When I remembered that, the idea just kind of popped into my head that we can do the same thing for you, but as a fake wedding date."

"I love it!" Darcie said. "So, since you said *we*..."

"I would totally be your fake date!" Rylea said. "It would be *so* much fun!"

Darcie felt as if a long dormant evil side of herself was waking up.

Having Rylea be her fake date actually made the scheme even more brilliant! The main reason for that was because Jeannette *hated* being in her thirties! She was one of those women for whom having a three as the leading number of her age was a tragedy on par with some of the great maritime disasters in history. And she was only thirty-three now! Darcie used to tease her that she didn't want to be around when Jeannette turned forty, and deal with all *that* angst. She used to then add that when Jeannette turned *fifty*, she'd go on holiday to Japan and let Jeannette wallow in her misery alone here in Cornwall.

Well, as it turned out, Darcie mused now, she *wouldn't* be around for Jeannette's fortieth or fiftieth. Those two milestone birthdays—and the freakouts Jeannette was bound to have—were now Miss Katelynn Jefferson's problem. The point was, arriving at the wedding with a *younger* woman on her arm would really make Jeannette stop and take notice. Not only that, but it was also bound to haunt her sleep for quite a while as well.

"God, she will *hate* that I am there with you!" she exclaimed.

Rylea laughed.

"Any particular reason why?" she asked.

"Two, actually," Darcie began. "One, she knows you, and knows how young you are! Two, you're just so incredibly beautiful." She held up her right hand, with the thumb extended. "So, young…" She then extended her forefinger. "…and beautiful."

Rylea laughed.

"Well, Jeannette is rather beautiful herself, if I recall," she pointed out.

"Yes," Darcie said, grabbing hold of both of Rylea's arms, "but she is *thirty-three!* You are, what, twenty-four?"

Rylea nodded.

Darcie cackled.

"Oh my god, this is just too awesome!"

"So…good idea?" Rylea asked, teasingly.

"Better than the fucking lightbulb," Darcie replied. "By the way, I hope you don't mind me using you for, you know, your youth and your beauty."

Rylea spread her arms, displaying her body. Darcie couldn't help licking her lips. Rylea was outfitted simply enough, in an ensemble very similar to her own: skinny jeans and a sweater. But Rylea was…well, Rylea, and thus very fetching.

"My youth and beauty are at your disposal, Darce," Rylea said.

Darcie *wanted* to believe Rylea was flirting with her but knew better. Nonetheless…

"Promises, promises," she said, making sure to add enough snark in her voice to indicate that she was joking. Then, to change the subject, she quickly asked, "So, how do we go about doing this?"

Rylea shrugged.

"Well," she began, "we need to—Oh, bugger!"

"What?" Darcie asked. "What's wrong?"

"We burned the bloody invitation!" Rylea exclaimed. "We don't know when or where the wedding is!"

Newquay Royal Arms. A week from today. 11:30 a.m. start time.

Darcie hated that her eyes had seared that information into her brain when she had first seen the invitation, but they had. In any case, it turns out it was for the best.

"I know all the details," she assured Rylea. She looked at her watch. "Bugger! Our fifteen minutes are just about up! The last thing I need is Mr. Trelawny jumping down our throats. Let's continue this after the game!"

Rylea huffed.

"You know, if I had known you were so bossy, I would have *never* agreed to start dating you!"

Darcie had to put off heading back to their table because she was laughing so hard.

***

The Geezers and the Girls ended up winning tonight's trivia contest. The prize, as always, was a coupon for a free dessert for everyone on the winning team. When he had been handed his, Mr.

Trelawny stood and waved it over his head in the direction of Pete Fisher's team, sneering the entire time, until his wife told him to stop acting like a child.

The Trelawnys and Mrs. Kelly left then, with Mr. Trelawny telling Darcie that she was welcome to join them anytime, and to watch out for Pete Fisher, who might try to convince her to join *his* team.

"Would you like another glass of wine?" Darcie asked Rylea after saying goodbye to their teammates. They had decided to stay at the pub to talk about what was now referred to as "The Plan."

"Love one," Rylea said.

Darcie managed to catch the attention of Sheila, the Ladle & Spoon's waitress, telling her "Same again, please, ta!" when she came to their table.

"So," Darcie began, "you're sure you don't have anywhere to be?"

Rylea laughed.

"Sadly, no," she said. "Am I pathetic for someone my age?"

"Yes," Darcie stated, keeping her face straight. She was joking, but she was also kind of not joking.

A woman's twenties were meant to be for backpacking and shagging her way through Europe, like she had done. Then, coming home and then shagging her way through Cornwall. Well, until Cleo showed up.

"You should be shagging your way through Cornwall!" she decided to tell Rylea.

Her friend shrugged.

"Not my style," she replied. "Too messy. I mean, you're a lesbian…have you not noticed that women are crazy?"

Darcie pretended to think.

"Now that you mention it, I seem to recall that being an issue," she said. "Beats the alternative, though."

"Cheers to that," Rylea replied. They both lifted their wine glasses, which still had a few sips left in them, and touched them together. "In any case," Rylea went on, "I'm happy running my business and living a drama-free life. One day, I'll find a girlfriend and, who knows, maybe she'll end up becoming my wife. But until then, I'll stay away from shagging my way through Cornwall, or any part of England. Better chance of preserving my sanity that way."

Sheila arrived then with the two new glasses of wine, dropped them off and departed.

"Which reminds me," Darcie began. "We need to work out the details of The Plan. Certainly before you end up getting a real girlfriend."

Rylea, after taking a sip of her wine, nodded.

"To start with," she said, "we need our origin story."

Darcie, nodding, picked up her phone and opened the Notes app.

"Origin story," she repeated, typing that phrase into her phone.

"What are you doing?" Rylea asked.

"Making our to-do list," Darcie answered.

"You're making a list?"

Darcie looked at her.

"I live with and am responsible for a ten-year-old child," she said. "Of course I'm making a list. Anyway, aren't origin stories for, like, superheroes? I've had to watch all those comic book films lately because of Cleo."

"Well, yeah," Rylea replied, "but it equally applies to lesbian relationships too."

"So, what's our origin story?" Darcie asked, considering the matter. "Did I just walk into The Bean one day and you suddenly realised how incredibly gorgeous I am?"

Rylea shook her head.

"No, no," she began, "that can't be it."

Darcie gasped.

"I beg your pardon!" she exclaimed. "And why couldn't that be it?"

Rylea, seeming to realise her faux pas and put a placating hand on Darcie's.

"I didn't mean it like that," she said. "I just meant that it's too…basic. If we're doing this, let's do it with style!"

"You mean, come up with an epic tale," Darcie suggested, and then typed *Epic* into her notes. "Like the way Superman was born on Krypton but then sent off to Earth before his home planet exploded."

Rylea stared at her.

"Like I said," Darcie told her. "Every. Bloody. Film."

Rylea, laughing, said, "Well, yeah, we need an epic origin story, but obviously one that doesn't include an exploding planet."

"Something funny," Darcie added, musing.

"But cute," Rylea said. "We want that 'Aww' factor."

"Oh, that's going to kill her!" Darcie said, smiling, adding *Aww factor* to her list.

Her and Jeannette's origin story didn't have any *Aww* factor. They had met when Jeannette had come into Shelf Life one day, soon after buying her cottage on Priory Lane. They had instant chemistry, sure, but there was nothing epic about the story. After Jeannette chatted her up a bit, she had said, "Fancy a drink one night?", and that was it. Origin story.

"What else?" she asked. For some reason, she felt like trusting Rylea with making sure they ticked all the boxes when it came to planning this charade. Maybe because Rylea was still so young, and this whole fake date thing seemed like a young woman's purview.

Rylea bit her bottom lip. Darcie quickly looked away from the sight. It was ridiculous, really…she had seen countless women do that exact same thing, but when Rylea did it, it seemed as if it was sexier somehow.

Rylea suddenly snapped her fingers.

"Wardrobe!" she exclaimed. "What do you want me to wear?"

Darcie shrugged.

"I'm sure you have plenty of nice dresses," she said.

But Rylea gave her a stern look.

"Darce," she began, "you need to have a killer instinct about this. In other words, stop being British. Yes, I have plenty of nice dresses, but is *nice* what we're really going for here?"

"Sorry. As opposed to…?" Darcie prodded.

Rylea sighed.

They hadn't moved seats after the Trelawnys and Mrs. Kelly left, so they were still sitting next to each other. Now, Rylea leaned a little closer to Darcie.

"I have plenty of outfits that are just perfect for a respectable occasion such as a wedding," she said. "*Or*…I have a rare handful of dresses that are perfect for respectable occasions, but which will also make every living, breathing Christian soul within a ten-mile radius want me."

Darcie licked her lips. Inside her bra, her nipples hardened.

"Yes, well," she began, "that's the option I want."

Rylea was right, after all. Why show up with a woman who just looks *nice*, when she could show up with a woman who looks…well, way more than nice. She added *Decide wardrobe* to the new list on her phone.

"Tell you what," Rylea began, "I'll send you options later tonight via text. Sort of a…selfie fashion show. Then, you can tell me which outfit you like best."

Darcie smiled.

"Thank you," she said. "I'm sorry to make you go to so much work, though."

Rylea waved that off.

"Are you kidding, Darce?" she asked. "I am excited about this little revenge project of ours and I am all in! Besides, as your official relationship exorcist—one of them, anyway—I consider it my duty to ensure that your needs are met."

Darcie crossed her legs.

She blamed the combination of the wine and the fact that she had neglected to masturbate before coming to the pub tonight for making her mind go directly where it needn't bother going. But as her nipples tightened even more, and her clit began quivering, she started thinking of several *needs* she wanted Rylea to meet.

Chapter 10

At home following her night out at the Ladle & Spoon, Rylea went upstairs and quickly changed out of her clothes and into her pyjamas. It had gotten much chillier by the time she and Darcie had left the pub, and now, pulling on a favourite pair of fuzzy socks, she heard the patter of rain on her roof.

Walking back downstairs, she smiled. She'd had a really good time with Darcie tonight, and she was glad she had come up with that scheme to be her friend's fake date to Jeannette's wedding. Okay, it was a bit of a childish thing to do, but the American cow deserved it. Besides, Darcie apparently thought it was one of the best ideas ever!

"That and the light bulb," Rylea said to herself as she reached the bottom of the stairs.

In her kitchen, she filled her kettle, switched it on and put a bag of Twinings in her favourite mug. Then she stood with her arms crossed, trying to determine what to do with the rest of her night, other than drink tea.

"Read, or Netflix?" she asked the empty kitchen. "Or Netflix *and then* read?"

She rolled her eyes and sighed.

Darcie was right. How come a young and attractive woman such as herself had nothing better to do on a Saturday night than decide between reading about women falling in love on her Kindle, or watching them fall in love on the telly?

She thought of Jemma and her offer to set her up with that mate of hers from uni…

Whose name is…?

"Lauren!" she exclaimed, glad she had dredged it up from her memory.

Maybe she'd give Jemma the go-ahead to make that happen.

Well, *after* her fake date a week from today. Otherwise, it would oddly feel like cheating on Darcie if she went on a *real* date with Lauren.

Or should that be the other way around? It would feel like cheating on Lauren if she went on a *fake* date with Darcie?

She shrugged, whichever way around it was meant to be, it was best to wait until after the wedding to do anything with Lauren, even a phone call.

The water boiled quickly and soon after she had her tea steeping, casting her eyes quickly at the kitchen clock and noting the time. Her mother had taught her that tea should steep for five minutes. Not four minutes; not four minutes and fifty-five seconds; not five minutes and two seconds.

Five minutes.

Of course, Mrs. Wallingford two doors down insisted tea be steeped for only three minutes; and Mr. Trelawny was adamant that six minutes was the right number. But Rylea had been taught five minutes, and she didn't need her mother's ghost haunting the kitchen, chastising her.

When the five minutes were up, Rylea took her tea into the living room and turned on the telly. She had just made herself comfortable on the sofa when she sat upright again.

"Bugger!" she exclaimed.

She was meant to send Darcie photos of herself wearing possible outfits for their date next Saturday.

Fake date.

Right, fake date; that's what she meant.

She looked towards the staircase, wondering if she should go back up and start the fashion show.

Instead, she picked up her phone.

Can the fashion show I promised you wait until tomorrow? LOL!

Once a woman was in pyjamas and fuzzy socks, after all, it was kind of hard to get her out of them.

Though, she considered now, Darcie wouldn't need to do much coaxing to convince her to shed the pjs and socks. And the underwear. And any lingering inhibitions.

Her phone pinged.

Pmsl, of course not! (Gives me something to look forward to tomorrow!)

Rylea smiled at Darcie's text. She was tempted to write back, maybe get a text conversation going that would last well into the night. But in the end, she decided against it. Darcie probably wanted to unwind and enjoy the rest of the night in peace. After all, this was her last night without Cleo. Darcie couldn't be blamed if she wanted to spend it on her sofa, drinking wine and watching rated 15 films until she fell asleep.

"I'll leave her be," Rylea said, placing the phone back on the coffee table.

***

Rylea groaned when her brain sufficiently surfaced from the depths of sleep enough to make her aware of what was going on.

The fake date scheme was a good one, sure, but it had wreaked havoc on her dreams last night! Her subconscious had certainly come up with rather erotic scenarios involving she and Darcie becoming *a lot* closer during next week's wedding. So much so, that it had gotten to the point that now between her legs she was so soaked she wondered if she had actually come during the night.

Whimpering at how good the slickness in her knickers felt, she rolled over onto her belly, slipping her hand into her pyjama pants and underwear.

She gasped at feeling her swollen clit, and how ready it was for the contact with her finger.

"Oh shit…" she murmured.

Pressing her shoulders into the mattress and raising her hips a bit, she started rubbing the button rapidly but then stopped, unsatisfied.

The clothes she still had on were not helping, and so she rolled over and quickly shucked the pyjamas and the underwear off in one go, gasping again when the slight chill of the bedroom air caressed her wetness, making goosebumps rise on her thighs.

Back on her belly, with her arse slightly raised.

Much better.

Not only could her hand move more freely, but she could imagine Darcie behind her, going at her with a strap-on. Hard. So hard because Darcie would know that Rylea liked being pounded.

"Pull my hair!" she grunted, and in her mind, Darcie did just that.

The pressure beneath her mound increased and continued increasing.

She opened her mouth, little choked mewls escaping from her throat before…

"*OhhhhhhhhhhhhhFuuuuuuuuck!*" she called out with the explosion, and her pussy became awash in pleasure. She felt her opening contracting rapidly, rivulets of her come being squeezed out all the while.

When the climax reached its crescendo and her vagina began its downward slide back to normalcy, she dropped her hips and lay flat on the bed.

"Bloody hell," she exhaled between laboured breaths. She couldn't remember many of the details of her dreams last night, but whatever they were, they had made her centre primed for release because that had been a *good* orgasm.

She gave herself a few minutes to enjoy how the pleasure dissipated throughout her form before finally getting up and off the mattress.

After showering, she put on her plush bathrobe and then stood in front of her wardrobe.

Hands on her hips, she looked at the section where she hung her posh dresses.

"Well," she began, letting her robe fall to the floor, "no time like the present."

Chapter 11

On Sunday morning, as she was having a simple breakfast of yoghurt and granola, Darcie's phone rang.

"Hey, mum," she greeted Irene.

"I'm acting as an emissary on behalf of Cleo," Irene began.

Darcie rolled her eyes.

"Uh-oh," she said.

"Cleo would like to know if she can stay here another night and play with Chester Two some more?"

"Really, mum?" Darcie said. "Chester Two? You couldn't come up with a more original name?"

"Merely a placeholder until we come up with something else," Irene replied.

"Well, I've always thought Winston was a fitting name for an English bulldog," Darcie told her.

Obvious, but fitting.

"Hm," Irene hummed thoughtfully. "But you don't think it might be too political?"

"Political?" Darcie asked, barking a short laugh. "Mum, the man's been dead for something like three-hundred years! Who cares now what his politics were?"

"Excuse me!" Irene exclaimed. "I was seven-years-old when Churchill died, and I assure you I'm not anywhere near the three-century mark!"

Darcie made a mental note that on her mum's next birthday, she'd decorate the cake with "Happy 300th!"

"Merely using humour for effect, mum," she said. "But I do think Winston is the winning name."

"I'll discuss it with your father," Irene told her. "Anyway, back to the question of Cleo…"

Darcie shrugged, though her mother couldn't see it. She had tried to get Irene onboard with FaceTime once her parents had joined the twenty-first century and gotten iPhones, but Irene had said that if she wanted to see someone while she was talking to them, she would just pop 'round for a visit.

Darcie didn't mind if Cleo stayed another night, although it meant she'd have to bring Cleo's school stuff over to her parents' place later.

"Fine by me," she told Irene. "If it's okay with you and Dad."

Her mother assured her it would be a delight, and Darcie promised to bring the school items and more of Cleo's clothes by later today.

When the call ended, she set about trying to figure out what to do with the rest of her unexpectedly free day. She decided that she would run the errand to her parents' now, and then go for a run. Running would help her come up with other plans for her Sunday now that Cleo was sorted with her parents.

Upstairs, she had just stripped out of her pyjamas and the underwear she had slept in when her phone pinged. Figuring it was her mum again, texting her the year of Churchill's death and pointing out that it *wasn't* three-hundred years ago, she lifted the phone off the dressing table where she had laid it and saw that it was a text from Rylea. Opening it, she gasped and then sat down completely nude on the edge of her bed.

Let the fashion show begin! read the message.

Accompanying that was a selfie of Rylea in a cocktail dress. *Wow!*

Darcie stared at the photo. Even on a hanger the dress would be hot. But on Rylea, it was scorching! And yet…it was still appropriate for a wedding. A one-shoulder, glittering knee-length affair in gold, it hugged Rylea's form perfectly. She must have set her phone on a stand of some kind, or propped it against something, and then set the timer, because the photo showed all of Rylea, posing like a model in the dress. She had even taken the trouble to put on the high heels that she would pair the dress with—classy, open-toed black sandals.

Darcie swallowed.

Her phone pinged again and suddenly another photo of Rylea appeared, wearing a different dress.

Red, kind of retro, with a neckline that showed her cleavage. It was a pencil dress, and it flattered her hips amazingly well. This time, Rylea had chosen simple black pumps to go with it. Overall, it was sexy, eye-catching and still fit for a wedding.

Biting her bottom lip, she was admiring how lovely Rylea's calves were when—*ping!*—another photo arrived.

Darcie couldn't help but think of the word she heard her father say often…

Blimey!

Dress #3 was a blue, sleeveless lace cocktail number with lace trim on the hem of the skirt. Cut a little higher than the previous two, Darcie crossed her legs at seeing the lower portions of Rylea's thighs, and she tried to imagine how smooth that skin would feel under her tongue. This led her to thoughts of sitting in a tub with Rylea and shaving her legs for her. Very slowly, very methodically, making sure she did a thorough job so that after the bath, when Rylea's legs were wrapped around her, she would feel nothing but buttery smoothness as she—

She closed her eyes and shook her head briskly. She forced herself to breathe deeply for a count of five.

So not appropriate!

She went back to examining the photos.

What amazed Darcie was how confidently Rylea posed in all three them—as if she were a woman in fashion adverts. She herself *hated* taking selfies, and thought she looked goofy in them, but then realised that was probably because most of her selfies were taken with Cleo, and when taking such pics with a ten-year-old, it was almost a biblical requisite to make silly faces.

She continued staring at Rylea's photos.

She didn't know about every living, breathing Christian soul within a ten-mile radius, but she did know that *she* wanted Rylea.

Suddenly, she became aware of her nudity, and how she wished she could share with Rylea the fact that she was enjoying this "fashion show" without wearing a stitch of clothing herself. In an almost trance-like state, she circled the nipple of her right breast with her left hand, the nipple tingling and tightening in reaction to her touch. She snapped out of it when she felt her core warming up, making her cross her legs the other way.

I love them all! she typed.

She then bit her lip, considering how to say this next bit without coming off too flirty. *You look amazing in all of them! Like…wow!*

She sent the message before she could overthink it. Besides, it was only a compliment, a simple woman-to-woman compliment.

Thanks! Do you have a winner picked out?

Darcie didn't have to even think on that. All the dresses were fabulous, but the one that would drive a dagger into Jeannette's psyche was the first one…the gold, glittery, one-shoulder number. It was not only appropriate for the occasion, but it was youthful—the dress of a confident twenty-something woman who knew she'd look good in almost anything.

The first one, please.

Rylea's reply came back quickly.

Your wish…my command. LOL! I'll save the others for the next woman you want us to crush together. LOL!

Darcie laughed. In her mind, she started running through the list of all her exes, going all the way back to when she was sixteen, wanting to "fake date" each and every one of them, provided Rylea was the fake date.

***

"You're *going* to the wedding?" Irene asked.

Darcie was at her parents' house, having dropped off Cleo's things. After spending some time with Cleo playing with the new puppy—now officially named Winston, though Cleo insisted on calling him Winnie—Darcie was with her mother out in the garden. She had just explained about Jeannette's wedding, asking if Cleo would be alright to stay with them again next weekend.

"I am," she answered her mother. "Jeannette invited me."

Irene scoffed.

"Well, that's hardly reason enough to go!" she exclaimed. "If Mussolini invited me around for pizza, I'd tell him to bugger off!"

"Right, well, I'm fairly certain I'd tell a fascist dictator to bugger off as well, mum," Darcie replied. "Anyway, it will be good closure for me," she added, knowing her mother would have no response to that. After all, Irene was from the generation that had invented the concept of closure.

Sighing, Irene said, "Very well. And of course Cleo can stay with us. Your father and I have no plans next weekend. Besides, Cleo keeps the puppy entertained."

"Thank you," Darcie told her.

"But are you going alone?" Irene then asked.

Darcie had anticipated this question. On the short drive over here, she had mentally girded herself for answering it, and then answering the numerous other questions her first answer would engender. It was tempting, of course, to lie and say, yes, she was going alone, but that would have only worked if they lived in London or New York, not in tiny Tremont.

"No, mum," she began. "Rylea is coming with me."

And let the games begin...

Darcie knew the routine that was about to commence. Over the years, she had even named each step.

The Furrow.

The Repeat.

The Deeper Furrow

The Unnecessary Identification.

The Still Deeper Furrow.

The Why.

Sure enough…

Irene furrowed her brow as if trying to figure out who this Rylea was that her daughter spoke of, even though there was only one Rylea in town.

"Rylea?" she repeated the name.

"Yes, mum."

Irene's brow furrowed deeper.

"The one who runs the coffee shop?" she asked unnecessarily, seeing as the only Rylea in town also owned the only coffee shop in town.

"Yes, mum."

The furrow deepened yet again. Her mother had a real talent for that, Darcie considered.

"Why on earth is *she* going with you to the wedding?" Irene asked.

Darcie launched into the answer she had prepared earlier.

"I happened to mention the wedding to her," she began, "and we thought it would be fun to go together, that's all. Free food, dancing, and cake."

"I didn't know you were that close to her," Irene said.

Darcie rolled her eyes.

"She hardly has to be my soulmate to come with me to Jeannette's wedding, mum," she replied. "She's my friend. It's more of an emotional-support-slash-girls-day-out kind of thing. A…break from the routine."

Irene, Darcie knew, wouldn't understand the notion of a fake date. She'd probably claim it wasn't British.

Thankfully, though, Irene didn't press any further or somehow work Mussolini into the conversation again.

***

Darcie was running her usual route through Tremont. After parking her Focus back at her cottage, she had set off down her street, turned left towards the centre of town, ran along Tretherras Road, Tremont's high street, including past her own bookshop, crossed Lewisham Creek via the Old Bridge, and then wended her way through the northern part of the village. Running along Wilbur Lane took her past St. Anthony's church and its cemetery, and past Mrs. Beckley-Hopworth's house. She ended up on Creek Trail, a dirt footpath that followed Lewisham Creek and which would eventually lead her to Duke's Circle, the road she would then follow back home.

She hadn't gotten far on Creek Trail when she noticed another running figure up ahead, approaching her. Even from a distance, she was able to see that it was a woman, and that her ponytail was swishing behind her as she ran. As the gap between them was reduced, she began smiling.

Rylea.

"Hiya," she greeted when they met, pulling the AirPods knock-offs she had found on Amazon out of her ears.

"Hey, Darce!" Rylea replied, giving Darcie a pretty smile. She was dressed much like Darcie was, in skin-tight athleisure pants and a yoga crop top. Whereas Darcie's clothes were all black, however, Rylea's were a soft pink, which flattered her auburn hair.

"I didn't know you ran this trail!" Darcie said. Both women were lightly jogging in place, to prevent their muscles from tightening. "I've never seen you."

"I was about to say the same about you," Rylea said. She hooked a thumb over her shoulder, back in the direction she had come from. "But I usually get started earlier. For some reason, though, today I got a late start." She smiled impishly. "Must have been the Fates wanting us to run into each other."

Darcie laughed.

"I think so, because usually I don't go running on Sunday," she told Rylea. "I'm only out today because Cleo is still with my parents." She then explained about the new puppy.

"Oh," Rylea began, "well, you'd better get used to that, huh? You will always lose out to a puppy."

Darcie had to concede her friend was right on that score.

"So…" she began, "where do you usually finish your run?"

Rylea nodded in the direction from which Darcie had just come.

"Centre of town," she said, "right at my shop. Then I walk home as a cool-down." She smiled. "Do you want to finish with me?"

Darcie's clit pulsed.

She used to date a woman at uni, Conny, who referred to having an orgasm as *finishing*. So, naturally, Darcie's mind went *there*.

Why, yes, Rylea…I would love to finish with you! Over and over and over…

"Sounds great!" she said. "I would love the company."

"Good choice," Rylea said. "You never know…" she then added in a conspiratorial whisper, "Jeannette might have spies here in Tremont, and so it would be good for us to be seen doing something fun together. You know, to sell our fake romance come Saturday."

Darcie nodded as if she had just been passed valuable state secrets.

"Excellent idea, Philby," she said, wondering if Rylea got the reference.

Rylea laughed.

"I love it!" she exclaimed. "I always enjoy talking to a woman who can use somewhat obscure references humorously. In fact, I can see it now, Darce: Saturday. At the wedding. Me talking to Jeannette the Cow. 'Well, I think, Jeannette, that it was Darcie's intelligence which drew me to her to the most, while we both were rescuing children from the burning orphanage.'"

Darcie roared with laughter.

"That's our origin story, is it?" she asked.

Rylea shrugged.

"Either that," she began, "or we use the classic accidentally-handcuffed-together-by-some-kid-practising-a-magic-trick."

"I like either one," Darcie quipped, "but keep in mind, I'm also a woman and therefore would not be opposed to you telling Jeannette it was my fabulous bum which caught your attention."

Darcie watched Rylea's eyes light up and how she then seemed to struggle—very briefly—with whether or not to say something.

She wants to flirt! Jesus…

Her heart rate—already elevated because of her run—increased some more.

Darcie decided to let her off the hook.

"Shall we?" she asked, indicating the way back to the centre of town.

Again, Rylea seemed to have ideas pop into her head that she *wanted* to utter but was deciding against doing so.

"Absolutely," she said, and then took off. Darcie easily fell into step beside her, still feeling a schoolgirl-ish tingle at the *something* which had just passed between the two of them.

Chapter 12

Shall we?

As they ran in the direction of Tretherras Road, Rylea considered the last two words Darcie had said.

Shall we?

Shall we have a bit of a cuddle? Yes, Darce, that would be fabulous!

Shall we snog? Yes, Darce, that would also be fabulous!

What's that, Darce? Shall we go back to mine and fuck each other senseless? Yes, Darce, I think that is a splendid idea!

Running, she shook her head briskly.

Out of the gutter, Miss Morgan. Get your head out of the gutter.

She was quite happy she had encountered Darcie today. When she had first spotted her running towards her on Creek Trail, she had felt a warm feeling come over her that didn't have anything to do with lust. Rather, it was the kind of warmth created when unexpectedly meeting someone she truly enjoys spending time with. It had brightened up her Sunday, which up until the creekside encounter, had been quite ordinary.

They ran side by side past the church and cemetery, and then along Rylea's usual route into the centre of the village, Darcie letting her lead the way. Even though they were next to each other, it was as if Darcie was perfectly in tune with her, seeming to know when she wanted to turn left or right, and never accidentally bumping into her.

When they reached Tretherras Road, they stopped in front of Bean There/Done That. They stood there for a few minutes in silence, both of them with their hands on hips, and catching their breath. Rylea felt her runner's high kick in, immediately relaxing her while simultaneously giving her a feeling of euphoria. Often after a run, she was horny, and today was no different, but she forced her mind to ignore that. The last thing she needed was her centre doing all of her thinking for her while Darcie was with her and then making her say something that would cause her friend discomfort.

Eventually, they started walking, heading in the direction of both their homes.

"Thanks for joining me," Rylea said. "I enjoyed the company."

"Thank *you*!" Darcie replied. "This was fun! Maybe we should do it again. After all, I've read that exercising with a partner makes you more accountable."

Rylea let out a theatrical groan.

"Urgh!" she muttered. "Accountable? Then how am I supposed to continue lying to myself about running ten miles when I really only ran eight?"

"That's okay," Darcie replied. "I do the same thing. I'm fairly certain that by the end of tonight, I'll have convinced myself I ran all the way to Newquay today. So, we'll just be enablers for one another."

"Consider it a deal, then," Rylea said.

They continued in silence for a bit. There were several other people out, enjoying a Sunday stroll. They ran the gamut from young families with small children to old-age pensioners, the latter all dressed warmly despite it being a rather pleasant day.

"You haven't changed your mind about Saturday, have you?" Darcie suddenly asked.

"Of course not!" Rylea assured her. Change her mind about going on a fake date with Darcie? As if! Considering it was the closest she'd ever get to *actually* dating her, she wasn't about to pass up that opportunity.

"In fact," Rylea went on, "I think I'd better ask you some things about yourself in case I end up in a conversation in which Darcie 101 stuff comes up."

Darcie laughed.

"Darcie 101 stuff?" she asked. "Okay, then…my birthday is in August."

Rylea scoffed.

"I knew that already!" she stated.

"Did you?"

Rylea shrugged.

"Small town," she said, blushing.

And I used to have a massive crush on you and had some pretty filthy ideas about how we could spend your birthday together.

She considered now how inventive her teenaged mind was back then, especially as her only proper sexual experiences then mainly consisted of her and her first girlfriend, Imogen, somewhat clumsily fingering each other in her bedroom when they were supposed to be studying for maths exams.

"Okay, then," Darcie replied. "Let's see…let me give you girlfriend intel. The kind of stuff a proper girlfriend would know."

They turned off Tretherras Road and onto Mawgan Lane. This put them in sight of the Ladle & Spoon.

Darcie put her hand on Rylea's arm.

"Let's pop in, shall we?" she suggested. "I could use some water, and we could order some fruit juice to go with it."

"Okay," Rylea agreed, "but you still owe me that girlfriend intel."

Inside, they found the pub rather busy; not surprising seeing how it was one of the few establishments open on Sundays. However, they found a table easily and in a few minutes Sheila, the waitress, had brought room temperature water and two glasses of orange juice for them.

"Right," Darcie began. "Girlfriend intel. Well, apparently I snore, though I refuse to believe it."

"Hm," Rylea hummed. "I'll have to decide just how badly you snore should the topic come up." She made a show of looking Darcie up and down. "You strike me as a right chainsaw snorer," she added.

"Oh, fuck you!" Darcie replied, laughing.

"Anyway," Rylea went on, "I doubt the topic of snoring will come up. What I need is more along the lines of day-to-day-being-Darcie's-girlfriend kind of stuff."

"Hm, okay…" Darcie started. "Well, first of all, how long have we been dating? It can't have been long because Jeannette only left me five months ago."

"Two months?" Rylea suggested.

Darcie seemed to consider this.

"Perfect," she said after a moment. "It means Jeannette can't automatically assume that you're just a rebound relationship. Okay, so this means that if we've only been together that long, I haven't done much to integrate Cleo into our relationship yet."

Rylea raised her eyebrows. She just assumed Cleo was part of the package.

"Is that right?"

Darcie nodded.

"Mm-hm," she confirmed. "I don't like the idea of her forming attachments to women who might not stick around. Which made it doubly hard when Jeannette left. Cleo had gotten used to the idea of Jeannette being in our lives, and she and Jeannette had been getting comfortable with one another. It seemed as if the three of us living together was going to work out quite nicely."

Darcie's face suddenly took on a sad aspect, and Rylea, without thinking, reached across the table and took her hand. She suddenly felt very protective of her—and of Cleo, who was a good kid! It was awful that Jeannette could callously walk away from both of them like that, hurting a little kid's feelings in the process!

"Is Cleo okay?" she asked.

Darcie gave her a wan smile.

"You know something?" she asked. "You're the first person to ask me that."

Rylea blushed. Meanwhile, Darcie was staring at her with what seemed to be a mix of gratitude and…invitation.

"Um…anyway," Darcie went on, giving her hand a little squeeze, but not letting go of it, "yes, Cleo is fine. She didn't really understand at first what had happened, but then again, neither did I. But she's a tough kid and bounced back nicely. But now, of course, I need to be extra careful when it comes to dating."

"Got it," Rylea told her. She made a mental note to not mention fun dates with Darcie *and* Cleo should Jeannette ask. However, what Darcie just related caused a question to appear in Rylea's mind. "So…" she began, "…if we're dating, but you're keeping Cleo out of it…how do we actually…you know, *date*? And…do other things?"

Darcie laughed, but Rylea noticed the blush that coloured her face and neck. With her free hand, she took a sip of her orange juice.

"My parents, silly," she said. "They're my dating helpers, for lack of a better term. They either come to mine to babysit, or I take Cleo to theirs. And before you ask," she went on, "yes, that includes *overnight* babysitting."

Now it was Rylea who blushed again as she imagined future conversations in an alternate universe…

Hey hun, can your parentals watch the little astronaut tonight? I just went shopping and I think you'd like what I have for you to strip me out of later…

She cleared her throat.

"So, anything else I should know about?" she asked.

"I love Italian food," Darcie said. Her eyes lit up and she squeezed Rylea's hand again. Rylea, amazed that they were still holding hands, smiled.

"Ooh!" Darcie exclaimed. "Should it come up, we'll mention that we just *love* going to Cacciatore's in Newquay! That's my favourite restaurant, and it was kind of mine and Jeannette's place."

"Excellent!" Rylea enthused. "This means you're using me to overwrite Jeannette in your life! What used to be *her* things with you are now *my* things with you. Us women *hate* that!"

Darcie laughed.

"You seem to be looking forward to this!"

"I'm loving our evil plan," Rylea admitted. "In fact, I think that's how I'm going to refer to it from now on…our Evil Plan. Okay, what else? I want to have lots of ammunition! Oh, hello Mr. Trelawny!"

Mr. Trelawny had just materialised as if by magic at their table.

"Hello, Mr. Trelawny," Darcie said.

"Ladies," the older gentleman said in greeting. He then cleared his throat and shuffled his feet a bit, seeming a little uncomfortable with something.

"Something the matter, Mr. Trelawny?" Rylea asked.

"No, no!" Mr. Trelawny quickly said. "Just that…well, of course it's none of my business, and I'm happy for you both…but I just hope that your new romance won't in any way interfere with your ability to participate in Trivia Night each week. I find you both to be assets to our team."

Rylea stared at him, wondering what he was on about. She shared a look with Darcie and determined that she was equally confused. But as they were looking at one another, it seemed to hit them both.

They were still holding hands!

In a crowded pub.

In a small village.

In full view of everyone.

They quickly separated their hands.

"No, Mr. Trelawny," Darcie said, "you see, the thing is…"

"We're not…" Rylea added.

"Right," Darcie continued. "We're not…"

"It was more of a moral support hand-holding," Rylea explained.

"You know how women are!" Darcie pointed out with a small laugh.

Mr. Trelawny seemed to relax a bit.

"Oh, I see!" he said. "Well, then, good show and carry on."

After he left, Rylea and Darcie burst into laughter.

"Do you hear that sound, Rylea?" Darcie asked. "That's the noise of the rumour mill starting up."

Rylea nodded.

"Christ, they'll have us married by midweek," she said.

"And I'm sure one of us will be pregnant by the weekend," Darcie added, making them both burst into a new round of laughter.

Chapter 13

On Monday night, after Beavers, Darcie and Cleo arrived home following their respective Beavers and Scouts meetings at the Village Hall.

Darcie had been a volunteer leader for the Beavers since shortly after gaining custody of Cleo. She herself had been a Beaver, then a Cub, and then a Scout when she was a little girl, and because she loved working with little children, had eagerly welcomed the chance to give something back to the organisation. Now, she was a Beaver Leader, complete with the coveted wood beads attached to her necker, which showed that she had completed all the necessary training to have earned such a lofty position.

"So," she began, as she and Cleo entered the cottage, "My Beavers are going to be working on their space badge next, Cleo. I am considering inviting you to attend one of our meetings so you can give them some interesting facts about outer space."

Cleo's face lit up.

"Okay," she said enthusiastically. Now she was bouncing and walking backwards in front of Darcie as they headed towards the living room. "I can teach them a lot!"

Darcie smiled.

"I know you can, luv," she said, looking at their path ahead, making sure that Cleo—who was completely *not* paying attention to where she was going—wasn't about to smash into anything dangerous. "But please turn around so you don't collide into an asteroid or something like that."

Cleo gave her an exasperated look but did as she was told.

"Auntie, there are no asteroids on Earth. Those are way out in space between Mars and Jupiter."

Darcie rolled her eyes. Sarcasm was often wasted on ten-year-olds.

"In any case," she went on, "I think it will be good for the Beavers to see that a kid like you knows so much about space."

In the living room, they sat on the couch, and with Cleo's help, Darcie made sure that her niece had everything she would need for school tomorrow, packed in her backpack.

As they worked, Cleo, evidently still excited, kept talking about Darcie's idea.

"I can teach them all about the planets, and nebulae, and escape velocities, and what the Sun is made of, and Lagrange points, and—"

"The what points?" Darcie asked.

"Lagrange points," Cleo said. "Those are points in space where the gravitational pull of two large bodies—like the Earth and the Sun—are kind of evened out, so that when you put something in orbit there, it stays put. That's where they put the James Webb Space Telescope."

Darcie blinked.

"Um…" she began, "…that sounds fascinating, Cleo—and I'm very impressed that you know that—but remember, we're talking about small children here. I was thinking perhaps you could talk about the constellations, maybe! Or perhaps we could go out one night and find a planet and you can tell them all about how far away it is. Things like that."

"Oh yeah, right," Cleo said. "Like, did you know that it would take twelve years to get to Neptune on a spaceship, but if we were riding a beam of light, it would only take us four hours?"

Darcie considered that. She thought her Beavers were clever enough to grasp that concept. Maybe.

Some of her own learning from her school days came back to her.

"But we can't see Neptune with the naked eye, can we?" she asked.

"Nope!" Cleo stated. "It's too far away."

Giving her Beavers facts about something so far away that it was invisible would probably be too abstract for them to grasp and retain, Darcie considered. Conversely, facts about something the little ones could see would be more likely to stick

"But we can see Mars," Darcie said. "So how long would it take a spaceship to get to Mars?"

"About seven months, maybe a little more," Cleo answered, and Darcie was impressed with how certain she was. The kid really did know a lot. "But light only takes between twelve and twenty minutes, depending on where Mars is in its orbit."

"Fine," Darcie told her. "We'll use Mars. And Venus too." She remembered that on nights when it was out, Venus was the brightest object in the sky, save for the Moon.

When they had finished with the schoolbag, Darcie clapped her hands sharply.

"Okay, kiddo," she began, "upstairs, shower, pyjamas. When you're done, we'll put on your new show. Scoot!"

Cleo's new show was an American documentary series Darcie had found on Amazon Prime, all about the solar system. In light of their discussion tonight, she considered she might want to sit with Cleo and pay attention to the show as well, rather than doing her normal tidying up around the house. If she was going to help her little Beavers earn their space badge, it would make sense if she started boning up on her astronomy knowledge.

A few minutes later, after hearing Cleo's shower turn on, Darcie went to her bedroom and removed her Beavers gear, which tonight consisted of a purple t-shirt with the word "Leader" printed on it, and her necker. She swapped her jeans for sweatpants, removed her bra, and then pulled on a plain black tee. She'd shower after Cleo was tucked in bed.

Heading back downstairs, her phone rang. Emma, her best mate.

"Hiya," she greeted, heading into the kitchen.

"Hiya," Emma said.

They had been friends since nappies, and both of them had decided that Tremont was home for them—despite how much they used to grouse about it when they were teens, fantasising about moving to London or Liverpool.

"What are you up to?" Darcie asked.

She heard her friend sigh dramatically from her house four streets over to the north.

"Up to here with Roy and the little monsters," Emma answered.

Darcie smiled but said nothing. "Roy and the little monsters" complaints were part and parcel of any conversation with Emma.

"Anyway," Emma began, "what's this I hear about you and Rylea Morgan being an item?"

Darcie, reaching for the electric kettle in order to turn it on, froze.

"Are you bloody kidding me?" she exclaimed. "Where on earth did you hear that?"

Emma then launched into a forensic account of how gossip spreads in a small village such as Tremont. Naturally, it all started with Darcie being seen holding hands with Rylea yesterday at the Ladle & Spoon.

Darcie didn't bother paying too much attention to what Emma told her, but it didn't matter. What it amounted to was that several Mrs. Somebodys in the pub that day witnessed the hand-holding, and then told other Mrs. Somebodys who *weren't* in the pub what they had seen. Those other Mrs. Somebodys told their sisters, who then rang up additional Mrs. Somebodys, who then spread the word to additional sisters, cousins, and various other relations, all of whom—of course—knew even more Mrs. Somebodys who would just hate to be left out of this intelligence.

When it was done, Darcie sighed.

"Rylea Morgan and I are not an item," she stated. "And we told Mr. Trelawny that!"

"Oh, well that was your mistake," Emma replied. "You see, *Mr.* Trelawny is a man, and men are useless in these situations. The old bugger probably went back to his table and resumed talking about the next Truro City match with the other old buggers. You needed to tell one of the *women*. In fact, what you should have done was stand atop your table at the Ladle & Spoon and announce that you and Rylea are not a couple."

"Or, people should just mind their own business," Darcie lamented.

Emma laughed.

"Maybe people mind their business in London or New York," she said, "but this is Cornwall."

"Rylea and I are not a couple," Darcie reiterated. "We were just doing a bit of strategising about this coming Saturday. She's agreed to be my fake date for Jeannette's wedding."

Emma squawked, and Darcie belatedly realised that she had forgotten to tell Emma about the invitation.

"Jeannette's wedding?" Emma practically screeched. "How is this the first I'm hearing about *that?*"

"I'm so sorry, Em," Darcie said, genuinely feeling like a bad friend. She went on to explain how the invitation had taken her by surprise, and how before she had gotten her head around it, Rylea had come up with the fake date idea, and then it just slipped her mind to tell her.

"Sorry," she repeated.

Emma scoffed.

"Please," she said. "I've got too many other silly things to deal with daily to be concerned about that. Today, for example, Roy Jr. got not one, but *two*, Cheerios stuck up his nose. Takes after his father, that one does. But now, of course, you will tell me *everything* that happens at the wedding as soon as it is over!"

Darcie smiled.

"Will do," she assured her friend.

"God, why do people do that?" Emma mused, irritation in her voice. "I mean, invite exes to their weddings? What is that meant to prove?"

"I don't know," Darcie admitted, turning the kettle on, and then pulling out her tea bags from the cupboard. "I suppose it's meant to prove that you're emotionally mature enough to invite your past to bear witness to your future."

"Very poetic," Emma said, "but a load of bollocks. Perfect choice bringing Rylea, though. Knowing Jeannette as I do and her preoccupation with age, it will be like throwing garlic at a vampire. Walking into that wedding with a teenager will drive her crazy!"

Darcie sighed.

"If Rylea was a teenager, I would not have agreed to the fake date!" she pointed out.

"The point is," Emma began, "that Rylea is closer to being a teenager than Jeannette ever will be again, so this will be quite a coup on your part."

Darcie leaned against the countertop. Her trained ears informed her that the shower upstairs had stopped, which meant Cleo would be down again soon.

"Anyway, don't tell anyone about what Rylea and I are up to with regards to the wedding," Darcie pleaded.

"My lips are sealed," Emma assured her.

"Do you think I'm doing the wrong thing?" Darcie then asked. "I mean, with this fake date. Is it absurdly childish?"

"No!" Emma exclaimed. "It's bloody brilliant! And *so* un-British! It's sneaky and underhanded and deceptive and revenge-driven! It's bloody French is what it is! I will never speak to you again if you *don't* go through with it!"

Darcie laughed.

"Heaven forbid," she said. "Otherwise, how would I know what to do if Cleo ever gets a Cheerio stuck up her nose."

"You'll never have that problem," Emma sighed. "Girls are far more sensible with their food."

***

The next morning, Darcie stopped into The Bean for her morning Americano.

Rylea was nowhere to be seen, so Darcie figured she must be in the back of the shop tending to whatever it is coffee shop owners tend to.

"Hey, Darce!" Bridget greeted her. "The usual?"

"Yes, please," Darcie answered.

Bridget nodded and immediately set about preparing her drink. Darcie frowned. Usually, the process here at The Bean was to pay first. Darcie even had a fiver in her hand, ready to do so. But she mentally shrugged. Nothing wrong with a shop employee mixing things up process-wise every now and then. Well, unless it was a bomb-making shop, Darcie supposed. Things could get rather messy in that case.

When Bridget was finished with her drink and had handed it over, Darcie tried giving her the fiver, but Bridget waved it off.

"On the house, Darce," she said, and then winked. "VIP and all."

Darcie blinked.

When did she become a VIP?

"Um…thanks?" she said. Once again she held up the fiver. "Are you sure I can't…?"

Again Bridget waved it off.

"No need," she said.

Puzzled, Darcie wanted to ask what was going on, but she needed to get across the street to open her shop. She'd question Rylea later.

"Okay, um…do me a favour, will you?" she asked. "Tell Rylea I said hi."

"Sure thing," Bridget assured her. She then gestured over her shoulder. "She's in the back on the phone with one of our suppliers at the moment."

"Yes, well, thanks for the coffee, Bridge," Darcie said. She held up her money again, deciding to try once more. "Are you sure I can't...?"

Bridget scoffed.

"Absolutely not!" she insisted. Then she winked again.

Darcie really had no idea what was going on, but she decided it was best to make her exit before things got any stranger.

It wasn't until late in the afternoon that it all got explained.

A little after three p.m., Rylea walked into Shelf Life. Darcie, seeing her, smiled broadly, feeling happy. In fact, she felt a little alarmed at how happy she felt. But she quickly reasoned with herself that she would feel just as happy if it was Emma who had just walked in.

Sort of.

"Hiya!" she greeted. "How's business today?"

"Very well, thanks," Rylea answered. "Yours?"

Darcie nodded.

"It's been good," she answered. This was true. A new instalment of a popular bodice ripper romance series had just been delivered this morning, and quite a few of the female denizens of Tremont, young and old, had been in to purchase it, many of them seeming quite anxious to get the book home and start reading it.

Darcie only knew the series by reputation. She had never been able to read hetero romances, and she certainly had no interest in reading the books in this particular series which, according to her sources, were quite descriptive with their sex scenes.

"So, what brings you in?" Darcie asked, realising belatedly that she had somehow decided to use her flirting voice. She cleared her throat. "I mean, so what's going on?" she asked in her normal voice.

"Oh nothing," Rylea said. "Just thought I'd drop in and say hello. After all, I was starting to feel guilty that I haven't been in your shop all day to see how my *girlfriend* is doing."

Darcie laughed, rolling her eyes.

"Oh my days, I take it you've heard, huh?"

"I have!" Rylea replied, also laughing. "Bridge seemed rather proud of herself that when you came in this morning, she gave you the VIP special without me needing to say anything."

The free coffee!

"Bugger!" Darcie exclaimed. "I had no idea that's what that was about! I was thinking maybe it was some sort of frequent-customer deal. I'm so sorry! Here, let me get my handbag and I'll—"

"Darce, relax," Rylea said. "I don't care about the free coffee." She looked down at her feet. "I guess I was more interested in making sure you were okay. I mean, nobody likes to be the subject of gossip, and you've had your fair share of that already the past several months."

So bloody sweet!

Darcie smiled.

"I am perfectly fine, thank you," she said. "Besides, there are worse things I can think of than to be rumoured to be Rylea Morgan's girlfriend."

Mentally, she chided herself. That last part had come out of her mouth because it somehow bypassed her brain's speech filter.

But Rylea didn't seem bothered by it. In fact, she smiled rather becomingly, her cheeks tinting pink with a blush.

"Weirdly enough," Rylea began, "that is actually one of the coolest things anyone has ever said to me."

Now Darcie looked down at her feet, shuffling them a bit, suddenly feeling like a thirteen-year-old kid talking to the cutest girl in school.

"Well, I meant it," she said. "Anyway…"

"Yeah, anyway…" Rylea repeated. "We should probably nip this in the bud."

"Exactly," Darcie agreed. "To that end, I've already told Emma last night, which means that she'll tell her mum, which means her mum will tell Mrs. Harringford—"

"Which gets the info to the Ladies Auxiliary at St. Anthony's," Rylea cut in. "And I've already straightened things out with Bridge, which means she'll tell Mrs. Stokes—"

"And Mrs. Stokes will get it sorted with the Bainsworth sisters, because they're thick as thieves, which means they'll tell Mrs. Trent-McManus and Mrs. Beckley-Hopworth—"

"And she'll tell her knitting circle…" Rylea went on.

"The knitting circle birds will tell the bridge club ladies…" Darcie said, picking up the thread.

"And…let's see…that gets the news to Mrs. Benton, who will tell Sheila, over at the Ladle & Spoon," Rylea suggested.

Darcie's eyes lit up.

"Which is where this whole thing started!" she exclaimed. "Full circle! I like that!"

"Fabulous!" Rylea said. "I think that will squash the rumour well and good!" She stuck out her hand. "Well, Darce, it was lovely being your official girlfriend for about forty-eight hours!"

Darcie shook her hand.

"Yes, quite lovely," she replied. "And not one argument between us."

Rylea shrugged.

"It's because we get along so bloody well," she said.

Darcie laughed.

Chapter 14

Saturday arrived.

Time to put the Evil Plan into motion.

Rylea awoke early that morning, being sure she was giving herself plenty of time to get ready before she had to leave to pick up Darcie.

In the shower, after washing, she shaved her legs very carefully, keeping in mind that the dress Darcie had chosen showed them off quite a bit. She also did a touch-up shave on her armpits—again, the dress—and then ran her fingers over her vulva, determining that she wanted to shave that nice and smooth also.

She was halfway through that task when she stopped and blushed.

The fact was her fingers had told her that she probably could have waited another day or two before shaving down there. *Sans* girlfriend, her typical schedule for making herself nice and silky smooth between her legs was three days, sometimes four. But she figured her mind was in date mode this morning, and that was what had made her want to neaten things up.

"It's a fake date, Rylea," she told herself aloud now. "Operative word: fake."

But then she shrugged. Since she had already started, she might as well finish the job. What was the point, really, in having one half of *down there* shaved, and the other not? Ergo, in another couple of minutes her vulva and her mound were date-ready. Well…*fake* date-ready.

This reminded her…

Yesterday, Jemma had come into The Bean, practically fizzing with excitement. Once the Rylea-is-dating-Darcie rumour had been proven false, Jemma had reached out to her friend Lauren, telling her about Rylea. And, apparently, Lauren had given Jemma the green light to provide Rylea with her phone number, which Jemma had.

Rylea hadn't used it yet, still believing it would be best to wait until after the Evil Plan had been executed. If she had contacted Lauren last night and it had gone well, then she'd most likely be thinking about Lauren throughout today, maybe even planning their first date. After all, her freshly shaved privates were ready for it.

But today was about helping Darcie get a little revenge on Jeannette. She was a relationship exorcist, after all, and this is what relationship exorcists do.

After applying lotion to her legs—the kind that added a bit of shimmer to them—she padded out of her loo and then tried to wrestle with the underwear dilemma.

This had been bugging her since last night.

The cut of the dress—one-shoulder—meant that she could go braless, because the bodice of the dress had support built-in. And because the dress fit so snugly and her boobs weren't ginormous, she didn't have to worry about her girls popping out at inopportune moments.

This left the question of knickers…

And last night, she had twisted her mind into knots trying to decide what to do.

She had, after all, seen *Bridget Jones's Diary…*

She and Tamsin had watched it months ago on Let's Laugh at Straight People in Films Saturday, where they watch silly romcoms about straight people, laugh at how moronic they all are, and then fantasise about the hot women in them.

Rylea seemed to recall finding Renée Zellweger pretty in a comforting kind of way. As in, the type of woman she'd like to curl up with in front of a fire drinking hot chocolate. She couldn't help feeling that although the sex might be a bit dull, Renée as Bridget Jones would always be waiting for her when she got home each night.

Tamsin, however, couldn't stop gushing about Embeth Davidtz. She also decided that if Colin Firth was silly enough to choose Renée Zellweger over Embeth, then Colin's character was, in fact, gay, and needed to shag Hugh Grant's character.

In any case, ever since watching that film, Rylea couldn't help but wonder just how intricately connected Fate and a woman's choice of underwear were.

On the one hand, this being a fake date and all, she could choose comfort over style. She had a handful of basic, cotton briefs that were about as far from sexy as a pair of boxing gloves. But they were comfy and up for just about any job.

However, to her it seemed to be poking the bear of Fate to choose such unflattering knickers. Fake date or not, she was certain that if she chose her granny pants, Fate would guarantee that she and Darcie ended up having sex today. And then Darcie would see her £5-for-3-at-Asda knickers and quite possibly lose any interest in things progressing past that stage.

On the other hand, choosing ultra-sexy knickers—of which she had plenty—risked Fate laughing at her hubris and snatch away any chance at all of having sex with Darcie today.

Nonetheless…

"Better safe than sorry," she said to herself, pulling out a black lace thong. "Not that I *plan* on having sex with Darcie," she continued, tossing the thong on the bed, and returning to the en suite to work on her makeup. "But I mean, who am I kidding? I wouldn't *turn down* having sex with Darcie. Not that it could possibly happen." She started applying blush to her cheeks. "It can't *possibly* happen," she continued as she worked. "For starters, we're just friends. For another thing…I'm talking to myself and I'm sure Darcie doesn't fancy lunatics."

Chapter 15

"Thong or brief?" Darcie asked herself, alone in her bedroom. "Thong or brief?"

Darcie *hadn't* seen *Bridget Jones's Diary*, but she did know that Fate loved a good laugh.

Don't shave your intimate area before a blind date, and the blind date turns into a shag-fest.

Don't take a shower first thing after getting home—when you've been wearing tight jeans all day—and your girlfriend wants to go down on you before supper.

Wear boring knickers that an old lady would own, before a fake date with Rylea, and Rylea ends up with her head under your dress.

This was the calculus Darcie was performing now, while deciding on her choice of underwear.

"Of course," she continued aloud, giving a short laugh, "Rylea is *not* going to end up with her head under my dress." She paused, biting her bottom lip. "But if she does…"

She pulled out a rather sexy lace thong.

She rolled her eyes at her silliness. That had been a lot of mental energy expended on a moot point, really. This was *not* a date! It was a *fake* date, and Rylea was only being super-sweet and super-fun, helping her get a little revenge on Jeannette. Her choice of knickers really did not matter today!

She was about to stuff the lace thong back in the drawer when she stopped, considering.

She shouldn't start letting her guard down around Fate now. Fate loved sloppiness like that. In fact, Fate *welcomed* such sloppiness. No…It would be good to maintain her vigilance against it by choosing to wear the sexy knickers.

That settled, she showered, shaving *everything* (again…Fate), and then set to work blow-drying and styling her hair. She was going to set it in a way that she knew Jeannette particularly liked. Likewise, she planned on doing her makeup in a way Jeannette always preferred. This was a strategy she had learned just last night while reading an article online entitled "How to Make Your Ex Realise He Made a Mistake."

(The world being what it is, the article was, of course, written for cishets. But seeing how it was written *for* women, Darcie figured the concepts mentioned could be used against lesbians as well.)

Tip #7 was "Show up for an event with your new beau, but with your hair and makeup done the way *your ex* likes it. It will drive him crazy!"

Darcie had taken a picture of that tip on her laptop's screen and texted it to Rylea, who had written back saying she thought the idea brilliant because whatever would drive a straight man crazy, would drive a lesbian completely, stark-raving bonkers, because, well…women.

Eventually, she was done with her hair and makeup, having given her brown locks some curl and bounce, and surrounding her hazel eyes with a sexy, smoky shadow that brought out the gold flecks in her irises.

She removed the towel she had been wearing, and, sitting on the edge of the tub, began applying lotion to her legs and arms. It was the good stuff, from The Body Shop, only brought out on special occasions, which is why it had lasted for two years.

As she was finishing, she heard her phone in the next room ping, and her heart stopped.

What if it was Rylea, cancelling? Bugger! There was no way she would go to the wedding alone, which meant all this hard work would be for nought!

Putting the lotion down on the sink counter, she hurried, nude, into the bedroom, and then breathed a sigh of relief when she read the message. It was Rylea simply telling her that she would arrive at her house in thirty minutes.

Darcie placed a hand over her heart and breathed a sigh of relief.

Thirty minutes was plenty of time. All that was left was to pull on her dress—a spaghetti strap, form-fitting number in teal, with a high slit and a cleavage-revealing neckline, a feature that Darcie felt was particularly potent since she couldn't possibly wear a bra.

Jeannette had never seen her in this dress, though Darcie had bought it while they were still together. But the event she had bought it for—ironically, another wedding—had gotten cancelled when the bride discovered the groom *in flagrante delicto* with her mother.

Before getting dressed, however, she sent a message to Irene, telling her that she would be leaving soon. Cleo was already over at her parents', having spent the night there, intent on spending the weekend teaching Winnie new tricks, and Darcie always liked keeping her parents informed of her whereabouts whenever they were watching her.

It was overkill, really. Her parents were more than capable of managing just about anything which could possibly come up with Cleo, even—god forbid—an emergency of some sort. What's more, this village being what it was, there was no shortage of people nearby whom they could rely on for help. But Darcie had learned that nothing made her more overly cautious than being responsible for another person's life.

A few minutes later, with the dress on, Darcie examined herself in the full-length mirror.

Wow!

She had forgotten that she could look like this. Of course, she knew she was an attractive woman, but village life in Cornwall rarely created opportunities for her to look like *this*. At least, not now she was single. In the Jeannette era, there had been plenty of chances to dress to the nines like this. They had often enjoyed going to Newquay for a nice night out or spending long weekends in London. What's more, the company Jeannette worked for frequently hosted posh dos throughout the year.

But now she had trouble remembering the last time she had put on a dress such as this, let alone high heels. And the makeup and the hair? It seemed forever ago.

It was a shame, really. She *enjoyed* this.

The sound of a car coming to a stop in her driveway pulled her away from her musings. Rylea was here.

After one last look in the mirror to make sure everything was where it should be, she grabbed her small handbag and headed downstairs.

Chapter 16

"Bugger!" Rylea exclaimed.

"Bugger!" Darcie said at the exact same time.

When Rylea had pulled up in front of Darcie's house, parking her Mini next to Darcie's car, she got out and was stepping up to the door to ring the bell when it opened, and Darcie stepped out.

Rylea didn't care that she was probably about to make a fool of herself.

"You look amazing!" she stated.

An understatement, really, but then again, she wasn't a wordsmith.

"Like, holy fuck, Darce, you really do look incredible."

"Me?" Darcie asked, and Rylea was finally over her initial shock to feel thrilled at how Darcie was checking her out. "You are stunning! I love that dress!"

Rylea smiled and pirouetted daintily on her heels, giving Darcie the all-around view.

"I think you made the right choice," she began. "If I do say so myself."

Meanwhile, she was trying to figure out exactly what kind of Faustian bargain she would be willing to make in order to turn this fake date into a real one.

I mean, do I really need sight in both eyes? I think I could make do with the left one going dark...

"Anyway," she went on, "once Jeannette gets a look at you, I think the wedding will be called off."

Darcie laughed, but blushed deeply, and Rylea thought the colour went well with her dress.

"Well, if that happens," Darcie began, "I would simply tell Jeannette, 'I'm sorry, but I'm absurdly loyal to Rylea.'"

Rylea wiped fake sweat off her brow.

"Whew!" she exhaled. "I'd hate the idea of needing a relationship exorcism to get over you."

That might have been a little too flirty, she considered, but hopefully, Darcie would take it as a joke.

"Anyway, shall we go?" she suggested.

"Yes," Darcie replied, but then she snapped her fingers. "Oh wait! I almost forgot! Just one sec!"

She reopened the door to her house. Whatever it was she needed must have been right in the entryway because she only leaned in. This caused her dress to tighten along her hips and her bum, and Rylea wanted to groan out loud.

"Got it!" Darcie said, straightening up and shutting the front door behind her.

In her hand was an expertly gift-wrapped box.

Rylea frowned.

"You're bringing a wedding present?" she asked. She knew the British, as a people, were prone to be on the nice side, but this was going overboard. It was like giving a book of matches to the arsonist who burned down your house.

Darcie, however, smiled. But it wasn't a "nice" smile. It was an every-evil-queen-in-a-Disney-film smile.

"Not as such," she said. "You see, the other night, I was rooting around in my wardrobe looking for a sweater I haven't seen in a while, and I came across one of Jeannette's old nightgowns that had somehow escaped the purge.

"I thought about burning it, but then decided, why not give it back? On her wedding day? I even popped a little note in there saying, 'You left something behind.'"

Rylea laughed.

"That is bloody brilliant!" she exclaimed. "And evil! I can see it now: Jeannette opening the gift, thinking you got her something outrageously expensive she registered for, and instead she finds it's a big box of 'Fuck you!'"

Laughing, they got in the Mini.

Pulling away from Darcie's house, Rylea made sure she drove very carefully, not wanting Darcie to believe she was a menace behind the wheel. She wasn't—at least, she didn't think so—but she would admit that she often took some turns too quickly because cornering in a Mini was fun.

"Is your shop squared away?" Darcie asked her.

Rylea nodded. Bridget was going to run Bean There/Done That today with help from her mother. Bridget would handle making the coffees, her mother—who used to work at Asda—would handle the order taking and the till. It was an arrangement that had been used in the past a few times when Rylea had to leave Tremont for one reason or another.

"Bridge is on it," she said. "Yours?"

Darcie scoffed.

"I think dad secretly relishes the chance to be running the show again at the shop," she said. "I am sure he will have a list for me when I get back, of all the things I'm doing wrong."

Rylea laughed. As she navigated the car to the A39 and then settled in on that road, she couldn't help daydreaming a bit, imagining that she and Darcie were proper girlfriends, heading into the city for a proper date, dressed nicely and chatting amiably as she drove.

It was a lovely image, especially when she enhanced it by imagining the two of them holding hands near the gear stick.

"What are you grinning about?" Darcie asked with a smile.

Rylea blushed at having been caught out like that.

"Nothing," she lied. "Still thinking about how devious your wedding present is, that's all."

***

"…and that was the end of Sarah-Jayne," Rylea concluded. "She moved to Liverpool, and I stayed here in Cornwall. I love it here too much to leave. Liverpool, London, Amsterdam…all great places to visit, but I'm a Cornish gal all the way through."

"Same," Darcie replied. "Although, I'm concerned about Cleo, long-term."

Rylea glanced over at her.

"What do you mean?" she asked.

"Well, let's face it," Darcie began, "Cornwall—and especially Tremont—isn't exactly the most *diverse* place on Earth. I'm not sure I want Cleo growing up with such a limited view of the world. I would love it if she had some Black friends, for instance, or Indian, or Japanese, or…you name it. I want her exposed to other cultures, and religions, and learn that different people—particularly non-white people—have different perspectives on how the world works and treats them. And that's where big cities have an advantage over places like Tremont."

Rylea nodded, considering that. Darcie had a point. Cornwall was lovely, but it was absurdly homogeneous; and when one has a child to raise, one has to take such a factor into account when determining what kind of adult that child will become.

"I see your point," she told Darcie.

"Do you?" Darcie asked.

"I do, really," Rylea assured her. "Kids today *need* to be exposed to a wider range of people and cultures. Besides, we're never going to get better as a species if groups of us just keep isolating ourselves with others who look and think like us."

Darcie reached over to her right and placed her hand on Rylea's leg. It was all Rylea could do to keep from jerking the steering wheel suddenly at the jolt of sensation which shot through her body then.

The touch was ever so brief. It was simply the kind of touch one woman gives to another to show anything from appreciation to comfort to understanding. But even when Darcie removed her hand, Rylea could still feel it.

"That was very well said," Darcie told her. "I guess you really do see my point."

"Oh, that's not something I'd lie about, Darce," Rylea replied. "I know how important the little astronaut is to you. It's pretty amazing what you've done for her, by the way. I don't think I've told you that before. She's lucky you're her auntie."

"Thank you," Darcie said. She then mumbled something else, but Rylea was unable to make it out over the noise of the engine.

"I'm sorry, what was that?" she asked.

"Oh, nothing!" Darcie answered. "Just…talking to myself. Ignore me. I'm a lunatic."

Chapter 17

"Why couldn't this be a real date?"

That was what Darcie had muttered under her breath, and she still couldn't believe she had said it out loud. Well, not out *loud*; out *quietly*…but still. The fact was the words had escaped her lips when all she thought she was doing was thinking them!

But the feeling had been *that* strong, she surmised, that her brain just couldn't keep it to itself.

Rylea was bloody amazing! Not only was she mouth-wateringly beautiful, but she was kind, funny, intelligent, and great fun to be with.

And she was single!

Like, how does that happen?

Really, why couldn't this be a real date? What she would give!

Do I really need hearing in both ears?

She considered a loss of hearing on one side was a worthy price to pay for this becoming a real date.

Especially since…

It was probably her imagination, but she was certain she had detected glimmers of interest from Rylea over the past several days, along with signals of invitation, as if trying to convey to her that she was open to being…approached.

Glimmers and signals. She was certain she had seen those! Well, maybe not *certain*, but at least *kind of* sure.

Of course, what did she know? Her senses about these things couldn't be trusted anymore. She knew she was woefully out of practice. A year with Jeannette, followed by months of being miserable during which she knew she had developed something of a shell, closing herself off from being receptive to any woman's signals because, really, what was the point? Women were cold-hearted bitches who would leave you the first time an American so much as said "Howdy."

She *was* kind of thawing in regard to that, though. She supposed it was true what they said about time healing all wounds, because over the past month or so she had started feeling more like herself. Nonetheless, she wasn't sure her Glimmers and Signals Receptors were fully operational yet, and therefore, the last thing she needed to do was make a fool of herself by suggesting a *real* date to the woman who was currently her *fake* one.

About twenty-five minutes after they started this drive, Rylea steered her Mini onto North Quay Hill in Newquay and slowly approached the Newquay Royal Arms.

The hotel was a fairly recent build, and thus looked far sleeker and more contemporary than most of the city's hotels. Newquay, Darcie knew, was really trying to make itself even more of a destination, and hotels like the Royal Arms were part of that plan.

It was typical Jeannette to want to get married here. As much as she loved what she called the "simplicity" of Cornwall, she was still a New York City girl who had a toffee-nosed side.

As Rylea manoeuvred the car into a parking space, Darcie saw what she guessed were other wedding guests arriving, heading into the hotel.

It suddenly became very real to her.

She was here, and soon she would see Jeannette for the first time since that day she left for New York.

She had to close her eyes and take a deep breath as the nerves took over. She suddenly felt very scared.

A warmth on her shoulder made her open her eyes and look to her right. Rylea had reached over, her hand now grasping her shoulder gently.

"Are you alright?" Rylea asked, and Darcie could tell just by the level of concern in her friend's eyes that Rylea understood what was troubling her. "You know," Rylea went on, "we don't have to…"

Darcie smiled.

"No, I need this," she stated, feeling some of her resolve come back. "Closure. I need to see her and realise that I can survive it, and that she's harmless. Otherwise, I'll be constantly looking over my shoulder, worried I'm going to run into her at Sainsbury's, or at your bloody coffee shop."

"If she comes into my coffee shop," Rylea said, "I will refuse to serve her!" She paused, her lips pursed and her eyes looking off to the side. "Okay, that would probably be a bad idea because, you know, the economy being what it is," she went on. "So…I *will* serve her, but I will do it spitefully!"

Darcie laughed. In a dreamworld, she would lean over and kiss Rylea deeply for making her feel better.

They got out of the car, Darcie carrying the box with her "gift," and were walking towards the hotel's entrance when suddenly Rylea stopped.

"Oh, shit!" Rylea exclaimed.

"What?" Darcie asked, alarmed. What if Rylea suddenly remembered a super-important appointment she needed to be at?

"Um, how do I put this?" Rylea replied.

Bugger!

It *was* a super-important appointment she needed to be at! God, she'd never be able to feel safe going into Sainsbury's again!

"What?" Darcie asked once more.

"Um…PDA," Rylea said. "Like, how do you want to handle that?"

Darcie blinked. Her still-panicked mind was having trouble deciphering exactly what Rylea was referring to. But after a moment, she caught on.

"Oh!" she exclaimed. "Right! PDA."

Shit! I hadn't thought about that.

"I mean," Rylea began, "there has to be *some*, right? We're trying to sell the fact that we're a couple…"

"Of course!" Darcie replied, feeling her heart rate speed up. The idea of doing even the simplest gestures of affection with the woman next to her was making her feel a little lightheaded.

She chuckled nervously.

"Well, um," she began, "we should definitely hold hands a lot."

"Okay, makes sense," Rylea agreed.

Darcie considered. Holding hands wouldn't be enough, she felt. Fine, Rylea looked devastatingly beautiful in that dress and in the way she was styled—that alone should certainly prick at Jeannette's heart, no matter how much she was in love with Katelynn Jefferson. But Darcie wanted Jeannette driven to the point of distraction by seeing her with Rylea today. She didn't want her ex to merely feel a sting of loss, she wanted the cow to feel gutted.

"But hand-holding isn't enough," she stated to Rylea.

"Okay, what else?" her fake date asked. "You're the boss today, so…whatever."

"Well, I don't want to make you uncomfortable…" Darcie quickly pointed out.

Rylea smirked.

"If you want to make me uncomfortable," she said, "force me to sing in front of a crowd. Now, what else do you have in mind?"

Darcie swallowed.

"Well, are you okay with doing something like this to me?" she asked, stepping closer to Rylea, and placing her hand on the small of her back. The gesture brought their bodies closer together, making contact at their hips and breasts. Immediately, Darcie started getting wet while her nipples became marble, but she made sure her face didn't reveal any outward signs of how her body was reacting.

Rylea licked her lips, and Darcie wished to god she could kiss them.

"Perfectly fine with it," Rylea whispered, and Darcie swore her friend stealthily took a deep breath.

"Great," she said. Another image popped into her mind. Something Jeannette used to do quite often and which, if she noticed Rylea doing the same thing, would drive her mad. She swallowed again. "And what about when we're sitting, you do something like this to me occasionally?"

Reluctantly, she removed her hand from Rylea's back and then repositioned herself, so she was standing next to her. In her mind's eye, they were now sitting next to one another. She then brought her hand up to the nape of Rylea's neck and very gently, almost sensuously, started playing with the super-soft curls back there.

Transfixed with what she was doing, she saw Rylea close her eyes, her lips parting ever so slightly as well.

Darcie couldn't prevent her mind from wandering, from imagining doing this for real; letting Rylea—her *real* girlfriend— feel her touch so she'd know she was being thought of, and that Darcie simply wanted to have an intimate contact with her.

And then…

Darcie bit her bottom lip as another side of her kicked in, because something was telling her that Rylea would gasp in pleasure if she were to extend her fingers, wrap them around Rylea's throat, and give a little squeeze…

"Um…yeah!" Rylea suddenly muttered, breaking Darcie's reverie. "I can do that, too."

Darcie snatched her hand away.

"Great!" she said. "I think that should cover it."

"Wait!" Rylea responded. "What about something like this?"

Still standing side by side, she took Darcie's hand.

"Now, imagine we're walking together somewhere—maybe to the bar to get a drink…"

"Okay," Darcie replied.

"And I do this…"

Rylea brought their joined hands up to her lips and kissed the back of Darcie's, very briefly.

It might have been only a mere peck, but Darcie's clit began shivering and the floodgates were beginning to open a little more in her vagina.

"I love it," she told her friend, realising that she was speaking the truth. She *did* love Rylea kissing her hand. "I mean, as long as I can do the same to you!"

"Totally!" Rylea replied. "I mean, that's what real couples do, right?"

And a hell of a lot more…

But Darcie kept that to herself, because the *hell of a lot more* she was thinking of was really *a hell of a lot more.*

***

"Oh my days…" Darcie began. "This is lovely!"

She hated to admit it, but Jeannette and Miss Katelynn Jefferson had chosen a terrific spot for their nuptials.

It was in the atrium of the hotel, a large, glass-enclosed space towards the back of the building, with soaring ceilings, and filled with an assortment of plants and trees and flowers, making her feel like she was no longer in dreary Cornwall, but in the tropics somewhere. Tahiti, perhaps.

The atrium had been further decorated with strings of fairy lights, lending a kind of otherworldly air to the space, as if magical things were about to happen.

Rows of white folding chairs were arranged before a garlanded archway, while further back, Darcie could see another arrangement of many round tables covered in white tablecloths, each with gorgeous floral centrepieces.

"Nice!" Rylea exclaimed.

"May I take that for you?"

A middle-aged gentleman in a suit had approached. He looked down at the box Darcie was holding.

"The gift table is in the other room," he said, "I'll gladly place yours with the others."

"Yes, of course," Darcie said, smiling and handing him the box. She and Rylea shared an amused look. When the man had gotten out of earshot, Darcie added, "Yes sir, you *may* take my big box of 'Fuck you.'"

She and Rylea burst into laughter.

Darcie looked around. She recognized some of Jeannette's work mates but was fairly certain none of them remembered her. Jeannette had kept her work life and private life separate, to the degree that people she worked with were just that, colleagues, as opposed to friends that were part of her and Darcie's relationship. Their mutual friends were all in Tremont. Darcie didn't know if any of them had been invited to this do, but if they had, she was happy to see they had all stayed home, presumably out of solidarity with her.

A young female server wearing a white shirt and black bowtie appeared carrying a silver tray with flutes of Champagne. Darcie and Rylea each took one, and when Darcie swallowed her first sip, she felt herself calm down even more.

It was then she noticed that the two of them were making quite the impression.

This being a lesbian wedding, it was no surprise that the majority of the guests were women, and Darcie felt rather gratified to see many of them checking her and her date out, some surreptitiously, others rather blatantly.

This was true of the many men who were in attendance as well. In fact, she witnessed one bloke earn an outraged smack on the arm from the woman he was clearly here with.

She leaned closer to Rylea, not caring that what she was about to say could not be construed as anything other than incredibly flirty.

"You are making me feel as if I'm the luckiest woman in this hotel," she whispered. "Thank you again for agreeing to do this."

Rylea smiled.

"Actually," she began, "you're the one who agreed. It was my idea, remember?"

Darcie tilted her glass of Champagne towards Rylea.

"So it was," she acknowledged.

"Besides, I'm the one who feels lucky," Rylea added. "I think every woman here wants to go home with my date, even the straight ones. I haven't felt like that in a long time."

"Well, they can't have—" Darcie stopped herself. She was about to say "Well, they can't have me because I'm yours," but that would have been going too far. Panicking a little, she tried to save herself.

"Well, they can't have any dances with me, because I'm imagining my fake girlfriend is the jealous type and wouldn't dare let another woman touch me," she said breezily.

Rylea laughed.

"Absolutely not!" she exclaimed in mock seriousness. "Well…except for any country music dancing. I can't stand it, and so feel free to dance with another if you must."

***

Eventually, a bell was heard tinkling, silencing the conversations in the atrium.

"If you would all please take your seats," a tall, imposing woman, standing in front of the garlanded arch, called out. She was dressed in a black pantsuit, and had her hair pulled back into a very severe bun.

"Show time," Darcie muttered.

"You still good?" Rylea asked quietly as they made their way towards the seats.

Darcie took her hand as they walked—they were supposed to be girlfriends, after all—and nodded.

"I am," she said. "Besides, I really like shopping at Sainsbury's. I cannot let Jeannette take that away from me."

Rylea laughed.

Darcie led them to a row of seats in the back. It was purposely symbolic. If Jeannette even noticed her during the ceremony, Darcie wanted her to see that she thought so little of this affair that she felt no need to be any closer to the proceedings.

She and Rylea had just sat down, crossing their legs, and Darcie was admiring just how absolutely perfect Rylea's ankles were, when she suddenly felt something on the back of her neck and she yelped, starting in her seat.

She batted at her neck, thinking it might be a creepy-crawly from this veritable jungle in here, who had mistaken her hair for a fern. But she felt nothing.

Then she saw Rylea staring at her, aghast. What's more, Rylea's arm was on the back of her chair, her hand raised at about neck-level.

"Sorry!" Rylea whispered. She looked at her hand. "I was just doing that thing we talked about in the car park. You know…" She waggled the fingers of her hand. "On your neck…?"

Darcie felt completely foolish, and immediately it was as if her entire body was blushing. This was compounded by seeing that others nearby had been alerted to her mini freak-out and were looking over at her in that very British way of looking but trying to seem *not* to be looking.

She settled back into her seat, sighing deeply, and looking down at her hands in her lap.

"Sorry," she said. "Erm…it just startled me, is all. I'm afraid I'm not used to anyone touching me like that anymore. I thought you might be a beetle."

Rylea laughed.

"I rather like beetles," she said. "And that's a damn sight better than you thinking I was a cockroach."

Despite how embarrassed she still was, Darcie chuckled.

"Anyway, Darce," Rylea went on, "should we just eighty-six the whole back-of-the-neck touching scheme?"

"No!" Darcie immediately said, softly but urgently. "I want you to touch me."

Let her read into that whatever she wants.

"Okay," Rylea replied. "I'm about to touch the back of your neck. This is just me, touching the back of your neck. I'm about to bring my fingers to—"

"I swear to God, I'm going to kill you," Darcie said.

Rylea laughed.

"This is good!" she exclaimed. "We sound like proper girlfriends already."

And then…

Darcie sighed when she felt Rylea's fingers make contact with the soft skin at her nape, disturbing the wispy curls of hair there, the fingertips gently rubbing circles.

She missed this. She missed these kinds of touches from a woman. The kinds that weren't meant to lead to any clothes coming off but were instead meant to remind her that she wasn't alone, and that *somebody* wanted to simply touch her.

Fuck my life, I need to start dating again…and get laid.

***

Surprisingly, the wedding ceremony was rather ordinary. Darcie had expected more from Jeannette.

The two brides materialised from somewhere, the tall woman who looked like Darth Vader's psychiatrist said some words, the brides exchanged vows and then lit a unity candle, and…that was it.

Jeannette, of course, looked gorgeous. Her blonde hair practically glowed, and her shapely form was sheathed in a stunning sleeveless dress of white, which came all the way down to her ankles.

When she had appeared, Darcie did feel her respiration kick up a notch along with a desperate yearning for her ex. This was accompanied by a frightening mental descent reminiscent of the days and weeks immediately following her abandonment, when she had started wondering what she had done so wrong to drive Jeannette away.

By then, Rylea had switched to holding her hand, and she had felt her friend give it a reassuring squeeze. And at that moment, it was as if a switch had been thrown.

She hadn't done anything wrong! Certainly nothing to merit what Jeannette had done to her.

If anything, *she* had escaped! After all, if Jeannette was capable of being so heartless, it really was only a matter of time before she had hurt her in some other way, even if she had never met Miss Katelynn Jefferson.

It was, in fact, remarkable that she and Jeannette had had a whole year together without Jeannette torpedoing their romance in some fashion.

I'm over her! And I got lucky!

Having made that realisation meant she had been free to examine Miss Katelynn Jefferson during the brief ceremony.

There was no denying the American was beautiful. Several inches shorter than herself and Jeannette, with curly brown hair, she was rather buxom and had a tattoo of some sort on her left arm, but Darcie was too far away to make out what it was.

Darcie realised that it felt good to finally see this woman. She'd had so many different iterations of what the woman Jeannette had left her for looked like over the past several months. Finally having that question answered was a bit of a relief. But it was also like facing a fear head-on and discovering that there was nothing really to be afraid of.

Katelynn Jefferson was just a woman. Pretty, yes, but not spectacularly so. Her boobs were bigger than her own, but so what? That just meant they had further to fall in about twenty years. Quite frankly, Darcie preferred being taller. Katelynn's hair was lovely, but then again, it was her wedding day.

She was just a woman, and there was nothing—superficially at least—which screamed, "This is why Jeannette left you for me!"

When the ceremony ended, and the happy couple had been pronounced, the assembled guests burst into applause. As Jeannette and her new wife walked up the aisle, Darcie kept her eyes on her ex, curious if she would notice her among all the other well-wishers, many of whom were taking photos with their mobiles or reaching out to briefly grasp either of the women's hands.

It happened when the pair were about three rows from the end.

Jeannette, smiling her grand smile—the one that could melt ice—happened to look to her right and—*bam!*—her blue eyes connected with Darcie's.

For the splittest of split seconds, Jeannette's eyes widened with delight and her smile—though no one would believe this was possible—got even more radiant. But then, Darcie saw Jeannette's eyes spot Rylea standing next to her. And Rylea really was *next* to her.

Her fake date had her arm around Darcie's waist, holding her close in a very *she's my woman now* kind of way. And Darcie registered how Jeannette's smile faltered, and how her eyes suddenly hardened a bit, and even lost some of their American cockiness.

Katelynn, who had been continuing to walk, holding Jeannette's hand, turned in surprise because Jeannette's own step had faltered, and she had fallen behind. But Jeannette quickly recovered and caught up with her bride.

The tiniest of smiles upturned the corners of Darcie's mouth.

The blow had been struck.

Chapter 18

"Was that too much?" Rylea whispered to Darcie after Jeannette and the other American cow passed. "I mean, having my arm around you?"

Darcie looked at her, and Rylea was thinking perhaps she needed to repeat the question, when suddenly, Darcie grabbed her head with both of her hands and planted a quick, closed-mouth kiss on her lips.

"Are you kidding me?" Darcie asked. "That was bloody brilliant! Keep it up!"

Rylea had to take a deep breath, her lips still feeling Darcie's on them.

"Erm, yeah," she said. "No problem!" Especially if her reward was going to be more kisses. "She did seem a little tripped up when she saw us."

"You noticed that too?" Darcie whispered.

Rylea nodded. It had actually been rather gratifying to notice that Jeannette, upon seeing her with Darcie, had seemed taken aback.

"I did," she answered Darcie. "Now we just have to continue the ruse."

"Exactly," Darcie said. "And remember, be sure not to look a day over twenty-five."

"I'm not a day over twenty-five," Rylea reminded her. "Or twenty-five, full stop."

"I know," Darcie assured her. "I'm just reminding you!"

Rylea smirked.

"This silly schoolgirl enthusiasm you have for revenge must be why I decided to date you," she said. She looked behind them and groaned. "Ugh, they're doing a receiving line?" she asked, noticing guests queueing up. "Really? Why? Those are so bloody stupid!"

Her theory about receiving lines was that couples used them to take note of who showed up for the wedding, which she imagined was important information when it came to determining who didn't bring a gift.

They joined the back of the queue, and Rylea was secretly thrilled when Darcie not only held her hand but would also rest her head on her shoulder from time to time, as if impatient with how slowly the line was advancing.

"We've got her attention," Rylea told Darcie softly. She was referring to how Jeannette would frequently look to her right, over her wife's head, to peek over at them.

"Oh, I know," Darcie replied, just as softly. "She was always terrible at subtlety, especially if she was bothered by something. She probably believes no one can see her doing that."

After taking another few steps closer, Rylea asked, "Right, so how do you want to play this when it's our turn?"

"Softly nibble on my earlobe while fondling my left breast," Darcie replied.

Rylea laughed, with Darcie joining in. This had the effect of making Jeannette, yet again, steal a glance over at them while greeting one of her guests.

"Just be yourself, Rylea," Darcie said. "You're already fabulous; just remember that you're fabulous *and* my girlfriend."

"I should bloody hope so if I get to fondle your tits," she snarkily retorted.

More laughter. Rylea couldn't help but realise that she was having more fun with Darcie than she'd had with many of her past *real* girlfriends. She just felt so at ease with Darcie, and she had a very strong suspicion that Darcie was feeling the same way.

It was too bad this whole charade wasn't going to lead to anything more, but she was feeling rather happy that it appeared as if she would come out of this with a really good friend.

Finally, it was their turn to give obeisance to the newly-minted wives.

Rylea watched Jeannette smile warmly at Darcie, as if she was just another guest. The cheek of it made her blood boil a bit.

"I'm so glad you came!" Jeannette said, giving Darcie a hug. "Really, I am glad to see you, Darce."

Rylea examined Darcie's face for any signs that she was about to crack, either into a weepy emotional mess, or into a raging volcano. She hadn't told Darcie this, but last night she had strategized on ways to pull Darcie off Jeannette should Darcie launch herself at her, ready to claw her eyes out. She had even watched a YouTube video called "How to Break Up a Fight Between Two Women"—not at all surprised anymore that such vids even existed.

Step One: When women fight, nails become claws, so control the hands first by getting behind one of the fighters and wrapping her arms in a bear hug.

To that end, Rylea now very subtly repositioned herself so that she was still *next* to Darcie, but also slightly *behind* Darcie.

But all Darcie said—rather pleasantly, considering—was, "Congratulations."

Jeannette then said, "Darcie, I'd like you to meet my wife, Katelynn. Katelynn, Darcie is an old friend of mine from Tremont."

Bugger! Old friend?

Rylea assessed the limberness of arms, judging them primed and ready to wrap around Darcie, keeping her from using her claws.

But her friend seemed to be handling things perfectly fine.

"So lovely to meet you!" Darcie enthused.

Katelynn smiled and even brought Darcie in for a hug.

"So nice to meet you too!" she said. "Thank you so much for coming!"

Rylea had to admit, Katelynn seemed very poised for a woman who just had to know that this was Jeannette's ex, and that she was complicit in the destruction of their relationship. But then again, why wouldn't she be poised? After all, Jeannette had chosen her over Darcie, which meant she was the victor.

"Jeannette," Darcie said, turning to her now, "you remember my girlfriend Rylea, don't you? From The Bean?"

Jeannette turned her attention to Rylea now, and though outwardly Jeannette was smiling and oozing charm, Rylea could detect a crack in her veneer. The woman was bothered.

"Of course," Jeannette said, and then leaned in to give Rylea a hug which had all the warmth of a Cornish morning in February. "It's so nice to see you again!" she continued when they separated.

"Lovely seeing you too!" Rylea exclaimed, smiling her best *I'm only twenty-four-years-old smile.*

Then she was in another hug, this time with Katelynn, a much warmer and genuine one.

"Thank you so much for coming," Katelynn said. "And I *love* your dress! You look gorgeous in it!"

"Aww, that's sweet of you to say!" Rylea replied. "And I should be thanking *you!* Do you know," she went on, looking between Katelynn and Jeannette, "this is the first lesbian wedding I've ever been to?"

"Really?" Katelynn asked.

Rylea nodded.

"Yep," she answered. "Twenty-four-years-old and no lesbian weddings! Like, how does someone get as old as twenty-four and not have any lesbian weddings under her belt?" She shook her head as if she herself couldn't believe what she was saying. "I mean, back when I was kid, I was *certain* that by twenty-four-years-old I'd have been to at least *one* lesbian wedding. But nope! This is my first! At twenty-four!"

Darcie, who had by now retaken her hand, squeezed it tightly, which Rylea construed as the signal to knock it off.

Katelynn laughed.

"Oh my god, I love you!" she said. "And twenty-four isn't old! I'm thirty! And my sweetie here…" She wrapped her arm around Jeannette's waist. "…is thirty-*three!*"

Rylea watched Jeannette's face, at how it ever so briefly looked as if she suddenly didn't want to be married to Katelynn anymore.

***

Following their duties on the receiving line, the two brides and their families spent time having their photos taken by the wedding photographer. Meanwhile, the DJ began playing music and other guests either started claiming spots at the tables set up for the reception, or mingled throughout the atrium with others.

"You're not horribly bored, are you?" Darcie asked. "You are!"

Rylea laughed.

"No, I'm not," she assured Darcie. "This is fun!"

She really was having a good time. Being the instrument through which Darcie exacted a measure of revenge on Jeannette was exciting. And it seemed to be working, which was awesome!

She had heard from her straight friends that men can't read women very well. Darcie could never understand that. Women were dead *easy* to read. Perhaps there was something in all the oestrogen coursing through their bodies which acted as a kind of radio receiver.

Whatever it was, Rylea had read Jeannette like a book, and it was clear she had been thrown off guard by seeing Darcie with her.

"By the way, I applaud you, Ms. Darcie Spencer," Rylea said. "You are holding up really well."

Darcie blushed.

"It's because of you," she replied. "Honestly, if I had come alone, I would probably be in the loo, crying my eyes out." She then smacked her head. "What am I talking about? I wouldn't have even bothered coming by myself! Instead, I'd be *home* crying my eyes out." She laughed nervously, as if embarrassed that she had revealed too much.

Rylea's heart broke for her friend. Without overthinking it, she pulled Darcie in for an embrace.

"I'm totally okay," Darcie said while they held each other. "But I could use a drink."

"Perfect," Rylea said, enjoying how their bodies melded together. "I happen to see a bar."

Darcie, keeping her hands around Rylea's waist, pulled away just enough to be able to look at her.

"Be sure to tell the bartender that you're twenty-four-years-old, though," she said. "And that, as a twenty-four-year-old, you're legally allowed to drink, because at twenty-four-years-old you're well over the minimum age, because you're twenty-four."

Rylea cocked an eyebrow.

"I'm just keeping my favourite exorcism client happy by reminding the enemy of how young I am," she said.

Chapter 19

Yes, it was true Darcie needed a drink, but she was amazed at how good she felt.

She had gotten her closure and had even gotten a bit of revenge in the process. It may have been five months back when she'd last seen Jeannette, but Darcie realised today that she still knew that woman and was still able to read her features and pick up on her signals.

It might have been un-Christian of her, but she was almost orgasmic at how much Jeannette had been bothered by seeing her with Rylea.

When she had asked if Jeannette remembered Rylea, that had been a completely needless question. Of course, Jeannette remembered Rylea! She had felt threatened by the incredibly beautiful Rylea ever since the younger woman opened Bean There/Done That across the street from Shelf Life Books.

Darcie knew that showing up here today with Rylea had been a knife thrust right at the heart of Jeannette's ego, and that her ex had gotten the message loud and clear: *You may have left me, but I'm doing just fine without you.*

She also knew Jeannette had been surprised to see her here at all—Darcie had picked up *that* signal when their eyes first connected right after the ceremony. Which meant Jeannette's invitation had only been her attempt to alleviate some of her own guilt.

Because of that, Darcie was planning to stay at this wedding until the very end, even if that meant her and Rylea escorting the two brides to the bloody honeymoon suite. Jeannette was going to see her enjoying her time with Rylea and she didn't care how ruthless or un-Christian it was.

As they walked to the bar, Rylea did that thing she had suggested in the car park: lifted Darcie's hand to her lips and gave it a kiss. It made Darcie's heart quicken. She was really enjoying being here with Rylea, so much so that she was beginning to wonder what the likelihood was of the two of them actually becoming something.

It didn't seem beyond the pale to imagine it. Not anymore.

One of the things becoming a de facto parent had done was sharpen her perceptive abilities. Because of this, she was reasonably certain that Rylea was just as attracted to her, as she was to Rylea, and that Rylea was…at least open to the idea of something happening between them.

But what manner of *something* would that be, Darcie wondered.

Rylea—only twenty-four and unfettered with a child—might only be interested in something discreetly casual, a friends-with-benefits kind of thing. But she *was* interested in something, of that Darcie was sure.

And if it was something casual Rylea wanted, Darcie was fine with it! The occasional, no-strings-attached shag once a week with the remarkable young woman who had just kissed her hand was enough to make her nipples—already hardened from that kiss—even harder.

She just needed to figure out how to approach it, without embarrassing herself or Rylea…

After getting their drinks, they sat through the god-awful speeches and the other ridiculous routines of a wedding. By the end of all that, Darcie was feeling rather impatient.

She wondered why people couldn't be more original when it came to their wedding receptions, why the same silly format had to be recycled again and again. What she would do differently, she had no idea, but if she did end up getting married soon, maybe she'd ask Cleo to plan the reception. After all, a child would at least be creative.

"Uh-oh," Rylea said at one point, after they both just sat down from dancing. "Bogey, ten o'clock."

Darcie blinked.

"Okay, I know I ought to be clever enough to understand it when you talk like a World War II RAF pilot," she began, "but what on earth do you mean?"

Rylea rolled her eyes.

"Jeannette is slowly coming our way, just over your right shoulder," she explained.

"Your hand. My leg. Now," Darcie ordered.

Another eye roll from Rylea.

"So bossy," she said.

Darcie gasped when Rylea then placed her hand on her left thigh, and then started stroking it slowly, sensuously.

The switch had been thrown. Inside her centre, she felt her walls swelling and becoming lubricated, and because it had been so long since a woman had touched her like this, she knew she was going to become very wet, very fast.

She held Rylea's eyes with her own for a heartbeat or two, and then glanced down at Rylea's lap. Like herself, her friend had one leg crossed over the other, which caused the hem of her dress to ride up and expose a lot of her right thigh.

Meeting Rylea's gaze again, she quirked an eyebrow and said, "May I?"

Rylea's cheeks coloured.

"I really wish you would, Darce," she answered.

Darcie's clit thudded.

She reached over and rested her hand on Rylea's leg, mimicking the stroking Rylea was doing to hers. She heard Rylea take in a deep breath at the same moment her eyes began smouldering.

What started as a way to further inflame the jealousy in her ex had now become something more.

A line had just been crossed.

"Fuck," Rylea whispered, "we're about to be interrupted."

"Hi there," Jeannette said, finally reaching their table.

Without removing her hand from Rylea's leg, Darcie looked over her shoulder at their visitor.

"Hi yourself," she greeted.

"Mind if I join you?" Jeannette asked, indicating an empty seat at their table. "I'm dying to sit!"

"Feel free!" Darcie invited. Now, she and Rylea removed their hands from one another's legs, but not before sharing a look in which both of them acknowledged silently to the other that the paradigm had shifted.

"Where's Mrs. Jeannette?" Rylea asked.

Jeannette smiled.

"Working the other side of the room," she answered. "We agreed to split the effort, so to speak. Sooooo…you two, huh?"

Darcie smiled, but try as she might, she couldn't help it from appearing a bit sinister.

"Yep, us two," she answered.

"That's great!" Jeannette enthused. "That's really great! Just…" She shrugged. "…great!"

Jeannette—one of the most articulate people Darcie had ever met…well, for an American—only became this inarticulate when she was perturbed.

"And, um, how long has this been going on?" Jeannette asked next.

"Two months," Rylea said, providing the agreed-upon answer to just such a question.

Jeannette smiled.

"Great!" she replied, and Darcie almost wanted to burst into laughter.

"Oh, yeah, my Darce is wonderful," Rylea went on. "I mean, the snoring can be a bit much, am I right?"

Darcie clenched her jaw and slowly turned her head to glare at Rylea.

"But at least we both love Italian food," Rylea added. "Cacciatore's…that's our place! Although, I try to keep her away from the fra diavolo sauce. Spicy food only aggravates the snoring later."

Darcie kicked Rylea's leg under the table.

"Yes, thank you, dear," she said. "I think we've heard just about enough on the topic of my snoring."

"So, Rylea…" Jeannette began, "I'm wondering if I can ask you a huge favour. Might I have a word with Darce, please? In private?"

Darcie met Rylea's eyes again and gave her a slight nod. In truth, she hadn't been expecting this. After the way Jeannette had skulked off in the night, so to speak, five months ago, with nary a word, revealing herself to be a coward, Darcie had expected the last thing her ex would want was a private word.

"Of course," Rylea answered Jeannette. "I'll just wander around the atrium admiring the foliage."

She got up, but not before giving Darcie's hand a reassuring squeeze.

Darcie made a point of watching Rylea walk away. In part, because she knew it would bug Jeannette; in part, because watching Rylea walk away was a treat for the eyes.

Then she turned her attention to the woman who had abandoned her and Cleo without even the courtesy of an explanation.

***

To her credit, Jeannette did seem deflated a bit, and not her usual confident self. Whether it was an act or not, Darcie wasn't sure.

Crossing her arms and sitting up with the kind of posture she hadn't used since she was a schoolgirl, Darcie stared at her, waiting.

"Rylea seems great," Jeannette said. "And you two seem happy."

"We are," Darcie replied. "And I'm fairly certain that if she decided to leave me, she'd at least tell me why."

Jeannette's body recoiled slightly, as if Darcie had physically struck her.

"Darce," Jeannette began, "I am so sorry! I never wanted to hurt you—"

"And Cleo," Darcie cut in. "Let's not forget the *child* who had started getting used to the idea of the three of us being a family."

Jeannette closed her eyes, seeming to take a moment to steady herself.

Well, Darcie wasn't about to let her get too steady. Mentioning Cleo as she had just done filled her with even more resolve. After all, in this confrontation that was five months in the making, she was acting as Cleo's champion as well.

"She made a banner for you, you know," Darcie went on. "'Welcome Home,' it said. We were going to hang it above the stairs so it would be the first thing you saw when you came back from New York to come live with us."

Jeannette swallowed. Her eyes were brimming with as-yet unfallen tears.

"How is Cleo doing?" she asked.

"Oh, she's grand," Darcie answered. "Thanks for *finally* asking."

"Darce…"

"Of course, now I'm wondering how long it will be before I let another woman get that close to Cleo again," Darcie continued. "A year? Two years? Or will I just wait until she's off at uni? I won't mind, you understand. I will happily sneak away when I can for a shag as long as Cleo is protected."

"Of course," Jeannette stated. "You're so good to her. It's one of your most attractive qualities."

Must put that on my Pink Cupid profile: Am not horrible to children.

"Listen, Darce, I behaved badly—worse than badly—and I'm hoping I can explain—"

Darcie cut her off with an aggrieved sigh. She realised now that she no longer cared what Jeannette's explanation was, which she took as a sign of growth and perhaps of finally obtaining some peace with what happened.

"You know what?" she began. "Don't bother. Please. I know that in your profession, both sides get to present their cases, but this isn't a courtroom. You did what you did; the damage is done, so keep your explanation.

"I will say, however, that whatever inadequacies I had as a partner did not merit what you did to me and Cleo, and you know that's true. What happened is solely on you!"

"I know that, Darce!" Jeannette hissed. "Don't you think I know that? What I did was perhaps the worst thing I've ever done to another human being, and I am not proud of it."

She picked up a napkin from the table and dabbed at her eyes.

"I was just hoping for an opportunity to give you an explanation of—"

"Of what?" Darcie interrupted. "Jeannette, I don't want to hear it! There is no acceptable explanation, don't you understand? And I refuse—refuse!—to have you put Cleo in the middle of this, by telling me that you weren't ready for an instant family! I didn't bloody well surprise you with her one day!"

"I would never do that!" Jeannette insisted.

"Fine," Darcie said. "So we have nothing further to discuss. You've apologised and, quite frankly, I'm happy leaving it at that because I am *so* done thinking about you. And me coming to this wedding was proof of that. I even brought you a lovely gift. Just tell me one thing, Jeannette."

Jeannette took a breath.

"What's that?"

"Where are you and Katelynn planning on settling?" Darcie asked.

"Here in Newquay," Jeannette answered. "Katelynn is a freelance journalist, so it was easy for her to relocate. Besides, I figured Tremont was out of the question."

Darcie scoffed.

"Understatement," she said.

"What are they calling me there?" Jeannette inquired.

"Oh, everybody is being very politely British about it," Darcie replied. "They're leaving it at 'American cow' and that's it. Anyway, I suppose Newquay is big enough for the two of us. Just look the other way if you spot me in Sainsbury's, especially if Cleo is with me."

"Jeannette, darling, your mother is asking for you."

This came from a young man in a suit.

"Tell her I'll be right there, please, Nigel," Jeannette said. When Nigel had gone, Jeannette stared at Darcie and smiled ruefully. "Well, when I sent the invitation, I said I wanted closure, and I've clearly gotten it. Loud and clear."

She stood and turned to leave, but then stopped and turned back to Darcie.

"For what it's worth," she said, her voice cracking, "I will always hate myself for what I did to you and Cleo. I don't expect you to do so, but please tell Cleo I'm sorry."

Before Darcie could even consider if that merited a response, Jeannette turned and hurriedly walked away.

Chapter 20

Rylea wandered around the atrium, appearing to be admiring the plants but in reality, plotting her next move.

The plants and trees were lovely, of course, but collectively they were all making her feel inadequate for the wilted or half-dead specimens of houseplants she had at home. So, rather than focus on her failings as a plant mum, she decided to focus on her and Darcie. The plants could sod off.

There was definitely something there between her and Darce! What it was, exactly, Rylea had no idea, but it was exciting and made her body feel tingly. Minutes earlier, when they had their hands on each other's legs, it felt as if they were silently agreeing that they both wanted one another, and all they needed was some privacy.

Bloody Jeannette! Coming over and interrupting them!

She and Darcie could be well on their way to sorting out…

Aargh! What, exactly?

Examining some beautiful but delicate-looking ferns, she told herself to look at it rationally.

Darcie was a serious sort. She was a mum, after all. Well, auntie-turned-mum, but same thing. And after what Jeannette had done to her, Darcie was bound to be extra-super-especially careful about getting serious with another woman.

Rylea was fine with that. All the time she had been spending with Darcie recently had made her realise that she only wanted to spend *more* time with her. And she'd be more than willing to take it at Darcie's pace.

And if Darcie only wanted something casual, without any expectations or strings attached, that would be fine too. Life was too short to turn away the Darcies of the world if all they wanted was a hot and heavy shag once a week to relieve the stress.

The question now was, how to proceed? What if bloody Jeannette had broken the spell somehow, and Darcie was over there now, having no recollection of the sparks they both felt during the hands-on-legs moment?

Even worse, what if Jeannette was over there upsetting Darcie anew?

Suddenly, she forgot about the possibility of hot and heavy once-weekly shags as concern for Darcie's well-being surfaced.

Maybe I shouldn't have been so quick to leave?

But, no…Darcie and Jeannette needed to have this confrontation, like Luke Skywalker and Darth Vader. Except…didn't Luke end up walking away from that conversation missing one hand?

Rylea glanced across the atrium at the table where Darcie and Jeannette were talking. Darcie still had both her hands—and what lovely hands they were, with long, thin fingers that could probably reach…

She shook her head.

Focus!

The point was, Darcie still had both her hands. In fact, Rylea considered, even from this distance it appeared as if Darcie was Darth Vader, and Jeannette was the one at risk of forever being known as Lefty.

Okay then…

Rylea decided it was safe for her to go to the loo if she could find it here in bloody Sherwood Forest.

Turns out, she needed to leave the atrium and make her way towards the lobby.

Remarkably, considering there was a lesbian wedding reception happening on premises, the loo was empty, save for one cubicle. After peeing, she emerged from hers at the same time as the other woman.

"Oh, hello!" Katelynn greeted her.

"Hi," Rylea replied, smiling, and starting to wash her hands. She still wasn't sure just how friendly to be with Katelynn but was finding it difficult to *not* be friendly. Jeannette's bride was one of those women who exuded warmth, openness, and a desire to get along with everybody.

Still, she had willingly conspired to destroy Darcie's happiness. In fact, Rylea could just imagine it…

New York City.

Katelynn meets Jeannette.

"Oh, you have a girlfriend back in merry old England? Well, forget her! I'm cute and bubbly and have the boobs of three women! Marry me instead!"

No, Rylea determined, she would be sufficiently British-polite to Katelynn, but she wouldn't pretend that everything was okay.

"Are you having a good time?" Katelynn asked, her face registering that she did really, really hope Rylea was having a good time.

"I am," Rylea answered. "You've chosen a lovely location."

They were done washing their hands and were now just chatting before the mirror.

"I had to rely completely on Jeannette for that," Katelynn admitted. "I've never been to Cornwall before. But now it's home."

"So, you're settling here?" Rylea asked.

Katelynn nodded.

"We are," she confirmed. "Do you live in town also?"

"No, I live in Tremont," Rylea supplied. "You know…where Jeannette *used* to live," she added pointedly. "It's about twenty-five minutes away, provided the roads are clear."

"Oh, that's not far!" Katelynn said. "Maybe we can all get together and hang out sometime!"

The cheek!

Rylea crossed her arms.

"Seriously?" she asked.

Katelynn nodded.

"I'd love that!" she said.

Rylea felt her Britishness cracking, but she managed to hold it together.

"I'm sure you would," she replied. "But you need to understand that Darcie only came here today because she wanted and needed the closure. And under the circumstances, I'm surprised at how well she's holding up, considering Jeannette's her ex and *you're* the one she left her for. No offence, of course."

Katelynn stared at her.

"I'm sorry?" she asked.

Rylea blinked.

How could Katelynn have *not* heard her? Perhaps she had mumbled.

"I was just pointing out," she tried again in a slightly louder voice, "that Darcie is holding up well considering that Jeannette left her for you."

"No, I heard you," Katelynn said, holding up a hand. She then took a deep breath. "What are you talking about?"

Rylea felt her mouth go dry and her heart drop to the pit of her stomach.

Bugger!

But how was that possible?

"Jeannette…" she began, her voice less forceful than it had been a mere moment ago. "Jeannette is Darcie's ex. They were together when Jeannette left for New York. When she met you!" She started feeling panicky, and suddenly it was as if her mouth was on autopilot. "They were going to move in together! Then Jeannette just never came back! No explanation! Nothing! Broke Darcie's heart! Next thing Darcie knows, she gets an invitation to your wedding!" She swallowed. "But surely you knew all this!"

But Katelynn's face clearly showed that, no, she did not know all of this. Her pretty features had morphed into a mask of barely contained anger, her pale skin now red and getting redder.

Fuck, what have I done?

Katelynn was no longer looking at her. Instead, her eyes were staring at a point beyond Rylea, and were rapidly moving back and forth, as if she was replaying scenes in her mind, watching them over again, searching for clues.

"Erm…I'm so sorry!" Rylea said. But it seemed as if Katelynn had not heard her, lost as she was in the visuals only she could see.

"Right…" Rylea went on. "Erm…"

Oh, the hell with it!

She quickly walked past Katelynn and out of the loo, hurrying back to the atrium.

When she arrived, she saw Jeannette stand up from the table where she had been sitting with Darcie. The blonde started to walk away, then turned and said something else before finally accompanying some bloke and leaving Darcie for good.

Rylea hurried over.

"We have to get out of here," she said to Darcie. She gently took hold of Darcie's arm and indicated that she needed to rise.

"What is going on?" Darcie asked. But thankfully, she stood, gathering up her handbag.

Maintaining her grip on Darcie's arm, Rylea started leading her out of the atrium.

"Rylea, what is the rush?" Darcie asked.

"*Jeannette Sommers!*"

Rylea's blood froze. Suddenly, all conversation in the atrium stopped.

Katelynn was storming in, and Rylea actually felt frightened. Katelynn was a small woman, but then again, a bomb was a small weapon. And Katelynn looked like a bomb whose fuse was lit.

"That's Katelynn!" Darcie said. "She looks upset!"

"Yeah, I wonder what that's all about?" Rylea replied. "Let's just keep walking, please."

"Rylea, what is going on?" Darcie asked.

Rylea sighed. They were crossing the lobby now.

"Let's just say that there's a cat—a very big cat—which has just been let out of a very big bag," she explained. "More details will be forthcoming once we are in the car, but for now, just trust me when I say we don't want to be here."

Just as they were exiting the hotel, Rylea could hear shouts and screams coming from behind them in the direction of the atrium, followed by what sounded like glass breaking.

"Must walk faster," she suggested.

Chapter 21

On the ride back to Tremont, Darcie absorbed what Rylea had just told her about her meeting with Katelynn in the toilet.

"That poor girl!" she said, meaning it. She tried to imagine what it would be like to find out—on her wedding day—that when she met her wife, she was already seriously involved with another woman, *and* was making plans to live with her.

It would mean that her wife was a liar.

It would mean that her wife was a cheater.

It would mean that she would have to question everything she knew about the woman she just married, including her ability to commit to the marriage long-term.

It would also mean that she could probably never trust her new wife.

What a shite way to start a life together.

"I swear, it was an accident!" Rylea insisted, again. She had started off the story swearing that what Darcie was about to hear was an accident, and then mentioned the accidental nature of her faux pas again somewhere in the middle of the tale.

Darcie looked to her right, at Rylea driving. Other people—blokes mostly, she figured—would consider this a funny story. But Darcie could see that Rylea was genuinely perturbed by her role, in what was starting to sound like World War III back at the Newquay Royal Arms.

She reached over and placed her hand on Rylea's shoulder, rubbing it gently with her fingertips.

"It wasn't your fault," she said. "You were right to assume that Katelynn knew. I mean, how could she not?"

She decided to take a chance and move her hand down to Rylea's leg, with the palm facing up, though. Rylea looked down, saw it, and took her left hand off the steering wheel to grasp Darcie's, their fingers interlocking like puzzle pieces.

They drove in silence for a while, with Darcie enjoying how companionable the quiet was.

"Thank you for today," she eventually said as she noticed them turn off the A39 and onto the road that would lead them to Tremont. "It was amazing."

Rylea took her eyes off the road just long enough to smile at her.

"Did it help?"

Darcie nodded.

"Yes, it did," she answered. "The dragon has been slayed."

This was true. Jeannette was now just a part of her past, a relationship that ended badly, but which had brought her joy while it lasted. She had learned much about herself during her time with Jeannette; she had even grown more as a person. And the fact that she was now able to acknowledge these facts meant that Jeannette no longer held any power over her. For five months, her ex had been a malevolent spectre in her life, making Darcie wonder—over and over—what was wrong with herself to have been treated that way.

Now, she realised it wasn't her fault. Jeannette had done what she had done because of something wrong with *her*. She finally felt at peace. And it was thanks to Rylea. She would never have gone to the wedding and confronted Jeannette if Rylea hadn't come up with this fake date scheme, helping her to slay the dragon.

Rylea had to release her hand to navigate the Mini through some sharp curves, but Darcie kept her hand on her friend's leg, stroking her thigh with her fingertips. She heard Rylea's breath quickening.

They were getting close to her cottage. Decisions needed to be made. And with her self-confidence restored, she felt a bit of assertiveness was needed here.

"Do you have anywhere to be?" she quietly asked Rylea. It was still early, after all, just getting on four-thirty in the afternoon. It was possible Rylea had other plans for today.

"Nope," Rylea said. "I'm all yours."

Darcie's clit pulsed.

"Are you?" she asked. She switched from rubbing Rylea's thigh with her fingertips to giving it a gentle squeeze. Her meaning needed to be clear.

Rylea inhaled sharply.

"All yours, Darce," she replied, her chest heaving.

They turned onto Corwin Lane.

"I take it I'm invited in, then?" Rylea asked, slowing the Mini to turn into Darcie's driveway.

Ooh, now who's being assertive?

"Absolutely," Darcie assured her. The car stopped and Rylea switched it off. For a moment they both just sat there, staring ahead, the sounds of their rapid breathing competing with the unseen chirping birds.

"Talk before, or talk afterwards?" Darcie asked.

"Talk afterwards," Rylea answered. "Definitely talk afterwards."

Darcie unfastened her seat belt.

"Let's get inside!" she urged.

***

They started kissing as soon as the front door closed, with Darcie pressing Rylea against the entryway wall.

Rylea's lips were soft, yielding, and opened immediately to allow Darcie to slip her tongue in. Their kissing was hungry but gentle, yet full of desire and passion. Groaning into it, Darcie realised just how much she had wanted this all day.

She let her hands roam down to Rylea's arse, giving it a squeeze and then feeling her clit flutter when Rylea moaned sexily. She then gathered up the fabric in her fingers and lifted the hem of the dress higher. At the same time, she split Rylea's legs with her thigh. Against her mouth, Rylea mewled as Darcie pressed her knee firmly on the young woman's centre. Darcie's eyebrows shot up upon feeling how wet Rylea already was. So much so that Darcie withdrew her leg and replaced it immediately with her right hand, needing to touch her.

"Oh fuck, Darcie!" Rylea called out, breaking their kiss.

Rylea's underwear felt like lace, and Darcie could tell they were tiny. And they were damp. What's more, Rylea's arousal had escaped the confines of the fabric, wetting the apex of her legs.

Darcie cupped her hand over Rylea's sex, over the knickers, while kissing her neck.

"Please take me upstairs," Rylea gasped. "Please!"

Darcie purred against Rylea's neck.

"Come along, then," she whispered.

Reluctantly, she withdrew her hand so that the both of them could hurry up the steps, their high heels clicking on the worn wood.

Darcie didn't care that her bedroom was slightly a mess—her bed unmade, her pyjamas from last night tossed carelessly on the mattress. In her anxiety this morning she just hadn't cared about being tidy. All that mattered now was her need for the woman who had come upstairs with her.

They were in each other's arms again the instant they crossed the threshold into the room, kissing desperately, Darcie's quivering pussy reacting to the warmth of Rylea's tongue on her own.

But she was getting bored with kissing…

She started walking Rylea backwards while maintaining their kiss. Eventually, she felt Rylea's legs encounter the edge of the mattress. She pulled her mouth away and grinned wickedly at Rylea just before placing her hand on Rylea's sternum and giving her a push.

With a yelp, Rylea fell backwards onto the bed, laughing when she landed. Darcie immediately joined her, topping her by straddling her waist. With her arms crossed, she grasped hold of the fabric of her dress at her waist and started pulling it up until she could lift the dress over her head and off entirely, revealing herself to Rylea.

"Oh my god!" Rylea gasped, her eyes riveted on Darcie's breasts. "You're even more beautiful than I imagined all these years."

Smirking, Darcie quirked an eyebrow.

"Imagined, huh?" she asked. "Years, huh?"

By now, Rylea had her hands on Darcie's waist, just above the waistband of the lace thong she was wearing. Now, she smirked.

"Trust me, Darce," she said, "I have fantasised about this for *years*."

Darcie's eyes widened. She really had no idea, and knowing it now was turning her on so much.

She leaned forward, supporting herself on her arms, bringing her chest to Rylea's face. Her breasts were dangling down, and she carefully positioned the left one over Rylea's mouth, allowing her to take what she had wanted all these years.

"Mmmmm," she moaned when her nipple was captured and sucked. "Oh my god!" It had been too long! With each pull Rylea made with her mouth, Darcie's clit pounded, and inside her vagina the flooding kicked up a notch.

Rylea gave one last hard pull before switching to Darcie's right breast and repeating the action, this time Darcie felt the edges of Rylea's teeth, very lightly, experimentally almost, as if asking for permission.

"Bite!" Darcie growled. It seemed silly, but she almost felt as if she were about to cry with how much her body yearned for everything Rylea wanted to do to her. "Bite!" she repeated. Then, *"Oh fuck!"* as sharp teeth clamped onto her hard nipple. The pain quickly shot through her breast and morphed into pleasure as it found its way to her core, making her inner walls flutter and swell more.

Rylea followed up the bite with soft and gentle sucks, and Darcie felt her take as much of the tip of her breast into her mouth as she could. After a few moments, Rylea returned her attention to Darcie's left breast, this time giving that nipple another sharp bite, but pulling on it as well, increasing that pain/pleasure factor. And while Rylea sucked and bit, Darcie switched to supporting herself entirely on her left arm, while bringing the fingers of her right hand up to her face.

They smelled of Rylea, of the musk of her pussy and of her perfumed lotion, and now she needed more of that.

When Rylea's teeth finally relented, Darcie pushed herself upright again and then quickly lay down beside her new lover, kissing her deeply. Meanwhile, her hand slid up Rylea's smooth thigh, Rylea opening her legs to accommodate her.

"Let me get this dress off," Rylea breathed.

Darcie smiled and then ran her tongue over Rylea's upper lip.

"Not yet," she said. "Ever since you sent me that picture, I've been dreaming of fucking you in this dress. Every woman at the wedding today wanted to fuck you in this dress. So you're going to keep the fucking dress on."

Rylea's eyes clouded over with lust.

"Anything you want…" she replied.

"Take your knickers off, though," Darcie instructed.

Removing her hand from between Rylea's thighs, she watched as Rylea brought her legs together, lifted her bum, and then pulled tiny black underwear off her legs and over the high heels she still had on, tossing them down to the floor.

"Shoes off?" she asked with an impish smile.

"Shoes definitely *on*," Darcie answered.

Rylea then scooched herself further back on the bed, Darcie doing the same.

"Oh my god, Rylea!" Darcie said when she touched Rylea's pussy. It was completely shaved like her own, and her smooth vulva was slick with arousal. Darcie kissed her in the same instant she penetrated her with two fingers which slid in without any resistance at all. With her fingers buried as far in as they would go, she pressed her palm against the hard button of Rylea's clit, making sure she had Rylea's attention.

"Tell me when you're close!" Darcie ordered, breaking the kiss just long enough to say that, before kissing her again.

"*Mmph!...Mmph!...Mmph!*" Rylea grunted into their kiss as Darcie began fucking her with her fingers, being sure to slap her palm against her clit with every inward thrust. Inside, Rylea was all warmth and cream, and Darcie felt some of it spray out with the action of her hand. She couldn't wait to taste it, to fuck Rylea with her tongue next and have her mouth completely awash with Rylea's flavour.

At one point, with her fingers deep inside, she curled them upwards, hitting the magic spot and making Rylea pull her mouth away in order to shout in delight.

"Oh fuck, Darce!" she called out! "Fuck! Darce! I'm getting close already!"

Without any preamble, Darcie ruthlessly pulled her fingers out of Rylea. This was not how Rylea was going to come. She then rolled onto her back.

"Sit on me, baby," she pleaded.

Rylea hurried to oblige. Darcie watched her hike up her dress so that it was bunched around her waist, and then carefully swing her left leg over so that she was now straddling her face.

Rylea's pussy was gorgeous! Swollen, glistening, her folds a dusky rose colour. There was a drop of arousal on one of them, looking as if it were about to fall.

Darcie took hold of Rylea's hips.

"Let the dress fall," she murmured. An instant later, the fabric collapsed around her head. In the semi-darkness of being under Rylea's dress, she lowered Rylea's pussy to her mouth.

This was how Rylea was going to come, Darcie thought. Wearing this dress that had made every gay woman at the Newquay Royal Arms today want her, and still wearing her sexy high heels as well.

"Darcie! Oh my god!"

The shout came when Darcie's tongue found Rylea's opening and slipped inside. Immediately, she was rewarded with liquid Rylea streaming out and into her mouth. She moaned at how good Rylea tasted, and she stretched her tongue as far as it could reach, until it started aching at the back, to get even more of what was trapped inside the tight passage.

Rylea began rocking her hips, fucking herself on Darcie's tongue. Soon, Darcie felt the entire lower half of her face coated with Rylea's wetness. She tightened her grip on Rylea's hips and then withdrew her tongue in order to circle the swollen clit that Darcie knew needed attention.

"Darcie!...Darcie!"

Darcie wrapped her lips on the hard button and began suckling rhythmically.

"Darcie! I'm gonna come! *Oh shit, I'm gonna come!"*

A moment later, she did.

Darcie almost came herself experiencing the sensation of Rylea coming on her face, feeling how her pussy quivered with the release, feeling how her opening gushed sweet arousal.

Releasing Rylea's clit, she shoved her tongue inside the climaxing passage once more. Rylea's pussy clenched it repeatedly, and Darcie simply revelled in swirling her tongue around, getting as much of Rylea's essence into her mouth as possible.

Chapter 22

Darcie Spencer just made me come! Holy shit, Darcie Spencer just made me come!

Rylea, her pussy still quivering and spasming from the orgasm, had her arms raised to her head, her hands entangled in her hair.

And I'm still dressed!

She couldn't believe it. She even still had her bloody shoes on!

She slowed the rocking of her hips as the detonations of pleasure continued and she went on with her cries and whimpers.

Remarkably, Darcie was showing no signs of letting up.

"*Oh my god…!*" Rylea mewled while Darcie's lips and tongue kept at it between her legs. "*Oh Jesus!*"

She leaned back and supported herself on her arms, her hands grabbing the stiletto heels of her shoes, and selfishly surrendered to Darcie's ministrations, feeling a little guilty for doing so. She should be tending to Darcie now. She'd had hers, after all. It was time to give back.

But Darcie's mouth had her under a spell and with more cries and shouts, she felt that pressure under her mound increasing again.

Switching her weight to her left arm, she used her right hand to pull up her dress and then was able to watch Darcie licking her shaven sex. Darcie's eyes were closed, and she was moaning as if what she was tasting was the most delightful dessert she'd ever encountered.

This visual amped up the rate at which her second orgasm was building, and Rylea started whimpering in anticipation of its release.

This was *Darcie Spencer*—her teenage crush—eating her out, licking her folds, sucking on her clit, about to make her…

"*Oh fuck!*" she squealed. "*Oh fuck, Darce! I'm coming!*"

And then…*BOOM!*

She gasped as if punched in the gut when the release came. Her pussy trembled and spasmed so hard that her entire body began quaking. Her eyes rolled back in her head, she turned her face to the ceiling and just let out a scream as the waves of pleasure rolled through her lower half.

She felt Darcie tighten her grip on her hips, keeping her sex right where she wanted it. By now, Darcie had thankfully released her hypersensitive clit, and was now just probing her tongue inside her flooded passage, and Rylea felt her opening clutching at it repeatedly.

Finally, the tsunami of pleasure waned, and her screaming morphed into mutters of "Oh my god!...Oh my god!...Oh my god!"

Darcie gently pushed upwards on Rylea's hips. Rylea took the hint and lifted herself off Darcie's face, only to collapse onto the mattress, the aftershocks of her climaxes still striking her.

Darcie let her be for a few moments, letting her enjoy the effects of the pleasure she had just been given.

After a while, she felt Darcie unstrapping her high heels and removing them. Rylea then forced herself to sit up, lifting her arms so Darcie could help her off with her dress, knowing that this was a momentous instant in time because Darcie was now going to see her undressed for the first time.

When the dress was pulled over her head, Darcie gasped.

"Oh my god, let me just look at you!" she whispered. She was kneeling on the mattress next to Rylea, and she now pushed Rylea back down, so she was lying flat once more. "Oh my goodness, you are perfect!"

Rylea couldn't believe it. Those words had just come out of her crush's mouth!

Darcie gently ran her left hand over each of Rylea's breasts. Then, she ran that same hand down over her midsection, passing over her abdomen. She caressed her left hip, where her tattoo of a hummingbird was. Then it was back to her abdomen before making the hand come to rest on her mound. Rylea gasped at the way heat bloomed in her pussy as her core anticipated more attention.

Darcie repositioned herself to lay beside Rylea, keeping her hand pressing firmly on Rylea's mound. She then started suckling on Rylea's left breast, her tongue circling the marble-hard nipple.

When she released it, she let out a breath, the expelled air cooling the wet nipple.

"Oh, how long I've wanted to do that!"

Rylea's heart soared.

This woman! Oh my god, this woman!

Before Rylea could get a chance to respond, however, Darcie had her other breast in her mouth, lavishing oral attention on it, making Rylea's clit pound.

"Mmmmm," Rylea moaned, after several moments of this had passed. "Oh fuck, please, Darcie! Let me have you!"

She felt her nipple pop out of Darcie's mouth.

The bookshop owner grinned at her and waggled her eyebrows.

"I like an eager woman," she said.

She then rolled over onto her back, taking Rylea with her so that Rylea ended up topping her, both of them laughing.

First, Rylea kissed Darcie deeply, tasting herself on Darcie's lips, which was definitely making her centre crave even more attention. But it would have to wait…she didn't want to be *that* greedy. Besides, the very idea of what she was about to do to Darcie was making her lightheaded with desire.

So hungry for it was she, that she decided there would be no faffing about. Darcie still had her knickers on, and normally, Rylea would spend some time kissing along the edges of the thong, building up anticipation in her lover, inhaling her scent. But she didn't have the patience for that right now.

Pushing herself up so that she was now kneeling between Darcie's lovely legs, she took hold of the underwear with her fingers. Darcie lifted up her bum to aid her in their removal, and Rylea slid them off her.

"Oh my god," she couldn't help muttering when Darcie's sex was exposed. And Darcie wasn't being shy at all. As soon as her knickers had come off, she raised her knees, placed her feet flat on the mattress and spread her legs, inviting Rylea to her.

Rylea didn't hesitate.

Lowering herself back to the mattress, she positioned her head between Darcie's legs and admired how gorgeous Darcie's pussy was.

And how wet she was!

Her pink folds were glistening, and a clear stream of her arousal was steadily leaking out.

And her clit!

"Oh my god," Rylea couldn't help muttering yet again.

Darcie's clit was swollen, out from its hiding place, and twitching, silently begging Rylea to give it what it needed.

Closing her eyes, Rylea inhaled Darcie's most intimate scent and then with a groan, brought her mouth to her folds, finally fulfilling a dream.

With the flat of her tongue, she licked the entire length of Darcie's pussy, feeling Darcie shiver as she did so.

"Oh fuck, Rylea!" Darcie gasped.

Darcie tasted fantastic, and Rylea groaned in pleasure and then repeated her lick, more slowly this time, the inner walls of her own pussy clenching with want as her tongue was completely saturated with Darcie's essence.

She withdrew her tongue back into her mouth and swallowed. Then went back for more. This time, however, she angled her head sufficiently so that she could slide her tongue into Darcie's vagina where it was instantly immersed in arousal.

Opening her eyes, she looked up, seeing that Darcie had both her breasts in her hands, fondling them, and that her head was turned to the side, with her mouth open. Her eyes were shut, and her brow furrowed as if concentrating on a really hard maths problem. From her mouth were escaping the sexiest cries and whimpers—the noises of a woman lost in pleasure.

I'm doing that to her!

Rylea still couldn't believe it. But now she really wanted to take Darcie to a higher plane of rapture.

Slowly licking Darcie's folds again, she stopped at her engorged clit and circled it twice before clamping her lips down on it and beginning to suck it rhythmically.

"Rylea! Oh Jesus!"

Instantly, Rylea felt a hand on the back of her head as now, Darcie's cries became louder and her grunts more strained.

"Oh fuuuuck!...Mmmmmmmph!....Mmmmmmmph!...Rylea, JesusfuckingChrist!"

With Darcie's hand holding her head where she wanted it to be, Rylea made the determination to give Darcie what she needed. She could sense the urgency of the woman she was eating out, so much so that even while doing what she was doing, she couldn't help wondering if this was the first time another woman had made Darcie come since Jeannette left.

If so, she wanted that honour.

Quickly.

With that in mind, each time she pulled on Darcie's clit, she swiped it rapidly with her tongue, knowing the end was near.

Sure enough…

"OHMYFUCKINGCHRIIIIIIIIIIIIIIIIIST!"

Chapter 23

Had it been this long?

This orgasm was *massive*!

She had no choice but to scream at the top of her lungs as her entire pelvic region just exploded in a storm of pleasure that made her vagina feel not her own, and that also made a bright white light burst behind her eyelids.

She screamed some more as wave after wave struck her, each building upon its predecessor, her pussy convulsing, clutching, spasming with the enormity of this release. It was so strong, she lifted her bum off the mattress, having the presence of mind to realise that Rylea—God bless her—kept her mouth right on her climaxing sex, not letting it get away from her, and not letting up with her attentions.

"*Jeeeeeeeeeeeeeeeeeez!*" she squealed as it kept building and building. She knew what was going to happen, and she wasn't sure if she was ready for it. But there was no stopping it…

Oh fuck…here it comes…

She came a second time and screamed to high heaven when she did.

Collapsing her arse back on the mattress, she arched her back instead while this new climax took over from the first one, not even giving her pussy time to recover. It was just as massive as the first, and Darcie no longer felt human with the way it spread beyond her centre, beyond her lower half, to instead consume her entire body.

It was so powerful, she actually started laughing—and that hadn't happened for a long time.

What was going on with her? She *came* all the time, not being a woman who had any hang-ups about masturbating.

But these were not her usual orgasms brought about by playing with herself. It must be because—

Oh FUCK!

Her mind almost had it, but now Rylea's tongue was penetrating her pussy, which was still in the throes of the climax, and she lost all ability to think or to reason. Instead, all she could do was clutch the bedsheets and tremble from the shocking jolts of pleasure she was experiencing.

"Oh god…Oh god…Oh god," she moaned repeatedly, as finally she began to come down from the peak.

Rylea coaxed her through it expertly, withdrawing her tongue and using her mouth gently on Darcie's folds, avoiding her clit, and even avoiding her opening, knowing as a fellow woman how sensitive the nerve endings there must be by now.

Darcie put her hand back on Rylea's head, stroking her hair. She was still whimpering, still experiencing aftershocks, some of which threatened to morph into yet another climax; but touching Rylea's hair was helping her to feel grounded once more.

"Come up here," she whispered some minutes later.

Rylea was lying beside her seconds later.

Darcie kissed her deeply.

"That was fucking amazing," she murmured when their lips parted. "Sorry for how loud I was."

Rylea laughed.

"Loud is hot!" she told Darcie. "I can't remember the last time I was so turned on by a woman in bed."

Darcie suddenly remembered what it was that her mind had almost grasped earlier.

Her orgasms were so intense tonight because it had been seemingly forever since another woman had made her come.

And she wanted more. Lots more.

"I hope you don't think I'm done, just because you shattered me a bit there," she stated.

Rylea quirked an eyebrow.

"Darce," she began, "I will keep going as long as you do. I guarantee it."

Darcie growled with lust and then immediately topped her lover.

Looking down into her eyes with a penetrating gaze, she said, "You have no idea what you just unleashed, sweet Rylea."

***

Gasping, Darcie covered her convulsing vulva with her hand, thus blocking Rylea's access to it.

"*Oh my FUUUUUUUUUUCK!*" she screamed, pulling her face away from Rylea's pussy above her.

They were sixty-nining, and Rylea had just made her come yet again. This time, however, Darcie's sex was telling her she'd had enough. This climax was potent not only in its level of pleasure, but in how sensitive her pussy now became. It just couldn't tolerate any more direct stimulation.

After her initial scream, Darcie brought her mouth back to working on Rylea's clit and her folds, making all of her subsequent noises against her partner's wetness, until about a minute later, Rylea came undone also in a trembling orgasm which made her shout lustily.

Still protecting her hypersensitive pussy with her hand, Darcie slowed her mouth's action on Rylea's genitalia, using slow licks with the flat of her tongue to catch all the come streaming out of her.

Eventually, though, Rylea lifted herself off Darcie, to lay beside her, but with her head down at Darcie's feet.

For several minutes, the only sounds in the bedroom were those of two women recovering from climaxes: heavy breathing, soft whimpers, startled gasps when aftershocks would hit, and sighed moans of pleasure.

"Bloody hell," Darcie finally said to the ceiling. She felt *wrecked*. She and Rylea had been going at it for quite a while, sometimes slow, sometimes hard and fast. It was dark outside now, but at some point during their activities, Darcie had managed to switch on her bedside lamp, and so the room had a soft orange glow in it.

Now that her body was finally recovered from the latest climax, she discovered how utterly starved she was.

As if on cue, she heard Rylea's stomach grumble, and she laughed.

"Just what I was thinking," she said.

Rylea also laughed.

"I guess we did forget to eat, didn't we?" she commented.

Darcie made a decision. She knew she might not get what she wanted—and she told herself it wouldn't be a big deal if she didn't—but she would at least put it out there.

"I'd love to cook for you," she said. "I have plenty of food."

"Mm," Rylea purred, kissing Darcie's right ankle. "I'd love that."

Darcie swallowed.

"I'd also like it if you stayed the night," Darcie added with a whisper. "I mean, you don't have to, obviously. But I have pyjamas you can wear…"

Rylea kissed her ankle again and then raised herself, so she was supported on both elbows.

"I live three minutes away, Darce," she said, smirking. "I zip home, toss my own pyjamas in a bag, I zip back."

"So you'll stay?" Darcie asked. Fine, it was still too early to determine what—if anything—this…*thing* with Rylea was going to turn into. But Darcie knew that Rylea was *not* a woman she wanted to just fuck and then send on her merry way. They had just shared something powerfully intimate together, and though Rylea may not be interested in having it turn into anything, Darcie wanted to at least let her know that she wanted to share her bed with her as companions and not just as playmates.

Rylea quickly repositioned herself, so they were now lying beside each other properly, heads aligned.

"I would love to stay," she said. "I was hoping I'd get an invitation."

"Were you?" Darcie asked, surprised.

"Mm-hm," Rylea confirmed. "Well, actually, I was hoping that we'd have sex to the point of utter exhaustion, and that you'd be forced to just let me crash here, thus fulfilling another fantasy of mine."

Darcie laughed.

"One day you need to fill me in on these fantasies," she said.

"Well," Rylea began, "you've already fulfilled about a few hundred of them. All that's left now is the sleepover part."

Darcie laughed again, but then gasped when a sudden thought occurred to her. It must have been Rylea's use of the word "sleepover."

"Oh my god! I used to babysit you!" she squealed, covering her face with her hands. Back when she was fifteen, maybe sixteen, and Rylea was just another little kid in the village Darcie could earn a bit of pocket money off of.

"And look at us now," Rylea said, a snarky tone to her voice. "Who would have thought?"

Darcie looked at her.

"Certainly not me!" she exclaimed. "Certainly not then!" she added, laughing.

"So when *did* you first start noticing me?" Rylea asked.

"Oh, not until this morning when you came to pick me up for the wedding," Darcie replied. "I had zero interest in you until then."

Rylea gasped, a shocked look on her face.

"Oh my god!" she exclaimed, laughing. "You are so mean!"

Darcie was laughing also, while simultaneously trying to fend off Rylea attempting to tickle her.

"Now give me the right answer!" Rylea demanded, settling back down on the mattress.

Darcie thought back, and then blushed.

"God, it sounds so creepy," she said, "but, I mean, I suppose when I got back from uni, I noticed what a beautiful woman you were turning into. But Jesus…you had to have only been sixteen or seventeen! But I mean, that's all it was!"

Rylea kissed her very quickly.

"Relax, Darce," she said. "I'm not thinking that you were scoping me out back then, with nefarious thoughts in your mind. There's nothing wrong with you determining that the little girl you used to babysit was becoming a good-looking woman. Just like there was nothing wrong with seventeen-year-old me seeing you about town and wanting to have *hours* of sex with you!"

Darcie burst into laughter, blushing hotly.

"You did not!" she stated, looking at Rylea.

"Oh, I totally did!" Rylea informed her, and Darcie was gratified to see that she was blushing as well.

Darcie quirked an eyebrow.

"Did you even know what lesbian sex was like back then?" she asked.

"I'll admit that I was lacking in a lot of *practical* experience," Rylea said, chuckling. "And that I was certainly not up on the more…advanced stuff. But…I used to watch *a lot* of porn! And, well…let's just say that while watching a video, I'd mentally replace the starring performers with…"

Darcie's mouth dropped open, and her pulse rate kicked up a few percentage points.

"Oh my god, this is simultaneously really hot, and really disturbing!" she said, laughing. "So…I suggest this is a good place to break for food!"

However, before Rylea had a chance to get up off the mattress, Darcie suddenly topped her.

Looking down at her, she said, "But we *will* come back to this conversation at some point. I'm very, very curious exactly what kind of videos your devious little mind had us starring in."

Chapter 24

Rylea hurried home to take a quick shower, change into fresh clothes and pack some pyjamas and clothes for tomorrow. The plan was for her to return to Darcie's for dinner and then…*to stay the night!* And not on the sofa or in a guest room.

In Darcie's room! In Darcie's bed!

With Darcie!

Unbelievable!

Out of the shower now and towelling herself off, she realised she was still on cloud nine.

What an incredible day, and what a spectacular night so far!

She and Darcie together were *amazing!* The sex had been out of this world, and Rylea's first instinct when she had completed the short drive home and entered her house was to ring Tamsin and begin what would certainly be a marathon phone conversation, about what having sex with Darcie was like—without providing too many details, of course.

But she had quelled that urge to call her best friend. In fact, thinking about it now as she used the hair dryer, she needed to quell any urge to say anything to Tamsin for the near future.

She and Darcie may be spending the night together, but that didn't mean she and Darcie were…

An item.

Better to hold off on saying anything to Tamsin just yet, out of respect for Darcie. This was a tiny village, after all. Tamsin wouldn't maliciously spread the gossip, but get enough drinks in her and suddenly the "slips of the tongue" became numerous. If Rylea felt the urge to blab about her carnal adventures with Darcie, she could Zoom call with her mate Sian in Romford, who never came to Cornwall.

She turned the hair dryer off as a new thought came to her.

Tiny village…

Rylea considered it probably wouldn't do to drive back to Darcie's and then leave her car in the driveway overnight, would it? If Mrs. Fitzroy-Kilgannon, who lived two doors down from Darcie, caught sight of her Mini in front of Darcie's house early in the morning—as Mrs. Fitzroy-Kilgannon was out walking her horrid poodle—then all those rumours would start up again.

Rylea could hear it now…

"That Morgan girl spent the night at Darcie Spencer's!"

"You don't say!"

"Saw her car parked there first thing this morning as I was out walking Tiddles. No reason for Rylea Morgan to be at Darcie Spencer's that early!"

"I thought that rumour was well and truly quashed, though."

"False flag operation, obviously! To throw us off the scent!"

Rylea sighed.

She did *not* want that happening! Not only for her own sake, but for Darcie's.

With that in mind, she determined she'd walk back to Corwin Lane. The way was well-lit, the weather was nice, and she'd be there almost as quickly as if she drove, thanks to the shortcut she'd be able to take on the footpath bisecting the greenway between Corwin Lane and Cardell Way.

That settled, she finished getting ready to leave. This time, the Knickers Question was much easier to answer. She had already told Fate to sod off *and* proven to Darcie that she did indeed own sexy underwear. Therefore, now she chose a playful and colourful pair of bikini briefs that were still alluring but most importantly comfy.

She did have to stop and take a breath when she wondered if her knickers would be staying on all night, though. Amazingly, despite how many times she had come earlier, now that she'd had a bit of a breather, Rylea felt she could go a few more rounds with Darcie—if Darcie were up for it.

And I hope she's up for it…

But she'd be fine if the opposite were true.

She recalled that moment in Darcie's bedroom from earlier…

I'd also like it if you stayed the night…

Rylea's heart had almost burst at how magical that moment had felt. It meant Darcie didn't view her as some quick lay who needed to go home and leave her be, once the orgasms had stopped.

How Darcie *did* view her as remained to be seen, sure; but Rylea was elated that for tonight, at least, Darcie *wanted* her to be there while she slept.

In any case, she wasn't going to overthink it now. She needed to finish getting ready and get back to Darcie's.

***

When Darcie opened her front door twenty minutes later in response to Rylea's knock, Rylea felt her heart warm at the smile Darcie gave her.

"I didn't hear your car," Darcie said after Rylea stepped inside.

"I walked," Rylea told her.

Darcie's brow furrowed, but then smoothed itself again as Rylea quickly saw comprehension dawn on her features.

"Because if you drove and parked overnight…" Darcie said.

Rylea nodded and gave Darcie her best *Mrs. Fitzroy-Kilgannon has a big mouth* smirk.

Darcie pulled Rylea to her and kissed her tenderly.

"You," she began, "are amazingly thoughtful. But I still feel guilty that you walked. Sorry."

Rylea shrugged.

"The perils of village life," she replied. "Anyway, what smells so good?"

Just before leaving her own house, Rylea had noshed on a handful of cashews to temper her hunger, but now her stomach rumbled again at the aromas in the air.

Taking her hand, Darcie led her into the living room. Rylea placed her small duffle bag on the floor beside the sofa, and then a moment later, Darcie pushed her down on that piece of furniture and then straddled her lap.

Rylea's heart started pounding.

Darcie was wearing loose-fitting blue sweatpants and a very clingy cami top, the fabric of which was conforming very nicely to her round breasts. And now those breasts were right in front of Rylea's face.

Looping her arms around Rylea's neck, Darcie said, "We are having trout which I had defrosted last night in anticipation of having dinner alone this evening. But there are two fillets, so there's more than enough. I am also making wild rice to serve with it."

"Trout," Rylea said. "Yum!" And then her eyes went right back to Darcie's chest, and she swallowed. The woman's nipples were so hard it looked as if they would poke through the cloth.

"We've still got ten minutes," Darcie said. Then, remarkably, she first eased one spaghetti strap off her shoulder, and then the other, freeing her breasts.

The salivating that had already begun in Rylea's mouth kicked up a notch, and she had to swallow yet again.

But that was nothing compared to what happened in her vagina just a second later when Darcie placed her hand firmly on the back of her head and guided Rylea's mouth to one of her hard nipples.

Yes, Darcie! Anything you fucking want, Darcie!

As she immediately began sucking, her passage started flooding. She was always quick to arouse. She had once joked to a girlfriend that she suspected her vagina had twice the lube-producing glands (or whatever they were called) than normal women's. This time was no different, especially with Darcie keeping that hand on the back of her neck. In seconds, she was *wet*.

"Harder, please," Darcie whispered, and then moaned when Rylea complied, sucking the nipple as far into her mouth as she could. Before long, she was adding bites, making even those harder when Darcie asked for/demanded it.

And so it went…

Rylea continued lavishing attention to each of Darcie's magnificent breasts, while Darcie moaned and even began grinding her pelvis on Rylea's lap.

But that's as far as it went.

Eventually, a *ding!* was heard, and Darcie used Rylea's ponytail to pull her head away from her breasts.

"Fabulous," Darcie sighed before giving her a quick kiss, pulling her shirt back up and hopping off Rylea before hurrying to the kitchen.

Meanwhile, Rylea remained seated on the sofa, panting, the taste of Darcie's breasts still in her mouth, thankful she'd had the foresight earlier to bring another pair of knickers to sleep in later.

The ones she had on now were soaked.

***

Dinner was delicious. Darcie was quite the cook, even for such a simple meal. After Rylea helped her clean up, they took their wine—including the bottle—into the living room and settled themselves on the sofa.

"I'm glad you're here," Darcie told Rylea.

"I'm ecstatic I'm here," Rylea told her after taking a sip of the Chardonnay Darcie had served with dinner. "But…I am wondering…"

On her walk over here, she had decided she needed to broach this subject. She'd be fine with whatever the answer was.

If this was just a casual one night thing, fine. Disappointing, but fine.

If this was just a casual friends-with-benefits thing, fine. She'd be fine with the occasional shag every now and then with Darcie.

If this was something more…official, definitely fine. No complaints would come forth from her mouth on that!

Darcie held up her hand, smiling.

"Just so you know," she began, "I'm wondering the same thing."

They both fell silent then, continuing to drink their wine.

"You go first!" they both said simultaneously, and then laughed.

Darcie sighed.

"I suppose as the oldest, I will go first," she said. Rylea thought she seemed a little nervous, which she found adorable. "So…" Darcie went on after taking a breath. "I've never really done *casual*, but if that's what you want, I'm fine with it. Except, in that case, we have to be like bloody James Bond with all the secrecy because I'd want to keep that away from Cleo.

"So, I'm *fine* with casual! But I'm actually…"

Darcie took another sip of wine. A big sip.

"Oh bloody hell, Rylea!" she exclaimed. "I'd love to date you, okay? There, I said it. I mean, I understand that I may not be the most appealing choice in Cornwall, considering I have a child I'm responsible for and you're still so young and—"

"I want to date you too!" Rylea blurted out. Was Darcie kidding? Not the most appealing choice? "Darce, I would love for us to give this a go. I mean, outside the bedroom. Casual isn't my thing either, okay? I want to be *with* somebody—not ambiguously, but officially. And you know that I think the little astronaut is fabulous!"

All of this was true.

She hated casual. The few times she had allowed herself to be talked into something casual with another woman, she always ended up developing feelings for that woman and then wanting *casual* to turn into *serious*. She didn't want to risk that happening with Darcie.

As for Cleo…

Remembering what Darcie had told her earlier, Rylea knew that dating Darcie would be a bit different than what she was used to. For one, Darcie's parental responsibilities would supersede all else. For another, it meant she might not be able to see Darcie as much as she was used to seeing a woman she was…well, seeing. She also remembered Darcie's edict against bringing women she was dating into Cleo's life, and how she was bound to be doubly wary about that since the Jeannette debacle.

But Rylea really did think Cleo was a fabulous kid. She wasn't naïve enough to believe that Cleo was *always* a fabulous kid, but from what she'd been able to see, Cleo was more well-behaved and better-mannered than a lot of other little humans running around England.

"I love that you call her the little astronaut," Darcie said now, laughing. "And so does she, by the way." But then her face became serious again. "But you do know that if we date, it will be a while before you and I do things together with her."

"Of course," Rylea assured her, trying to make sure her face conveyed her acceptance of that idea. She reached forward, placing her hand atop Darcie's free one, the one not holding the wine glass. "Look," she began, "I want to do this. I hate to tell you this, Darce, but for a while now I've thought about how lucky I'd be if I was able to call you my girlfriend."

Darcie let out a breath.

"Oh thank god you said that!" she replied. "I've thought the same about you! I was already planning on hating the cow whom you eventually started dating."

Rylea laughed.

"And now that's you!" she pointed out. Then, a sudden thought popped into her head. "Bugger!"

"Problem?" Darcie asked.

"Jemma!" Rylea exclaimed.

"Of Liz and Jemma?" Darcie queried.

"The same," Rylea confirmed. "Right this moment—well, maybe not *right* this moment—Jemma is setting me up on a blind date with a mate of hers…Lauren."

Darcie cocked an eyebrow as she took another sip of wine.

"Well," she said. "Looks like I'm going to have to march right down to that shop of Jemma's and tell her she needs to inform Lauren to sod off."

Chapter 25

This is more like it!

Sitting here on the sofa with Rylea, Darcie was realising that she felt more like her old self again.

For five months, Jeannette had taken that away from her—while being absent no less!

But now…

Darcie felt her old confidence returning. She could hear it in her voice, feel it in her soul even.

Ever since her confrontation with Jeannette earlier today in Newquay, Darcie had felt her old self returning bit by bit. It was as if her spirit were soaking in some kind of elixir that was slowly permeating into her being and returning Original Darcie back to whoever it was Jeannette had left behind.

She had really noticed it when she and Rylea were having sex earlier.

Darcie wouldn't term herself as a domineering lover, but she certainly wasn't afraid to take the lead or to demand what she wanted—to tell the new twenty-four-year-old woman in her bed, for instance, that she was "going to keep the fucking dress on."

Okay…maybe she was a *little* domineering.

In fact…

Rylea had just swallowed the last of her wine and was putting the glass on the coffee table.

"I like the way you're looking at me," Rylea said.

Darcie cocked an eyebrow. With her bottom lip between her teeth, combined with the way her eyes had been running over Rylea's figure, she could imagine that her guest could find the look she was giving her thrilling.

She held out her wine glass.

"A little more, please," she said.

When Rylea took her wine glass, Darcie scooted back on the cushions until her back encountered the arm of the sofa. She then lifted her bum off the seat and slid her sweatpants, together with her underwear, off her legs.

Rylea, noticing, chuckled.

"I thought you wanted more wine," she said, not looking at Darcie's eyes when she said this, but rather at the apex between Darcie's thighs.

Darcie reclined against the sofa's arm, her back cushioned by a throw pillow. Keeping her left foot planted on the floor, she swung her right leg onto the back of the sofa, spreading them and displaying what she knew Rylea wanted.

"I do want more wine," Darcie told her, reaching out her hand to take the newly refilled glass from Rylea. "And I'm going to enjoy it," she went on, "while you enjoy me."

She heard Rylea suck air between her teeth.

"Oh fuck, Darce," she murmured.

Darcie had been bringing the wine glass up to her lips, but she paused that motion and raised her eyebrows at Rylea.

"I'm pretty sure you meant to say, 'Anything you want, Darce,'" she stated. "Right?"

Rylea licked her lips.

"Yes, indeed," she said. "Anything you want, Darce." She tugged at the cable knit sweater she was wearing along with the jeans she had on. "Am I keeping my clothes on this time too?" she asked cheekily.

Darcie laughed.

"You do look adorable," she said. "Very Cornish Comfort. But those you can take off."

When Rylea was nude a few moments later, Darcie couldn't help but groan.

"You really do have a lovely figure, Rylea," she breathed.

Long and lean legs, a cinched waist, flat abs, and spectacular breasts that were round and pert with tiny nipples that were puckered and hard now.

Rylea got back on the sofa, laying down with her head between Darcie's legs.

She looked up at her and smirked.

"You've got a lovely figure also, Darce," she said, just before she started occupying her mouth with pleasing the woman she just addressed.

Darcie gasped as the sensations of having her pussy licked began spreading through her core.

Watching Rylea take care of her, Darcie brought the wine glass to her lips, controlled her breathing enough to take a sip, and then savoured the dual pleasure of her clit being edged by Rylea's tongue, while really good Chardonnay stimulated her taste buds.

Swallowing that sip, she took another, unable to stop herself from moaning as her core reacted even more strongly to what Rylea was doing.

With her free hand, she reached down and grabbed hold of Rylea's hair at the back of her head.

"I think I've just found my new favourite way to drink wine," she whispered/moaned, taking another sip while continuing to watch her new girlfriend service her.

***

"Auntie?"

Darcie's eyes fluttered open. She smiled at her niece, who was standing beside the bed.

"Mm," she hummed sleepily. She was still knackered. "Yes, luv?"

"Auntie," Cleo said, "Grandma wants to know where you keep the bloody waffle iron."

Darcie sighed. She knew Cleo was only repeating what her grandmother had said. In fact, she was almost certain her mum had told Cleo, "Go upstairs and ask your auntie where the bloody waffle iron is." Which meant she needed to have a talk with mum—again—about being careful with her phrasing around the child.

"Tell Grandma that the bloody—I mean, that the waffle iron is in the cupboard under the sink."

"Okay," Cleo replied.

Darcie felt a body shift next to her on the bed.

Wait a minute…

Her brain, still a bit foggy from sleep, was having trouble figuring out what was wrong with this scenario.

"Hi, Rylea!" Cleo said cheerily.

Rylea?

From behind her, she heard a voice say groggily, "Hey, little astronaut, good mor—Bugger!"

Wide awake now, Darcie sat up, her mind tack-sharp once more. She was also feeling grateful that she had put a t-shirt on to wear before falling asleep.

What the hell was Cleo doing here?

She looked to her right. Rylea was still lying down, but with the duvet pulled up to her chin, her wide eyes looking between Darcie and Cleo.

"Are you Auntie's girlfriend now?" Cleo asked.

"Erm…" Rylea uttered, looking now only at Darcie, her eyes pleading for help.

"Cleo," Darcie said to her niece, "go back downstairs, please. We'll…erm…we'll talk about that later, okay? For now, just tell Grandma where the waffle iron is."

"Okay," Cleo answered. "See you, Rylea!"

"And shut the door, please," Darcie told Cleo.

When they were alone again, with the bedroom door shut, Darcie scampered out of bed, and then blushed.

She may have remembered to put on a t-shirt last night, but not pyjama bottoms.

"Bloody hell!" she groaned, stomping over to her dresser, pulling open a drawer and removing drawstring bottoms. "I am *so* sorry!" she said to Rylea.

"No, I'm sorry!" Rylea replied.

"You have nothing to be sorry for!" Darcie told her.

"I guess that's true," Rylea said. "But I'm British."

Darcie went into the en suite. She could wait to pee, but she did swig some Corsodyl.

Bloody mum!

She had no idea why on earth her mother had come over, but of all days to pop by unannounced. It wasn't entirely unheard of, naturally , and Irene did have a key, but really…why today?

Still swishing the mouthwash, Darcie remembered—rolling her eyes at the irony of it—that she had meant to have a discussion with her mother about ceasing these unannounced visits once Jeannette moved in. Despite what American sitcoms might want the rest of the world to believe, Americans in real life were *not* big fans of people—even loved ones—just walking into their homes whenever the mood struck. Unfortunately, Jeannette had done her disappearing act before Darcie could have that chat with Irene.

Spitting out the mouthwash, she checked her appearance in the mirror, determining that she simply looked like a woman who had just gotten out of bed, and not necessarily like a woman who had spent the night rediscovering just how many times she could be made to come by a skilled lover.

In the bed, Rylea still had the duvet clutched to her chin, as if afraid the impressionable little child might walk back in at any moment.

"I'm going to find out what's happening," Darcie told her, sliding her feet into her slippers. "Erm…stay here, I guess? I am so sorry again!"

"No worries," Rylea said. "I'll just put some clothes on and wait right here."

That's when Darcie remembered that Rylea had turned in for the night topless, telling Darcie that's how she usually slept.

"Ta," Darcie replied, opening the bedroom door, stepping through it, and closing it behind her.

Downstairs, she found Cleo watching that bloody documentary about the solar system again, and her mother in the kitchen.

"Oh, there you are, dear," Irene greeted her. "Cleo thought it would be nice if we came over and made you breakfast, and so here we are!"

"Yes, mum, I see that," Darcie sneered. "How wonderful. But I really wish you would have called first," she added, using her best *I have a naked woman upstairs* tone of voice.

"Called?" Irene asked, looking up from mixing the waffle batter. "Since when do I need to call?"

Darcie rolled her eyes. Of course her mother wouldn't know the *I have a naked woman upstairs* tone of voice.

"Will Rylea be eating breakfast with us?" Cleo asked, appearing magically in the kitchen the way children do.

Irene, her brow furrowed, looked at Darcie.

"Rylea?" she asked, confused.

"Yes, mum," Darcie hissed.

The brow furrowed more deeply.

"The one who runs the coff—"

"Yes, mum!" Darcie hissed more urgently and with frustration. "The *only* Rylea in Tremont. *That* Rylea!" And she turned her eyes upwards to indicate that *that* Rylea was in the bedroom.

Cleo took a bottle of water out of the fridge and returned to the living room, apparently deciding to await the answer to her question in that room.

"Rylea is here?" Irene whispered, and she too turned her eyes upwards towards the bedroom.

"Yes!" Darcie confirmed.

Irene blushed.

"But I didn't see her car in front of the house!" she explained. "I mean, I had no reason to expect…And besides, you haven't been dating anyone, and so…And I thought it was meant to be a fake date!"

"It *was* a fake date, mum," Darcie said with a sigh. "But then it turned into a real one."

"And you've slept with her after only one date?" Irene asked. "Is that how I raised you?"

"Mum!"

Irene threw up her hands.

"Okay, okay," she said. After sighing, she then added, "Well, what do you want us to do? Shall I take Cleo back home?"

Darcie gave a sigh, which to her ears sounded exactly like her mothers, which alarmed her.

I'm too young to be turning into her!

"No," she said. "The damage is already done. I'll go upstairs and ask Rylea if she'd like to join us for breakfast." She then pointed menacingly at Irene. "But don't act weird around her!"

"Weird?" Irene asked. "Weird how?"

"Like…I don't know…scrutinising her! Like you're wondering how *she* was raised if she was willing to sleep with me on a first date."

"Darcie Diana, I am *not* the type of person you are making me out to be!" Irene whispered, apparently affronted.

"Just make sure of that!" Darcie reiterated, refusing to be cowed by her mother's use of her middle name. "Now, you can finish making breakfast while I go talk to Cleo."

"Very well, dear," Irene said, returning to what she had been doing.

In the living room, Darcie sat on the floor cross-legged next to Cleo. What it was about kids, that they preferred sitting on floors rather than actual furniture, was beyond her.

"Cleo, luv, do you mind if we talk for a bit?" she began.

"Yeah, sure, alright," Cleo said. She even—without prodding—used the remote to pause the show she was watching.

Darcie smiled. She really was a good kid.

"So, erm, about me and Rylea," Darcie said. "I'm sorry you found us like that. I hope it wasn't upsetting?"

"No, it wasn't," Cleo stated. "I like Rylea. I think she should be your new girlfriend."

Darcie laughed.

"Well, I like Rylea also," she told Cleo. "And we *have* decided to start dating, but you need to remember that sometimes it doesn't work out between two people in that way, no matter how much they like each other. So, as much as I may *want* to date Rylea for a long time, there's a chance we won't stay together that way. Do you understand?"

"Yeah, I do," Cleo replied. "Is that what happened with you and Jeannette?"

Darcie blew out a breath. When Jeannette had left, Darcie had been purposely vague with Cleo, only telling her that she and Jeannette had decided it would no longer work between them, and as a result, Jeannette would not be moving in. She determined now that Cleo deserved a better explanation.

"No, luv," she began. "Jeannette made a very…*selfish* decision while she was in New York. I'd like to tell you that it wasn't intentional, but unfortunately it was, and as a result, I ended up getting hurt, and so did you."

"I was more sad for you," Cleo told her.

Darcie's heart melted, and she pulled Cleo to her for a quick, sitting hug.

"You're amazing, you know that?" she said. After the hug ended, she went on, "Anyway, I've talked to Jeannette just yesterday and told her what a rotten thing she did. For what it's worth, she apologised to both of us."

"Alright," Cleo said. "And so now Rylea is your girlfriend?"

Darcie nodded.

"Looks that way," she replied. She wasn't one of those women who did all that silly nonsense of waiting until the "right time" to call a woman her girlfriend. She had always found that odd in the lesbian fiction she read. No…if she was dating a woman, that woman was her girlfriend, plain and simple. And she got the impression last night that Rylea felt the same way.

Speaking of Rylea…

"Listen, luv, I'd better get back upstairs to Rylea, and let her know it's safe to come down," she said.

"Maybe she'll want to watch this show with me and learn about the solar system," Cleo suggested.

"Maybe!" Darcie said with a smile. It was going to be odd, she considered as she rose from the floor. Having a woman she was *just starting to date*, interacting with Cleo, and in her home. But her hand had been forced by her mother showing up this morning unannounced, as she had. Besides, she further considered, Cleo really did seem to understand what she had told her earlier about how sometimes things don't work out between people who start dating.

Maybe I've been underestimating her a little?

She still wanted to be careful about exactly how much she integrated Rylea into Cleo's life, but perhaps she didn't have to be *too* careful. After all, part of dating her meant dating Cleo in some way as well. And as long as she was always open and honest with Cleo about how things were progressing with her and Rylea, then it should all be fine. Well, as fine as one can expect, in any case.

***

Upstairs again, she found Rylea dressed and sitting cross-legged on the bed, scrolling through her phone, which she put down as soon as Darcie entered.

Once more, Darcie closed the bedroom door behind her. She kicked off her slippers and then got on the mattress, sitting cross-legged in front of Rylea.

"Is everything okay?" Rylea asked, taking her hands.

Darcie smiled.

"Everything is fine," she assured her. "Sorry again about all that. In fact, you're invited for breakfast."

"Oh!" Rylea exclaimed.

"And it was Cleo who more or less invited you, so that's practically a royal decree," Darcie added.

"Lovely," Rylea said, but Darcie could hear something in her voice.

"What's wrong?" she asked.

"Nothing, per se," Rylea said, biting her lower lip. "But…will your mum be joining us?"

Darcie blinked.

"Of course," she answered. "She's the one cooking breakfast. Why?"

Rylea sighed.

"I'm sorry," she said. "It's silly, of course, but it just feels a little…odd, having to go downstairs and have breakfast with your mum when she's very much aware of, um…well, of what we've been up to. Again, sorry."

Darcie smiled. She knew there were only seven years between herself and Rylea, but this was one of those times when it seemed more like seventeen.

"We're grown women, Rylea," she said. "And my mother knows I'm not a virgin. In fact, I'm fairly certain that she's happy I've started seeing someone again. She wasn't thrilled that I was unhappy these past few months."

With that said, Darcie leaned forward to give Rylea a peck on the lips.

"Now, enough of this delaying, slowcoach," she said, getting off the bed. "Do whatever else you need to do and be downstairs in five!"

As Darcie was heading towards the bedroom door, Rylea said, "Oh my days, I can tell I'm dating someone with a child!"

Darcie turned, blushing.

"Sorry," she said sheepishly. "Bad habit, I know. The perils of having a little human in the house." She tapped the side of her head. "Must remember…Rylea is proper adult. Rylea is proper adult."

But Rylea cocked an eyebrow.

"Be that as it may," she said, and Darcie could already hear the sauciness in her voice, "perhaps one night you could treat me like a *naughty* proper adult and be a bit demanding."

Darcie gasped, her eyes widening with shock. She blushed even deeper at the same moment her clit began swelling.

"You cannot say things like that when we're about to sit down with my mum!" she whispered with a laugh.

Rylea put a perfectly innocent look on her face.

"But you said she knows you're not a virgin," she said, the innocence of her tone matching the innocence of her face.

Darcie crossed her arms, shifted her weight to one leg and glared playfully at Rylea. But before she had a chance to retort, Rylea spoke up again.

"You know," she began, "standing like that is only making me want you to give me a bit of a paddling."

Darcie burst out laughing, not caring if those downstairs heard it.

"Oh my god!" she hissed. "You are impossible, and I am leaving right now. See you downstairs!"

Chapter 26

So far, breakfast with Irene wasn't as stressful as Rylea had anticipated it to be.

Sure, it started that way—for her—but soon after they had all sat down, Irene seemed to have zero interest in whatever sexual antics her daughter and Rylea had gotten up to last night. Instead, she launched into the preparations she was making for next month's charity fundraising bake sale, which she was chair of. Apparently, there was some controversy brewing, in that both Mrs. Beckley-Hopworth *and* Mrs. Kelly wanted to bake lemon drizzle cake, and of course, two lemon drizzle cakes in the same bake sale was ridiculous.

However, each woman was steadfast in her belief that *her* lemon drizzle cake was the superior recipe, and thus would earn the most money for the Penhallow Women's Shelter in Newquay, and neither would back down.

"What would you do, dear?" Irene suddenly asked Rylea.

Rylea, surprised, swallowed the bite of waffle she was chewing.

"Oh…um," she began, considering. "Well, you're the chair, right?"

Irene nodded.

"So, your word is law then, no?" Rylea went on.

Irene nodded again, her eyes sparkling.

"Why yes," she said. "I suppose that does mean my word is law!"

"Oh no!" Darcie muttered.

Rylea and Irene looked at her.

"Oh no, what?" Irene asked.

Darcie was giving Rylea a *You have no idea what you've unleashed* look.

Tilting her head towards her mother, Darcie said, "She'll be calling the PM next, asking him to share the bloody nuclear codes with her."

Rylea laughed, but Irene gasped with indignation.

"I most certainly will not!" she squawked. "Really, Darcie, you act as if I'm mad with power."

"What are nuclear codes?" Cleo asked.

"Things your grandmother should never, ever have," Darcie told her. "Otherwise, we would have to find another planet to live on."

"But there are no other planets for humans to live on," Cleo pointed out.

"We would have to try really, really hard," Darcie said. "Anyway, I'll explain more about nuclear codes later. Please be sure to remind me."

Irene rolled her eyes and then brought her attention back to Rylea.

"Now, go on," she began. "What were you saying about my power as chair?"

Rylea went on.

"It's simple, really," she said. "You have Mrs. Beckley-Hopworth and Mrs. Kelly both bake their lemon drizzle cakes, and then present them to you in a blind taste test. Then you choose the winner, and *that* person gets to have her cake in the bake sale."

Irene's eyes widened.

"That's brilliant!" she exclaimed. She looked at her daughter and gestured towards Rylea. "Bloody Paul Hollywood you've got here," she said.

Darcie winked at Rylea.

"Thankfully without the beard and all the other bits I could do without," she said with a grin.

Irene winced.

"Darcie, really…there's a child present," she said disapprovingly.

"And the child is very much aware of the fact that men and women are built differently, mum."

"That's true, grandma," Cleo said, and then took another bite of scrambled eggs.

Irene scoffed.

"Kids her age are not supposed to know things like that!" she stated.

Darcie rolled her eyes, and then leaned over towards Cleo.

"Don't listen to her," she told the child. "*Grandmas* are not supposed to know things like that."

This made Cleo burst into a fit of red-faced giggles, and Irene to look heavenward as if seeking divine assistance.

Rylea was enjoying this show. It was nice to see Darcie, Irene and Cleo interacting, seemingly without being guarded about it at all, due to her presence.

When the meal was done, Rylea offered to help Darcie with the cleaning up. Irene, meanwhile, began saying her goodbyes.

"I'm sorry for interrupting your morning, girls," she said, addressing Rylea and Darcie. Then, apparently mindful that Cleo—who had absconded to the living room after placing her dishes in the sink—was only in the next room, and thus still in earshot, added in a whisper, "In my defence, I *was* led to believe it was a fake date!"

Rylea heard Darcie sigh next to her.

"It *was* a fake date, mum," she said.

"That's true, Mrs. Spencer," Rylea added.

Irene shrugged.

"Well, I'll be sure to call before coming around next time," she said.

"Thank you, mum," Darcie replied.

Rylea felt a chill go up her spine when she imagined now what would have happened had she and Darcie awoken earlier and then started having sex. Then she almost burst out laughing, envisioning what Irene's face would have looked like when, upon entering the house, she heard the kinds of noises Rylea now knew she and Darcie could produce together, coming from upstairs.

***

When the dishes were done, Darcie poured Rylea some more coffee, apologising that it wasn't as good as what was served at The Bean.

"So…" Darcie began once they had sat back down at the kitchen table.

Rylea's heart jumped nervously. The tone of that "So…" was that which is often immediately followed by, "Last night was a mistake" or "I think we should see other people."

But she told herself to stop panicking and to let Darcie finish what she was going to say.

"Cleo has been over at mum and dad's since Friday," Darcie went on, "and I should spend some time with her now that she's back. I'm sure she has all sorts of exciting stories to tell about Winnie."

Rylea blinked.

"The Pooh?" she asked.

Darcie laughed.

"The puppy," she said. "Anyway, as much as I want to continue spending time with you today…"

Rylea jumped in.

"I get it," she assured Darcie. This was what part of the whole *dating a woman with a kid* thing was going to be about.

"I'm sorry," Darcie said.

"No need to apologise," Rylea said, meaning it. "This is part of what being your girlfriend means, and I get that. I really do."

Darcie smiled, and then leaned forward and gave Rylea a kiss which started Rylea's heart racing, especially when Darcie slipped her tongue past Rylea's lips. Unfortunately, the kiss ended too soon.

Kid in the next room. Kid in the next room. Kid in the next room.

"So, I'm sorry about ending today early," Darcie said. "But I'm hoping we can make plans for our first date? A real date, not a fake one."

Rylea laughed.

"Love to," she said.

"Can I call you later?" Darcie asked. "Or are you going to be one of those girlfriends who prefers texting?"

"Definitely call me," Rylea told her.

"Will do," Darcie promised. And then Rylea could see that something else was on her mind, by the way her brow furrowed, and her lips pursed. "One other thing…" she began.

Rylea kept quiet, waiting.

"I know that because of how things developed this morning—thanks to mum—Cleo is aware of…well, the two of us, but I'd still like to give us some time before she becomes a big part of our relationship, if that makes sense?"

Rylea nodded. Reading between the lines, she knew Darcie was basically saying, *Until we figure out if we're going to last more than one night of incredible shagging.*

That was fair, she considered. She wasn't about to push for anything that could cause problems for Cleo down the road. In her mind, by agreeing to date Darcie, she was also agreeing to take on the responsibility of making sure Cleo didn't get hurt in the process.

Okay, maybe she and Darcie wouldn't have a happily-ever-after. Hell, maybe they wouldn't even make it past Real Date No. 1. But if that ended up being the case, Rylea knew she had to do her part in making sure a certain little girl didn't get buried in the wreckage.

"I completely understand, Darce," she said. "As far as Cleo goes, you're the boss, okay? You won't get any pressure from me to do things one way or the other."

"Bloody hell," Darcie muttered.

Rylea blinked.

"What?" she asked. "Did I say something wrong?"

"No," Darcie stated. "You said everything right." She leaned in towards Rylea again. Rylea expected another kiss, but at the last moment, Darcie detoured her head, bringing her lips to Rylea's ear. "Which fucking turns me on," Darcie breathed.

Rylea—mindful of there being a child in the next room—quietly sucked in a breath as her clit began thrumming.

"And now I'm supposed to leave, huh?" she whispered.

"Afraid so," Darcie purred in response, her lips still ghosting Rylea's ear.

Two can play at this game.

"Even though you've just made me very wet?" Rylea asked.

Darcie gasped, and Rylea felt her rest her head on her shoulder.

"You fucking bitch," Darcie said softly with a chuckle.

Chapter 27

Bloody hell! This hasn't happened in a while!

It was early the next morning. Monday. Darcie had awoken as usual, well before Cleo, so that she could go downstairs, make some coffee, and enjoy some quiet time prior to Cleo getting up and ready for school.

But this morning, it hadn't been her alarm clock that had woken her up…

"*Oh Christ!*" she squealed quietly, before sticking the knuckle of her left forefinger between her teeth.

Even before she managed to jam her right hand into her pyjama bottoms and her knickers, she was coming. *That* was what had woken up.

When her fingers touched her pussy, the orgasm ramped up in intensity, and she felt the entire length of her vagina spasm, the walls seeming to undulate as the waves of the climax coursed through her core.

"*Mmmmmmmmmmmmmmmmph!*" she squealed again, biting her knuckle, and trying to be as quiet as possible.

Between her legs, she was soaked, and she quickly began rubbing her clit with her middle and ring fingers, feeling how damp the fabric of her panties was with the arousal that had seeped out while she was sleeping.

She came again quickly, immediately shoving those same two fingers in past her opening, feeling her pussy clutch repeatedly at them as it climaxed with even more power than the one she had woken up with.

The knuckle wasn't going to do it this time.

Feeling the cry work its way up her throat, she took her finger out of her mouth, grabbed the unused pillow next to her and pushed it down onto her face, while placing her feet flat on the mattress and lifting up her pelvis.

"*NNNNNNNNNNNNGHOLYFUUUUUCK!*"

Her shout was smothered effectively by the pillow. Good thing, too, because she kept crying out as she began fucking herself with her fingers until the sensitivity of her opening's nerve endings couldn't take it anymore.

She collapsed her pelvis back on the mattress and set about coaxing herself through the remainder of the orgasm.

She stilled her fingers, and just let her vagina soak them in her come as her clit throbbed against the palm of her hand.

Remembering that she needed to breathe, she lifted the pillow off her face and gulped in a deep breath.

It really had been a while since this had happened, waking up mid-orgasm. Ironically, for her, it seemed to occur the most when she was *in* a sexual relationship, as opposed to enduring a dry spell. Jeannette used to joke that it must be her body's way of saying "Gimme more!"

Well, if her body was telling that it needed more of Rylea, then the message was received. What she had just experienced had been…satisfying.

She started chuckling as the aftershocks started hitting her. *Yep…when coming makes me laugh, I'd call that satisfying. Rylea…*

Last night, they had spoken over the phone and agreed that Tuesday evening would be their first date. Tonight was impossible, what with Beavers and then getting Cleo home to bed. Therefore, tomorrow night was the best option. She was certain her parents would watch Cleo.

However…

Though their first date wouldn't be until tomorrow, that didn't mean she and Rylea wouldn't get to see each other until then. Their shops were across the street from one another, after all, and Darcie still planned on getting her Americano from The Bean this morning.

But not until she got out of bed and started this day.

The storm in her centre had finally passed, and like all storms, it left behind quite a bit of a mess. Darcie was a little stunned at how wet she was. She only wished she could remember what it was her sleeping mind had been dreaming about that had woken her up so pleasantly, but she couldn't recall anything.

She removed her fingers from her vagina, sucking in air between her teeth at feeling the mix of pleasure combined with a still sensitive opening when she did so.

She should have just pulled her hand right out of her pyjamas. Instead, she slid her fingers upwards through her folds until they reached her still swollen clit.

"God damn it," she muttered, turning her head to the side and then clamping her bottom lip between her teeth.

She glanced at the alarm clock.

Turns out her needy core had woken her up *early*. She still had forty minutes before the alarm was set to go off.

"Oh god," she murmured, closing her eyes as her fingers began pulling those familiar sensations from her hard button.

Tuesday was still too far away.

And she had forty minutes to kill…

***

Walking into Bean There/Done That later that morning, Darcie couldn't help blushing when she and Rylea made eye contact.

The things she had thought about this woman while masturbating this morning…

"Hey!" Rylea said.

"Hiya!" Darcie replied. "Hey, Bridge," she added.

"Hey, Darce," Bridget greeted her. "The usual?"

"Yes, please."

"I'll take care of it, Bridge," Rylea said. "I think I heard Elmo pull up in the back. Can you help him get sorted, please?"

"On it," Bridget replied, making her way to the mysterious unseen area at the back of shop which mere customers like Darcie never got to see.

"Elmo?" Darcie asked, with a smirk. "From *Sesame Street?*"

"No, smart-arse," Rylea retorted, starting work on Darcie's coffee. "Elmo from Button Street, in Newquay. Appliance repair. Our walk-in is acting wonky."

"Sorry to hear that," Darcie said. Reason No. 153 why she was glad she was in the bookselling business and not the food service industry: Not having to deal with wonky appliances vital to her livelihood.

Her coffee was prepared quickly—an advantage of the Americano—and she held out a fiver.

But Rylea shook her head.

"On the house," she said.

Darcie, however, shook her head right back at her.

"Nope!" she replied. "I just finished reading a lesfic book where one of the ladies was dating a coffee shop owner, and she insisted on continuing to pay for her drinks. I decided I like that philosophy."

Rylea laughed, but she took the proffered money, and then made change for Darcie, who saw Rylea then take a quick scan around the shop before leaning forward on the counter.

"I missed you last night," she whispered, her eyes looking at Darcie's lips.

"I missed you too," Darcie said. She then decided to be a little naughty. Despite wanting this relationship with Rylea to be based on a lot of things, high up on the list was sexual excitement.

"I also missed you this morning," she went on. "Several times, in fact," she added.

She watched as comprehension dawned in Rylea's eyes.

"Christ!" Rylea said. "Thanks for that, Darce. Now how am I supposed to focus on running my shop the rest of the day?"

Darcie laughed.

"Sorry," she answered with a cheeky smile. "Couldn't resist."

"Really…several times?" Rylea asked.

Darcie rolled her eyes, remembering.

"Oh my days," she said, "you have no idea!"

It had actually been a reassuring experience for her.

Since Jeannette left, masturbation had taken on more of a functional quality. It had turned into something she did only because *not* doing it meant that at times she would be unfocused, or unable to sleep, or even downright snippy with people. So, she'd find some alone time and make herself come, just to get it over with so she could return to more important things.

But this morning…

What she had done this morning was proof again that she was returning to her old self—a woman who enjoyed sexual pleasures, even when it was herself providing them.

This morning, she had stayed in bed until the alarm clock rang, repeatedly taking herself to the heights of pleasure, only stopping for breathers in between. She had screamed into her pillow, over and over again, and by the time she was done with it all, she lay gasping on the mattress, staring up at the ceiling, feeling a touch lightheaded.

Her knickers and pyjama bottoms, which she had kept on the entire time had gotten soaked from all of her ejaculating, and when she had finally gotten out of the bed and looked down, she knew she'd be better off changing the sheets as well, on account of the wet patch she had left behind.

"Well, anyway," Rylea said now, "thanks again for putting *that* image in my mind!"

Darcie shrugged.

"It'll keep you interested," she suggested.

"Darce," Rylea began, "I was interested *way* before I ever got the privilege to even kiss you."

Just then, another customer walked in. Several, actually.

Darcie wished they would all go away—everyone, including Bridget and Elmo in the back. What Rylea had said was special, so much so that all she wanted to do now was kiss her girlfriend deeply and tenderly.

As if reading her mind, Rylea smirked.

"Later, I promise," she said.

Picking up her coffee, Darcie said goodbye and walked out of the shop, feeling as light as a feather.

Chapter 28

At half two, Rylea surveyed her shop.

The monthly meeting of the Tremont Mystery Book Club was underway in the far corner of the shop, near the window, in the section of seats Rylea always reserved for them on Monday afternoons.

Rylea wondered if any of the old ladies in the club actually read any books. From what she had been able to observe ever since the club had started meeting here, all the biddies ever did was sit around gossiping and laughing, and pouring gin into their coffees from hip flasks, thinking Rylea didn't see them doing it.

The books they brought with them, however, always remained unopened on the tables. Rylea often wondered if they were even mystery books.

But the women were a harmless lot, and didn't cause any trouble, so she allowed them their not-so-secret tipples.

Old Mr. Garrity was also in the shop, puzzling over the latest crossword in the *Times*. Nowadays, it felt odd to Rylea to see someone with an actual newspaper, but she supposed in Mr. Garrity's case, it was a generational thing.

All in all, the shop was in good order. This was often their slow period on a weekday, which was why Mr. Garrity enjoyed coming in to work on his crossword at this time.

"I'm going to pop across the street for a sec," Rylea told Bridget.

"Yeah, alright," Bridget replied, from over where she was cleaning one of the brewers.

Rylea removed her apron, stuffing it onto a shelf beneath the countertop, and then headed out of the shop.

Stepping into Shelf Life a few moments later, she saw Darcie look up from her seat behind the till and give her a smile that made Rylea's heart swell.

My girlfriend.

"Slow day?" Rylea asked as Darcie stood and came around from behind the counter to meet her more or less in the middle of the shop. When Darcie was stopped in front of her, she peeked over Rylea's shoulder, towards the picture window and the entrance.

Rylea wondered what that was all about, until Darcie draped her arms over her shoulders and kissed her deeply.

Rylea surrendered to the kiss, putting her arms around Darcie's back, and pulling the woman closer. Their lips slid against each other's smoothly, without hurry, but with plenty of passion, and their tongues played together, which only made Rylea's nipples harden even more.

When that kiss ended, they started another one, and Rylea felt herself lose all perception of anything other than Darcie in her arms, and how wonderful it was to be kissing her.

Breaking for air, Rylea said, "I can't believe I get to do that with you now."

Darcie smiled.

"My feelings exactly," she replied. "And I really hope you enjoyed it, because I have some bad news."

"Uh-oh," Rylea murmured.

"Nothing tragic, just…disappointing," Darcie amended.

"Hit me with it," Rylea prodded. They were still holding each other, and she could feel Darcie's breath caress her lips every time she exhaled.

Darcie sighed.

"I just got off the phone with mum," she began. "She apologises but she got her dates wrong way 'round. She *can* babysit tomorrow, just not overnight. Turns out, she and dad are leaving early the next morning for one of their marathon bike rides with some mates of theirs in Devon. They'll be gone until Friday."

Rylea thought fast.

"Disappointing, yes," she said. She had been really looking forward to another night of sleeping with Darcie. *Actually* sleeping.

Yes, she wanted the fucking too, and had been looking forward to that as well, but she also wanted what would come afterwards: falling asleep in each other's arms.

"What time will the little astronaut be brought back home?" she asked.

"I asked mum to bring her by at eight," Darcie answered. "Her bedtime is nine."

Rylea saw no problem—apart from *not* getting to sleep with Darcie tomorrow night.

Just outside of Tremont, to the north, was Marco's, a wonderful Italian place. If they left straight away after closing their shops, they would still have plenty of time for a lovely date.

She explained this to Darcie, who nodded as if she completely agreed with the logic of what Rylea was saying.

"Yes," Darcie said. "Lovely idea. However…"

Rylea frowned.

"However, what?" she asked, wondering what this new wrinkle would be.

Darcie looked at her evenly.

"Can I be completely frank with you?" she asked.

"Of course," Rylea assured her, having no idea what Darcie was leading up to.

"Well," Darcie began, "as lovely as dinner at Marco's sounds, going back to your place to fuck for a few hours sounds even more lovely."

Rylea shivered as the walls of her pussy began swelling…rapidly. The lubrication that had started when they were kissing now kicked up a notch, gravity making sure that it easily flowed out of her and into her underwear. Moreover, her clit started thumping, and it was just priming her centre even more.

"Bloody hell, Darce," she murmured.

"I don't want you thinking I'm just after you for only one thing, though," Darcie said.

"Even if you are," Rylea replied, "I'll get over it."

Darcie laughed.

"You're silly," she said. "But no, really…we have plenty of time for proper dates. Besides, what's the difference between two women talking and getting to know one another after sex, and them talking and getting to know one another in a restaurant?"

"Food," Rylea suggested.

"I'll bring a pizza," Darcie said.

"Deal," Rylea replied. "Anyway, I've been gone long enough. Best be getting back."

"After another one of these, please," Darcie said, bringing her lips to Rylea's for another kiss that made Rylea moan and wish to hell that tomorrow would hurry up.

***

The text message arrived soon after Rylea got out of the shower on Tuesday evening.

Please just eat something quick to hold you until after!

Rylea laughed while simultaneously her clit began tingling.

The message was from Darcie, who was presumably at home, getting ready to come over.

Will do! Rylea tapped out on her phone.

It was a brilliant idea, she considered, and one she was grateful for. Eating pizza when Darcie arrived would have taken time away from what it was obvious they were both wanting—especially since their time tonight would need to be abbreviated by necessity.

With that in mind, Rylea reconsidered what she had planned to put on after the shower…

Instead of jeans and one of her favourite house sweaters, she opted for a simple striped shift dress with a round collar, and which came down to mid-thigh. It was one she often wore around the house and had the advantage of being able to be pulled off incredibly quickly.

To further make things easier for Darcie, she chose to go braless beneath it.

Before leaving her bedroom, she checked to make sure it looked presentable, deeming that everything was where it ought to be, which wasn't always the case. Moreover, there were fresh sheets on the bed, and she had even taken the trouble to clean the two toys she owned—a g-spot vibrator and a very girthy, clear suction cup dildo—just in case things took a turn in that direction. She had placed the toys out of sight, but readily at hand, in her nightstand drawer, rather than their usual home, in a plastic storage box under her bed.

A glance at her bedroom clock told her Darcie should be arriving soon—like in ten minutes.

Hurrying downstairs, she opened her fridge, her eyes scanning the contents quickly before alighting on one of her go-to quick snacks: hard-boiled eggs. She had prepared a dozen on Sunday night, and there were about eight left. She had two peeled and salted quickly. Hardly a proper meal, but they'd keep her appetite at bay, and she ate them hurriedly.

Fuck!

Now her teeth felt eggy.

Back upstairs to the en suite for a quick brush and rinse. She had just finished spitting when she heard the knock on her door.

Back downstairs, her bare feet slapping the wooden steps as she rushed down.

Reaching the bottom step, she practically launched herself at the door, twisting the brass knob—burnished from the countless times it had been turned by countless hands over the decades—and pulling it open.

Darcie.

Darcie looking perfectly respectable in grey leggings, Nike trainers, and a blue sweatshirt. A woman just out for a walk on this surprisingly mild Cornish evening.

She stepped inside Rylea's house quickly, though Rylea really didn't care if any of the Mrs. Somebodys or Mrs. Somebody Elses who lived nearby noticed.

No words were exchanged…not even a "hello."

Rylea took Darcie's hand, and they quickly ascended the stairs, reaching the bedroom in moments, and Rylea kicking the bedroom door shut, though that was a completely needless thing to do in a house containing only the two of them.

They started kissing immediately, and Rylea was certain her lips would be bruised afterwards by how hard and hungrily their mouths were working together. As they kissed, she grabbed Darcie's dark ponytail, while Darcie fisted her hand in her still-damp locks and pulled.

Kissing was fine, but Rylea wanted this to progress quickly.

Keeping her lips on Darcie's, she let go of the ponytail and then grabbed the bottom edge of her girlfriend's sweatshirt and began pulling upwards.

Their kiss broke as Darcie allowed the garment to be pulled over her head, raising her arms to facilitate its removal.

Rylea groaned when she saw that Darcie had nothing on beneath the shirt. Her round breasts were right there for her eyes to feast on, and she couldn't help lowering her head to take one nipple as far in her mouth as she could, making Darcie moan as she did so.

Already, beneath her dress and between her legs, Rylea—who had chosen not to bother with knickers—could feel her arousal dripping out of her and onto her thighs, while beneath her mound a storm was brewing, a churning build-up of pressure just waiting for Darcie to release it.

Done with Darcie's breast for now, she guided her to the bed and playfully pushed her, so she'd fall backwards onto the mattress, reminiscent of their first night together, when Darcie had done the same to her.

Darcie toed off her trainers and Rylea immediately started yanking off her leggings, being sure to take hold of Darcie's underwear as well.

"Oh my god, you're so fucking beautiful!" Rylea gasped. With her hand, she indicated that she wanted Darcie to scoot back further on the mattress, and while Darcie did that, she quickly pulled off her own dress.

"Come here, baby," Darcie murmured, holding open her arms.

With a groan, Rylea complied, topping her, their breasts pressing together, her thigh between Darcie's legs, feeling how slick things already were down there.

"Fuck, I've missed you," Darcie said between quick kisses.

"I've missed you too," Rylea replied.

"I'm sorry I couldn't see you last night," Darcie went on, after raking her teeth along Rylea's jawline.

"Shh," Rylea hushed. "You're here now, and I'm so fucking happy." She then mashed her mouth against Darcie's, penetrating her with her tongue instantly.

Darcie's hips began rocking during the kiss, and Rylea felt how easily her pussy was sliding against her leg. And that's when she determined she wanted to feel it sliding against something else.

Ruthlessly breaking the kiss, she raised herself off the warm body beneath her.

She opened Darcie's legs wide, then draped her own left leg over Darcie's right hip, and with a few more well-practised movements, they were scissoring, their wet pussies pressed against each other.

"*Oh god!*" Rylea called out at the sensation.

"*Oh fuck, Rylea!*" Darcie exclaimed.

They started off slowly at first, finding their rhythm, discovering the perfect angle. They knew they had it when…

"Right there!" Darcie squealed.

"Right there!" Rylea also squealed, practically at the same time.

Supporting herself on her arms, Rylea, in the dominant position, bore down then and started grinding, looking down at their union, making sure she targeted Darcie's engorged clit with her movements, while keeping her own clit happy by ensuring it got the contact it needed as well.

For several minutes, the bedroom filled with their high-pitched noises and gasps of pleasure—mostly incoherent sounds that were randomly interspersed with an "Oh fuck!" or an "Uh-huh!" or a "Fuck, baby!"

Eventually, Darcie grabbed her breasts.

"Oh shit, I'm gonna come!...Right there!...Right there!....Holy shit, baby!"

Rylea concentrated on doing exactly what she was currently doing, not allowing her pussy's angle, nor the pressure with which she was rubbing it against Darcie's, to change in the slightest.

Darcie suddenly gave a surprised-sounding gasp, the kind of gasp a woman makes when she walks into her house to find a roomful of people waiting to wish her a happy birthday.

And then…

"Oh fuuuuuuuuuuuuuuuuuuuuuuuckinghellllllllllllll! NNNNNNNNNGH!"

"That's it!" Rylea encouraged, watching Darcie succumb to the orgasm. "Come on me! Come on me!" She felt her pussy sliding even more easily against Darcie's now, and heard the wet sounds of their tribbing increase, knowing both were caused by her girlfriend's come spraying out.

The storm beneath Rylea's mound was about ready to burst. She decided to help it along.

Balancing herself on only her left arm, she reached with her right hand between her legs and began rubbing her clit hard and fast, unleashing her own climax mere seconds later.

When it hit, she pressed her quaking vulva harder against Darcie's, wanting to *bathe* Darcie's sex with her arousal which she could feel was being forced out of her passage by the contractions of her vagina.

"*GaaaaaaaaaaaaahdDarceeeeeeeeee!*"

For several more moments, it was just screams and cries of pleasure as the two of them rode out their orgasms.

Chapter 29

"Tell me when, Darce," Rylea instructed.

Darcie nodded, though she knew Rylea probably couldn't see it, what with her head resting on her mound as she flicked her tongue over her swollen clit.

So, she squealed out something which, to her ears, kind of sounded like "Okay," and went back to surrendering herself to the pleasures Rylea's tongue was eliciting from her buzzing clit.

While her girlfriend was lavishing attention on the engorged button, the opening to Darcie's vagina was wrapped around the head of a clear dildo Rylea had produced some time earlier.

It was an impressive toy, much more so than the comparatively thin slimline vibrator she had at her own house, or even the pink strap-on dildo she also had, which had survived the break-up with Jeannette.

Tonight, Rylea had fucked Darcie well and proper with this toy, making Darcie's back arch at how solidly it filled her.

But now, Rylea had been engaging in a bit of teasing…

As badly as Darcie wanted to be completely penetrated once more by it, Rylea had only inserted the tip of it in past her opening, ruthlessly holding it there while sometimes slowly, sometimes quickly, she licked her clit, expertly building up yet another orgasm which Darcie felt might top the several she'd already had in its intensity.

"Oh fuck!" she gasped out as the roiling sensations of pleasure started…well, roiling more quickly. "Oh fuck!"

"Tell me when," Rylea said softly, and Darcie's eyes sprang open at the feeling of Rylea's warm breath caressing her clit.

"I'm so fucking close!" she said. "Oh fuck, please!...Please Rylea!"

Her vagina, wanting the full penetration of the dildo, was clutching at the bit of it that was inside her, as if trying to pull it in.

Meanwhile, Rylea's tongue began working faster and more firmly at its task, and Darcie knew her pussy was a runaway train now, heading to nirvana.

"Oh fuck!...Oh fuck, Rylea!" she squealed. "*Oh fuck!...Don't stop!...Don't stop!...Oh shit…Oh shit, baby!...Oh fuck, I'm coming! I'm coming NOW!*"

Just as the orgasm broke free of its cage, Darcie felt the dildo pushed all the way inside her, spreading her trembling and contracting walls on its journey along her passage.

"OHMYFUCKINGGODRYLEAI'MCOMINGHARD! HOLY SHIIIIIIIIIIIIT!"

She was right. This one topped the others.

Below her waist was an explosion of primal delights that was making her entire body spasm, while inside, her pussy came on that rigid dildo stuffing it, inundating it with her come, squeezing it with its contractions, unleashing the fury of this climax on it.

Even in her throes, she became aware of her girlfriend coming to lie beside her, and then of her left breast being sucked, the sensations of that adding new depths to her bliss.

Relentlessly, Rylea held the dildo inside her as the orgasm had its way with her, and as she continued sucking on her breast.

Eventually, the storm subsided, and her spasms stopped, allowing her to more or less lie still on the mattress.

When this happened, Rylea released her nipple from the warmth of her mouth, and instead started planting soft kisses on her shoulder.

After a minute or so, Darcie heard Rylea ask, "Out?"

Darcie nodded, and then winced and groaned with her lips between her teeth as the dildo was pulled out of her, sliding over the now ultra-sensitive nerves at her vagina's opening. She let out a deep breath of relief when it was finally completely removed.

"Oh my god, Rylea," she murmured. "Like, bloody fucking hell!"

Rylea chuckled.

"We are amazing together, Darcie Spencer," she said.

Trembling anew from the aftershocks of her climax, Darcie nodded.

"We certainly are, Rylea Morgan," she replied.

***

They cleaned up and then got back into bed, topless but with underwear on, because after everything they had just experienced, arousal doesn't just stop leaking out instantly.

In bed, they started talking about their days, and amusing interactions they each had with customers. Darcie also told Rylea about the night she'd had at Beavers yesterday. Her assistant hadn't shown up due to illness, and so Darcie had nearly a couple dozen little kids to manage by herself.

"Urgh!" she groaned now, remembering it. She loved her role in Beaver Scouts, and loved little kids, but even she had limits. "Cleo was a star, though," she added. "She decided to be my helper. Now, normally, when a ten-year-old offers to help, the word *help* often doesn't describe what they end up doing for you. But she actually *helped*."

"I'm glad," Rylea said, kissing Darcie's shoulder. After a few moments had passed, Rylea then asked, "So, are you going to be adopting her?"

Darcie smiled. She figured by now the entire village was wondering what would happen with Cleo.

Tremont knew the macro details, of course…

That Patrick, her older brother, ran away from home when he was sixteen, and Darcie was nine.

That he ended up in London and never seemed to stay out of trouble with the law.

That Darcie's family didn't hear from him for a few years until finally, her mother decided to do some sleuthing online (which had impressed Darcie to no end), discovering that her son was doing a stretch of ten years in HMP Belmarsh, a Category A prison in Eastern London.

That once released, Patrick fathered a child. Of course, the Spencers knew nothing about this child because Patrick hadn't said two words to his family since leaving as a teenager. ("It's almost as if we never had him," Irene had remarked one day to Darcie, after Patrick had already been gone for eight years.)

But one day, the phone at Darcie's parents' house rang. It was their son calling.

According to Irene's retelling of the conversation to Darcie, Patrick kept the call short, telling them he figured they didn't much want to hear from him.

He told them a woman would be coming by, but that she wouldn't be staying. The woman would have a child with her.

His child.

He wanted his parents to take the child. The woman would offer no objections, and besides, she wasn't fit to be a mother anyway.

He also told them that this time he was in for good. If they ever let him out, he'd be an old man.

It happened just as he said.

Two days later, a woman arrived. Darcie was at the house with her parents when she did. She had only recently returned permanently to Tremont and was preparing to take over Shelf Life from her father.

Cleo was four-years-old.

The woman—Cleo's mum—brought Cleo into the house, promptly turned around, and got in the taxi from Newquay she had arrived in.

And that was it. They never saw her again. A year later, a letter from HMP Whitemoor arrived. It was from Patrick, informing his family that he had just gotten word that Cleo's mum had died of a drug overdose.

Regarding his daughter, he included one line.

"No one is ever coming back for her."

***

"I believe I will," Darcie said in answer to Rylea's question of adoption. "My parents and I have shared guardianship over her, of course, but I think it would be nice to make her mine, officially."

"She can't do better than you, Darce," Rylea told her.

Darcie hummed contentedly, rolling onto her side to face the woman whose bed she was in.

"When you say sweet things like that," she murmured, "I just want to eat you up!" She bit her bottom lip, as something she had been worried about came to the forefront of her mind. "You realise that this isn't just a rebound thing, right?" she asked. "I'm *over* Jeannette. Seeing her on Saturday didn't change that. If anything, it only made me realise even more just how *over* her I am."

Rylea smiled and tucked a stray lock of Darcie's hair behind her ear.

"I wasn't thinking I was a rebound," Rylea said.

"Good," Darcie said, feeling relieved. "I'm in this for real," she added.

"You'd better be," Rylea said, "or I'll stop adding three shots of vanilla to your Americano each morning."

Darcie's brow furrowed.

"Three?" she began. "No, I only get one."

"Not for a while now, Darce," Rylea told her, and then she told Darcie about how she began adding two extra shots of the vanilla syrup as a way of making her feel better in the early post-Jeannette days.

Darcie burst out laughing.

"And I just thought you had gotten really good at making Americanos!" she exclaimed.

Rylea scoffed.

"A rhesus monkey with both hands tied behind its back can make an Americano, Darce," she said. "But *yours* tasted so good because of those two extra shots."

Darcie laughed again.

"Why is that, like, the most insane *and* romantic thing anyone's ever done for me?" she asked. She then kissed Rylea deeply.

When the kiss broke, Rylea said, "I hate to be the one to bring this up, especially because I'd like nothing more than for you to stay, but it's almost half seven."

"Bugger, is it?" Darcie groaned. She looked around for a clock, noticing it for the first time on Rylea's nightstand. She then let out a sigh. "I feel awful leaving you," she said, sitting up and bringing her knees to her chest.

"Don't," Rylea said, also sitting up, also bringing her knees to her chest. "This is just part of how *we* have to be *us,* for now."

Darcie smiled.

"And it's amazing you understand that," she said. "But I promise, we will wake up next to each other again soon."

She meant it too. She might not have all the details sorted right this moment, but she also knew she wanted things to happen with Rylea other than massive orgasms, and somehow, she was going to have to figure out how to bring those things about.

The next day, again at half two, Rylea said to Bridget, "I'm going to pop across the street for a sec."

"Say hi to Darcie for me," Bridget replied.

Rylea blushed as she opened the door to the street but didn't say anything.

She hadn't yet told Bridget about her and Darcie officially dating. She felt she owed that honour to Tamsin, and she was going to do that this evening.

As she approached Darcie's bookshop, Rylea could see that there were a few customers inside, and she wondered if she should bother going in. She didn't want Darcie to feel as if she needed to neglect other patrons just to chat with her.

But she decided to stop being silly. She'd pop in, say hello and at the very least let Darcie know she was thinking about her.

Walking into the shop, she said hello to Mrs. Lavisham and Mrs. Trevenson-Smythe, who were both browsing the titles in the biography section. She also said hello to Mr. Shackleton and Mr. Whitegate, two elderly gentlemen in the magazines section.

Darcie smiled at her from behind the till, where she was completing a purchase for Ellen Carter, Tremont's GP.

While her girlfriend was thus occupied, Rylea wandered over to the LGBTQ section of titles.

She did most of her reading on her Kindle, but Darcie also stocked a nice assortment of photography books, artist monographs, and travel books, all by gay creators, and even before she and Darcie started dating, Rylea enjoyed coming in here to see what was new, and if any were worth buying.

"Can I help you, miss?" Darcie said, appearing by Rylea's side as she was starting to flip through a book of photographs of gay pride parades around the world.

Darcie looked amazingly cute today, in a merlot-coloured midi dress, patterned tights and Mary Janes. And she was smiling at Rylea with the impish smile of a child who was up to no good.

Rylea cocked an eyebrow.

"Well, yes, in fact, you *can* help me," she said. "I am looking for a classic novel, but I do not see it on your shelves."

"Hmm," Darcie murmured. "And what is the name of this classic novel?"

"Beebo Brinker," Rylea told her.

Darcie's eyebrows raised.

"I'm impressed," she said. "Such a classic, and well worth reading. You obviously have great taste in literature."

"Among other things," Rylea said.

Darcie put her hand on her chin, as if thinking.

"You know…" she began, "I might have something in the back which you might enjoy. Would you like to come with me, and I'll show it to you?"

"Why, thank you, I would," Rylea told her.

As they both started walking towards the back of the shop, Darcie turned her head in the direction of the magazines.

"Would you mind keeping an eye on things, Mr. Shackleton, while I help this customer with something in the back?" she asked.

Mr. Shackleton waved and smiled.

"Gladly, Darce!" he said in his slightly wavering old man's voice. "Don't you worry about a thing!"

"I never do when you're around, Mr. Shackleton!" Darcie added.

A moment later, they passed through the curtain which Darcie had in the doorway leading to the back of the shop. Rylea had never been back here.

There were two rooms—well, three, if one counted the tiny toilet which would make anyone with claustrophobia pass right out.

The first room was clearly for storage, had walls lined with shelves and was full of boxes of books and shop supplies. The second room was smaller and at a glance looked to be outfitted as an office.

But Rylea didn't get an opportunity to examine her surroundings any closer than that, because as soon as they got back there, Darcie grabbed her hand and pulled her into the office-type room.

Before Rylea knew what hit her, Darcie pounced, capturing her lips in a hungry kiss, which Rylea returned just as hungrily.

Rylea marvelled at how perfect they were at this already. Kissing Darcie—which she had the privilege of doing only since Saturday—felt so familiar, as if they'd had years behind them of knowing how to move their lips against one another's, how much pressure to apply, how to make their tongues dance so synchronously that it seemed choreographed.

Breaking for air, Darcie said, "Sorry, it's busy here."

"That's okay," Rylea said, her breath a little shallow. "Sorry I can't stay longer."

Darcie ran her hands down Rylea's sides before grasping hold of her belt loops.

"God, I want you," she muttered. "Sorry. It's not all I want, of course, but…"

"Trust me," Rylea whispered, mindful that there were customers not far away, and not knowing how well sound travelled in this shop, "I know what you mean."

And then they were at it again…Two sets of lips that shouldn't be quite this practised with each other at this early stage, yet somehow were.

Darcie groaned. It was an animalistic sound, and it made Rylea's clit begin throbbing.

As they continued kissing, she felt hands taking hold of the bottom of her Depeche Mode t-shirt that she had found in a Notting Hill vintage shop.

What was happening?

Very quickly, the hem of her shirt was being lifted. She wanted to protest—there was no time for anything physical—but this was Darcie Spencer doing it, and Rylea was helpless.

She was pushed against a wall. Her shirt was lifted to just under her armpits.

Darcie broke the kiss and then hurriedly pulled aside the left cup of Rylea's white balconette bra, freeing her breast, and sucking her nipple into her mouth.

Rylea tilted her head back against the wall, her eyes shut, her mouth open.

"Oh fuck, Darce!" she said so softly, she wondered if Darcie even heard her.

Darcie's tongue toyed with her nipple, which by now was granite…by turns circling it slowly, and then flicking it rapidly. All the while continuing to suck, pulling on her breast with her warm mouth, each pull eliciting a sympathetic pulse in Rylea's clit.

And then came the first sharp little bite.

"Nnngh!" Rylea squealed, as quietly as a mouse.

Her core, already excited, now became very wet, and she knew she'd have to spend the rest of the day at The Bean constantly being reminded of this erotic interlude in Darcie's office.

The bite was followed up by a tender kiss on the still tingling nipple. She then felt her breast released and being covered again by her bra.

Playtime was apparently over.

"Wow," Rylea muttered, adjusting her boob so that it once more sat properly in its cup, before pulling her tee back down.

"Sorry," Darcie said, her hands back on Rylea's belt loops again.

Rylea looked at her, an eyebrow cocked.

"Are you really?" she asked.

"Of course not," Darcie whispered, and even in that low tone of voice, Rylea could hear the lust it contained. It matched the fire Rylea saw in her girlfriend's eyes. "In reality, I want to rip everything off of you and make you come."

Rylea squeaked out a surprised gasp.

"Jesus, Darce!" she said hoarsely. "I wish you bloody well would!"

"Maybe some other time," Darcie said with a grin. "But I am sorry about something, though."

"And what would that be?" Rylea enquired.

Darcie blushed, but her grin became wider.

"For the condition of things below your waist," she said. "I mean, *I'm* a mess, so I'm sure you are too."

"And saying things like *that* is not helping!" Rylea said with a laugh. "You are *evil!*" She then gave Darcie a quick kiss. "But I'd better get back," she added. "Call me later?"

"Of course," Darcie promised.

They exited the office together and in a moment were back out in the shop proper.

"Right!" Mr. Shackleton said upon seeing them. "Did our Darcie get you what you wanted?"

Rylea smiled, swallowing a laugh.

"Very nearly, Mr. Shackleton," she answered. "Very nearly."

***

"Bloody Americans!" Tamsin said, opening the door to her house when Rylea knocked.

Rylea stepped inside, following her best friend to the living room, where a bottle of wine was already opened.

"What did they do now?" Rylea asked, watching Tamsin pour her a glass and then hand it to her. They both took a seat on the sofa.

"You haven't heard?" Tamsin replied. "There are two of them at Lennox Hall."

Lennox Hall was a stately home north of Tremont, dating back to the 1700s, which historically belonged to Lord Thornton. This was back in the days when Tremont was part of the Thornton estate. It was stunningly beautiful and imposing and belonged to one of the oldest families of England.

The current Lord Thornton—the seventh male to hold that title—opened portions of the mansion for visitors one day a month, for guided tours. Moreover, because of his family's fortunes not quite being what they had been in centuries past, he also made the property and grounds available for weddings or other special occasions—for those who could afford it—as a way of offsetting the costs of being the present lord of Lennox Hall.

"Two, huh?" Rylea said. "Bloody D-Day invasion that. Shall we surrender now?"

"Or fight back!" Tamsin said.

"Tams," Rylea began, "there is nothing to fight over. Lennox Hall is very beautiful, and no doubt those American tourists have spent the day taking countless selfies in front of the mansion. In fact, they're probably brainless influencers posting about their travels on Instagram. Either that, or they're planning to book it for an event."

"*Or*..." Tamsin said after taking a sip of wine, "they're bloody well planning on buying the place!"

Rylea blinked.

"How did you get from hearing there are two Americans at Lennox Hall, to those same Americans buying the place?"

"Because it's what Americans do!" Tamsin said, her tone indicating that this was a sufficient explanation.

Rylea shrugged.

"Let them," she said.

Tamsin started choking on her most recent sip of wine.

"We can't let bloody Americans come over here to buy up our precious British heritage!" she exclaimed in a manner which Rylea felt would make Churchill proud. "Even if they are women!"

Rylea's eyebrows raised.

"Even better!" she said. "Women need to be buying more of our precious British heritage."

"Not American women!" Tamsin insisted. She then gasped as apparently another nefarious thought came to her mind. "Oh my god, can you imagine if they're gay?"

"Since when do you have a problem with gay women, gay woman?" Rylea asked.

"Stop being stupid!" her friend chided. "You know what I mean! If two American lesbians buy Lennox Hall, then two *more* American lesbians show up to buy a smaller house here in Tremont. Then, a bunch of *single* American lesbians show up and not only buy *more* houses, but start dating *our* Cornish lesbians, who will naturally fall for them because they're from exotic America!"

"I don't think exotic is a word ever used to describe America," Rylea pointed out.

"Well, *interesting* then," Tamsin amended. "The point is *our* Cornish lesbians will all be seduced by American *L Word* lesbians before you know it."

"Not this Cornish lesbian," Rylea said. "At least not for the time being. Darcie and I have started dating."

Tamsin gasped, her face lighting up with a smile, which Rylea took as a sign that her friend had now been distracted from the possibility of hordes of American lesbians descending on Cornwall.

But just as quickly as she smiled, Tamsin frowned, and Rylea girded herself for having to prove that Darcie was as British as the Queen.

"I thought those rumours were false," Tamsin said. "You mean we have to start all over?" she added with a wail.

"*Or…*" Rylea began, "…you and the rest of the gossip-mongers just keep out of it."

Even as she said that, Rylea knew the futility of the suggestion. She was fairly certain that Bridget suspected something was up between her and Darcie, despite the original *Rylea-is-dating-*

Darcie rumour being squashed. After all, Rylea was not in the habit of popping "across the street for a sec" two days in a row.

Moreover, who knew what intelligence Mrs. Lavisham and Mrs. Trevenson-Smythe had started spreading around after her and Darcie's trip to the back of the bookshop earlier today?

The point was, Rylea suspected the rumour was already out there…again. The only difference this time would be the degree of certainty and the speed with which it spread. The biggest rumour-mongers were no doubt being more careful, after having been proved wrong previously (a disaster in their business).

"Sooooo…" Tamsin began in that tone of voice which all women—even those in America, Rylea was sure—used to indicate they expected something juicy for their ears, "What's she like?"

Rylea smiled, suddenly feeling like a teenager again, but she didn't allow herself to slip into carelessness. In Tremont, providing details about…anything…was risky.

Therefore, although she told her best friend that Darcie was not only an amazing kisser, but also an amazing lover, she decided to leave out the fact that the last orgasm Darcie had given her—just last night—had made her feel dizzy enough that she could have sworn the bed was spinning.

Nor did she mention that, even though a few hours had passed now, she could *still* feel Darcie's mouth on her left breast, sucking on it, each pull making her clit throb…

Which it started doing now just thinking about it.

Crossing her legs, she forced Tamsin to give up her line of questioning about whether Darcie was more a top or a bottom, and instead told her about what it was like at Jeannette's wedding, including her run-in with Katelynn in the toilet.

Chapter 31

At Darcie's house that same evening, she and Cleo were having a dinner of roast beef, potatoes, and carrots at the dining table. At their feet was Winnie, the puppy, present because Darcie's parents were off in Devon, and had suggested that Cleo might enjoy having the dog at home to play with while they were gone.

Darcie considered that Winnie was a very wily puppy for one so young.

Rather than actively making it known that he would appreciate any scraps the humans happened to toss his way, he was instead taking a different tack. He was lying on the floor, acting as if he couldn't care less if he was handed any food.

Of course, Darcie wasn't about to give him any—and she had forbidden Cleo from doing the same. He was a puppy, and was still on a puppy diet, she had told her. To which Cleo had rolled her eyes, stating that she already knew that because "Grampa and Grandma already told me." Which was when Darcie realised that Cleo probably knew more about this puppy than she did, by having spent far more time with him.

Still though…despite the embargo on feeding the dog, Darcie felt a little offended at the animal's apparent lack of interest in her cooking.

Her roast beef smelled fantastic! Not only that, but it had come out perfectly! If she took a photo of it, she was certain it would be featured in a roast beef advert of some sort. Yet despite how wonderful it smelled, Winnie simply sat there, seeming as if he'd rather starve than eat what she had laboured to produce.

(Well, what the slow cooker had laboured to produce.)

It almost made her *want* to give him some, just to show him what he was missing.

Crafty bugger…

She forced her mind to forget about the dog. She had other things to think about.

"Cleo…remember our talk the other day?" she asked, taking a sip of water. Some wine would have been nice with her roast beef tonight. Something tannic, like a Syrah or a Malbec. But she didn't want to be one of those parents—because that's effectively what she was—who drank casually in front of her child. She did not want Cleo growing up believing that alcohol was a staple for every meal.

"Depends," Cleo said. "Which talk are you talking about?"

"The one about Rylea," Darcie answered. "Well, the one about *me* and Rylea."

Cleo nodded.

"I remember," she said.

"Okay, good," Darcie began. "In that case, what would you say if I invited her over for dinner tomorrow?"

Earlier, when Rylea had left Shelf Life, Darcie had determined that her new girlfriend deserved more than brief make-out sessions in her poor excuse for an office at the shop. And so did she, for that matter.

However, her parents weren't coming back until Friday night, which meant the earliest they would be willing to babysit Cleo again would be Saturday, and Darcie didn't want to wait that long. Besides, as far as Cleo was concerned, the cat was out of the bag, so to speak.

Darcie was beginning to wonder if what had happened Sunday morning had been a sign of some sort. Perhaps it had been the universe's way of telling her that in this case, she didn't need to concern herself with shielding Cleo from her relationship with a woman until she felt sure it was going to stick, the way she had done with Jeannette.

Besides, Rylea was not Jeannette. Even if it didn't last between them, she felt as sure as anything that Rylea would not callously up and disappear one day, leaving not only herself but Cleo with more questions than answers.

"Can we make pizza for dinner tomorrow?" Cleo asked. "I can show Rylea how to do it."

Darcie smiled.

"Well, we should first ask if Rylea is okay with eating pizza tomorrow," she said. "It's only polite."

"Yeah, alright," Cleo replied, as if she considered that a fair concession to make.

Then the child asked something which Darcie was completely unprepared for.

"Can Rylea sleepover on Friday night?" Cleo enquired. "And on Saturday morning, I can show her how to make pancakes."

***

"I'm shite at making pancakes," Rylea said with a laugh later that night when Darcie had her on the phone.

It was half nine, and Cleo was in bed for the night, already asleep. Darcie was in her en suite, putting on face cream, with Rylea on speakerphone.

"Well, Cleo is an expert," Darcie said, rubbing the cream on her forehead. "She will teach you everything you need to know."

"I'm not sure my ego can handle being schooled by someone in Year 6," Rylea replied.

Darcie laughed.

"Welcome to my life," she quipped. "Trust me, you don't know how much you've forgotten from your school years until you've lived with a kid, learning the stuff you've already forgotten."

"So…you're fine with Cleo's sleepover idea?" Rylea asked, and Darcie could hear the note of caution in her voice.

"I am," she stated, making sure her own voice conveyed the truth behind her words. "I think, in her own way, Cleo is telling me just how fine she is with the fact that you and I are dating."

"Well, that makes me feel good," Rylea said.

"Me too," Darcie told her. She was done with applying the face cream, and now needed to leave it on for five minutes before rinsing it off. While she waited, she leaned against the countertop with her arms crossed. "Besides," she went on, "it means I *finally* get to spend the night with you again."

"Mm," Rylea hummed. "I did enjoy falling asleep with you last weekend."

Darcie smiled, but then another thought furrowed her brow.

"Do I snore as badly as Jeannette suggested?" she asked.

Rylea laughed.

"To be frank, I have no idea," she answered. "You exhausted me on Saturday night, and I fell into a coma. You could have been snoring as loudly as a lorry engiine and I would have slept right through it."

Darcie rolled her eyes.

"I'm almost certain I'm not that bad!" she said. At least, she *hoped* she wasn't that bad. She wondered if she could get Siri to record her snoring one night, for playback in the morning.

"So…during this sleepover…" Rylea prodded.

"Yes, we can have sex," Darcie told her with a chuckle. "Of course, that being said, it would need to be *quiet* sex."

"Oh, fuck my life," Rylea murmured. "How am I supposed to do that? I was barely able to keep quiet when you were sucking on my boob in your shop."

Darcie's clit thumped at the reminder. Her mouth suddenly remembered the taste of Rylea's breast once she had freed it from the bra, and her tongue suddenly recalled the texture of her nipple.

"I swear to God, I wanted to fuck you right there," she whispered. "I don't know what came over me, but like I said, I wanted to rip all your clothes off and just…take you!"

She heard her girlfriend gasp over the phone's speaker.

"Ooh!" Rylea uttered. "Keep me tied up in your office, naked, only popping out to the front to help a customer every now and then?"

Darcie shut her eyes as a surge of erotic pleasure which started in her chest found its way to her core.

"I would have to stuff your mouth with something to make sure you don't scream out for help," she suggested.

"True," Rylea agreed. "Well, your knickers would do."

"God!" Darcie gasped. Her vagina had just clenched, and arousal was beginning to obey gravity and slide down her walls. "This is reminding me of a book I read recently."

"I suspect we read the same book," Rylea said. "Not too many of them out there featuring a tied-up lesbian kept quiet with her captor's knickers stuffed in her mouth."

"And the world is poorer for it," Darcie quipped. Then she couldn't help but add, "This conversation is going to make it difficult for me to fall asleep."

"Are you saying I've been a bad girl for bringing this up?" Rylea asked.

Darcie groaned. In the past couple of minutes, Rylea had managed to push certain buttons in her that hadn't been pushed in a long time, turning on aspects of her desire which she and Jeannette only rarely played with.

"You *have* been a bad girl for bringing this up," she said throatily, surrendering to the yearnings which felt as if they were taking over her entire body.

"I probably need a spanking to learn my lesson," Rylea suggested.

Darcie felt her knees weaken. She picked up the phone now from the countertop, knowing her voice was losing the strength to speak normally.

"Fuck…why are you doing this, Rylea?" she breathed.

"I thought we both agreed…I'm a bad girl," was the answer.

Darcie's pussy clenched again, and now her clit's pounding was matching her heartbeat.

"I can't spank you quietly," she said firmly. "I've never laid a hand on Cleo but trust me, when I spank a woman, she knows she's being spanked."

Now Rylea groaned.

"God, that's sexy!" she exclaimed. "And I would really like to know I'm being spanked by you, Darce."

"Trust me, you would," Darcie assured her. Heavens, she was so wet now.

"When can that happen?"

Darcie took a deep breath, trying to pull her mind away from the absurd idea of telling Rylea to get over here tonight so they could finish what they started with this conversation. It wasn't practical, after all. Cleo was in the house—they couldn't risk waking her with the sounds of Rylea pert bum being spanked. Moreover, it was already getting on for ten o'clock—she needed to be up in time to get Cleo fed and off to school, and Rylea needed to be up early to open The Bean.

This weekend, however…

With her parents back on Friday, perhaps they'd be willing to let Cleo spend the night on Saturday. Thus, if Rylea was still in this mood, she could be spanked that night to her heart's content.

She opened her mouth to say, "This weekend."

Instead, what she heard herself say was, "Be here in ten minutes."

***

Darcie, wearing pyjama shorts and an oversized sleepshirt, was waiting by the front door, tapping her bare foot on the wooden floor.

Finally!

She heard footsteps approaching, and she opened the door before Rylea could knock.

Rylea entered the house, Darcie closed the door behind her, and then they stood there looking at each other.

Rylea had the most devilish smirk on her lips.

"What are you looking so cheeky about?" Darcie whispered, her nipples hardening.

Rylea cocked an eyebrow.

"Because I won," she stated softly but…well, cheekily.

Darcie's breath hitched, and she narrowed her eyes.

"You fucking bitch," she hissed, taking Rylea's hand and leading her upstairs.

By her reckoning, the dining room was the farthest indoor portion of the cottage from Cleo's room. But if for some reason Cleo awoke during the next…however long this took—due to a nightmare, or Winnie doing something puppy-like—nothing could prevent the child from coming downstairs into the dining room.

Her own bedroom door at least had a lock.

"What's that?" Rylea whispered, spotting the device on the floor near the door.

Darcie blushed, locking the door behind them.

"One of those sound machines," she said quietly. "Sometimes, I have trouble sleeping and need help tuning out the world beyond."

"And it's by the door because…?" Rylea prodded.

Darcie glared at her.

"Because a certain woman I'm seeing made it clear to me she wanted a particular something tonight," she said, "and managed to get herself invited over here."

"Oh, that would be me," Rylea replied, that cheeky smirk back on her lips.

"Yeah, well…" Darcie began, indicating the machine. "Welcome to the practicalities of dating a woman with a child. I'm hoping this blocks the noise we're about to make."

Rylea suddenly looked contrite.

"If you're uncomfortable with this, Darce…"

Darcie bent at the waist and pressed the power button on the machine. Her bedroom was filled with the hissing yet soothing sound of white noise.

Standing upright again, she crossed her arms and stared at her girlfriend.

"Take your clothes off, Rylea," she ordered.

***

Bloody hell, Rylea was soaked!

Darcie was sitting upright against her headboard, with her legs stretched out before her, still wearing her nightclothes.

Draped across her lap was the nude Rylea, her arse raised by the pillow Darcie had placed under her pelvis.

The first round of spanking was done, and the alabaster flesh of Rylea's bum was red, with several distinct handprints on each cheek.

Now, Darcie had slipped her hand between Rylea's legs, encountering a pussy so wet it made her gasp. Without any prelude, she slipped three fingers inside Rylea's vagina, marvelling at how easily they entered her girlfriend.

"Mmph!" Rylea grunted into the pillow she had been using to muffle her cries from the spanking.

"So wet…" Darcie murmured. "You liked that, didn't you?"

Rylea nodded, keeping her face buried in the pillow. Eventually, she turned her head to the side.

"You told me I'd know when you spanked me," she murmured. "You were right."

Darcie didn't reply. Instead, she withdrew her fingers, found Rylea's clit and began rubbing it firmly and quickly.

"*Oh shit!*" Rylea squawked.

"Don't come," Darcie said, but she didn't let up on what her fingers were doing.

"*Darce!*" Rylea whispered urgently.

"Don't come," Darcie repeated, applying just a little more pressure. Her fingers were so wet with Rylea's arousal that they slid over Rylea's engorged clit effortlessly.

"*Darcie!…I'm so fucking close!*"

"Rylea?" Darcie cooed. "Behave."

"*Jesus Christ!*"

"Don't be bad," Darcie warned. "You know what happens to bad girls."

"*Oh shit!...Yes, I know!*"

"Be a good girl, Rylea," Darcie said sweetly as her fingers continued their ruthless stimulation. "Be a good girl, and don't come…"

Rylea gasped, and by the sound of it, Darcie knew the end was near.

"*I can't help it!*" Rylea squealed. "*Oh fuck!...I can't help it!...Oh fuck, I'm coming!*"

Again, she buried her face in the pillow just when the screams started.

Rylea's pelvis began rocking on Darcie's lap, and Darcie felt her hand sprayed with come.

"Wow!" she uttered, amazed at how wet Rylea's climax was. "That was a big one!"

She then palmed Rylea's sex, letting her girlfriend's orgasm run its course. When she sensed that Rylea was calming down, descending from the high, Darcie took her hand, now wet with Rylea's essence, out from between the other woman's legs, raised it, and then brought it down on Rylea's arse…hard.

"*Nnngh!*" Rylea grunted.

Again…

"*Nnngh!*"

Again…

"*Nnngh!...Nnngh!...Nnngh!...Nnngh!...Oh shit!...Nnngh!...*"

As her hand fell repeatedly, Darcie enjoyed watching the flesh of Rylea's tight bum quiver with each spank.

"Told you not to come," she said.

But she determined that her girlfriend hadn't learned her lesson.

Therefore…

Smack!

"*Nnngh!...*"

"Told…"

Smack!

"*Nnngh!...*"

"You…"
Smack!
"Nnngh!..."
"Not…"
Smack!
"Oh fuck..."
"To…"
Smack-smack-smack!
"Nnnnnnnnnnngh!..."
"Come."

***

With her right hand grasping the headboard, Darcie clapped her left hand over her mouth just in time.

The orgasm shattered her.

With her eyes squeezed shut, she screamed into her hand, grateful the sound machine was still running because she wasn't sure that even with her hand in place over her mouth, the shouts she was attempting to muffle wouldn't be heard beyond the bedroom door.

Her pussy was detonating with pleasure, right onto Rylea's face, which she was sitting on.

"Mmmmm…Mmmmm…" Rylea moaned, as her lips and tongue continued doing what had brought Darcie to this state.

Even in the violent throes of this climax, Darcie knew her pussy was giving Rylea plenty to taste. She could feel the come streaming out of her, helped along by the contractions of her passage, and by the fact that even before she sat on Rylea's face, she had been so turned on that her centre had been nothing but nectar.

"Mmmph!" she squealed behind her hand as she felt Rylea poke her tongue up into her opening, tightening the grip she had on her hips to hold her steady. *"Mmmph!"*

After the second round of spanking Rylea, Darcie had made her come again, wanting to follow-up pain with pleasure. That time, however, there had been no penalty exacted on Rylea's bum for daring to enjoy her release. Instead, Darcie had ordered her to lie down, and then immediately removed her nightclothes and straddled her face, needing her own release.

It hadn't taken long.

Darcie was almost embarrassed by how quickly she had come, but she was not at all sorry for how damn good this felt.

Rylea's tongue stayed inside her, swirling around throughout the duration of the climax, Darcie knowing that what her vagina was producing must be heading straight down her girlfriend's throat.

Finally, it was over.

Breathing heavily, Darcie lifted herself off Rylea's face, and quickly lay beside her.

"Bloody hell," she muttered, staring up at the dark ceiling.

"Bloody hell," Rylea agreed.

"My brain feels like it's short-circuiting," Darcie said. This was true. It was as if parts of it were threatening to shut off, as if there wasn't enough stored energy in her body to fuel both her mind and her centre, which was still experiencing microbursts of pleasure.

"Can I stay?" Rylea asked. "I'm knackered now."

"Oh, sweetie, of course you can stay," Darcie told her. She snuggled closer to Rylea, wrapping her left arm around her midsection. Then she kissed her shoulder.

"I'll need to leave early," Rylea said, and Darcie could detect the sleepiness in her voice. "The alarm is already set on my phone. I'll be sure to sneak out super quietly, so I don't wake the little astronaut."

Darcie chuckled.

"I still love your nickname for her," she said.

"Well, to be totally honest," Rylea began, "I've forgotten her name. Is it Chloë?"

Darcie laughed.

"You have *not* forgotten her name, liar!" Then she huffed with frustration. "I hate, hate, *hate* that you have to sneak out of here!" she complained.

"Darce, this was my idea," Rylea said. "I knew if you invited me over, I'd either have to leave straight away, or get out tomorrow without Cleo seeing me. I have no problem with sneaking out."

"I understand that," Darcie replied. "But just so you know it's *not* going to happen again. From now on, let's promise that when you're here, it's official."

"Meaning the little astronaut knows?" Rylea asked.

"Exactly."

"I'm fine with that if you are," Rylea said.

"You have no idea how fine I am with it," Darcie answered. "Now, let's get cleaned up before we pass out. I have pyjamas you can sleep in."

Chapter 32

"Wife keep you up all night?" Bridget asked Rylea the next morning.

"Shut up," Rylea mumbled after yawning for what was probably the twentieth time since she and Bridget had arrived and started prepping the shop half an hour ago.

"Here," Bridget said, handing a steaming 350ml disposable cup to her. "A red eye."

Rylea smiled, gratefully accepting the drink.

"Thanks, Bridge," she said, and then took a sip. It was strong…just what she needed. Almost instantly, she felt the effects of the two espresso shots.

"How's that going by the way?" Bridget asked. "Sorry if I seem nosy."

Rylea shrugged. Bridget didn't seem any nosier than anyone else in this village, but at least she knew that her friend wasn't asking the question *just* for the sake of spreading gossip. There was genuine friendship behind the enquiry.

"Any advice for dating someone with a kid?" Rylea asked, logging into the POS system which ran the till.

Bridget scoffed.

"You have it easy!" she said. "Cleo is ten, which means she's almost a normal human being! If she was a toddler, my advice would be to leave Darcie behind here in Tremont and move to the Midlands."

"Move to the Midlands," Rylea repeated, rolling her eyes. "Got it. Anything else?"

Like, practical?

"Well, I think you already know this," Bridget went on, "but dating someone with a kid means dating the kid too. Are you okay having dinners out with Cleo tagging along? Picnics in the park with Cleo tagging along?"

"You know what," Rylea said, "I am fine with that. And I'm having dinner at their house tonight. Apparently, we're making pizza."

"That's another thing," Bridget said. "I hope you like pizza. Kids eat a lot of pizza."

"*I* eat a lot of pizza," Rylea retorted.

"And you never put on an ounce," Bridget said petulantly. "Whereas I…if I so much as say 'margherita,' I balloon up a couple pounds."

"Must be tough being old," Rylea couldn't help quipping.

"Just you wait," Bridget shot back, "you'll get there one day too. I'm going to go check the loo." She then headed off in that direction.

"Ta!" Rylea said. She then smiled a secret smile, imagining herself growing old with Darcie, and the two of them complaining about pizza pounds together—but still ordering pizza, nonetheless.

But she briskly shook her head to dispel those thoughts. They were rather premature, after all. She needed to focus instead on just getting through the next few weeks and months—the way she would with any new relationship. She and Darcie still had a lot to learn about one another—far more than the fact that Darcie snores and likes Italian food. What's more, she and Cleo still had *everything* to learn about one another!

Rylea had only ever had passing conversations with the child, but she supposed practically everyone in Tremont could say the same thing. Cleo was an amazingly friendly kid and loved talking and showing off her knowledge about outer space.

Which reminds me…

Very early this morning, as she was walking back to hers from Darcie's, Rylea had come up with the notion that she should try to bone up on her own knowledge of outer space. She figured that between Wikipedia and YouTube, she'd ought to be able to glean enough facts to engage intelligently with Cleo about her favourite topic. Well, Cleo's favourite topic of the moment, anyway. This made Rylea consider that if she and Darcie continued dating for quite a while, she'd have to bone up on a lot of different topics to keep up with Cleo.

She shrugged.

At least that would keep her mind sharp. After all, she didn't want to eventually reach Bridget's age not being able to eat pizza *and* being a dullard.

***

Tamsin rushed into The Bean at a little after eleven o'clock, and straight away, Rylea knew something had her friend flustered.

"The Americans are coming!" Tamsin hurriedly said, coming up to the ordering counter, and slightly nudging Mrs. Jackson-Pembroke aside.

"Excuse me, dear," the elderly woman said, somewhat apologetically.

"Oh!" Tamsin said to her, as if noticing the tiny, retired schoolteacher for the first time. "Sorry, Mrs. Jackson-Pembroke! How rude of me. Please, allow me to buy your coffee!"

"Well, I was rather hoping for a herbal tea…" Mrs. Jackson-Pembroke said.

"Of course!" Tamsin replied. "How silly of me!" She reached into her handbag, withdrew a fiver as if by magic and slapped it on the counter near the till.

"Give her whatever she wants," Tamsin told Rylea. "Tea, coffee…whatever." To Mrs. Jackson-Pembroke, she then said, "You can wait for your drink over there, Mrs. Jackson-Pembroke. I'm sure Bridget will have it right out for you." And she started guiding the old woman towards the end of the counter, where orders were picked up.

"Oh, yes, dear, thank you," Mrs. Jackson-Pembroke said.

"What has gotten into you?" Rylea hissed. "A herbal tea, please, Bridge," she added, turning her head slightly to the woman behind her.

"Got it," Bridget said.

"The Americans are coming!" Tamsin repeated.

It took a moment, but the penny finally dropped for Rylea. The Americans who were at Lennox Hall the other day. The two women who were apparently the harbingers of doom for Tremont.

"Not this again," she moaned. "Are you warning me because they're armed?"

"Cheeky," Tamsin replied. "I'm just warning you as one gay woman to another!" She tilted her head back. "Oh my days, Rye Bread! Wait until you clap eyes on them!"

Rylea laughed, amused at seeing her friend with her head so obviously turned by two women from a country one would think she despised.

"Well, how do you know they're coming here?" Rylea asked.

"I ran into them at Jemma and Liz's shop," Tamsin explained. "You know, they were in there, being all confidently American, like…'We're American, and we're here to buy Lennox Hall and the rest of your lovely village!'"

Rylea blinked.

"Did they say that?" she enquired. Christ, was a Starbucks about to open down the street?

"Not exactly in those words," Tamsin admitted.

"Well, what *did* they say?" Rylea asked.

"Hello," Tamsin said, but then hurriedly added, "But you know how Americans are with their swagger. They say hello, and even that sounds like a demand to surrender your country."

Tamsin went on to explain that she learned the Americans were touring Lennox Hall, not to buy it, but because it was on their list as a potential wedding venue.

Rylea sighed.

"And you know they're coming here because…?" she prodded.

"Oh! Because one of them—the shorter one—asked if I knew a place in town with great coffee. I said no, but that The Bean is open just down the street."

"What?" Rylea said between clenched teeth.

"It was a joke!" Tamsin assured her. "And it worked! They both laughed so hard, Rylea, like I was bloody Sarah Millican. Who knows? Maybe one or both of them wouldn't mind opening up some Anglo-American negotiations with me if you get my meaning." She waggled her eyebrows.

"Unfortunately, I do," Rylea told her. "However, I doubt the two women who are here trying to plan their *wedding* would be interested in opening any kind of negotiations with you."

Tamsin shrugged.

"You never know," she said in a singsong voice. "Throuples are becoming more popular nowadays, among our kind."

Rylea rolled her eyes, but she didn't doubt that if anyone she knew would end up in a throuple, it would be Tamsin.

"I thought you hated Americans," she said.

Her best friend scoffed.

"Rylea, if this is what the American lesbian invasion looks like, then tattoo the bloody Stars and Stripes on my arse and call me Tex. You'll see! They are *gorgeous!*"

"I'm sure they are," Rylea said, "but I have a girlfriend already—a gorgeous girlfriend. Also, I don't want any more tattoos, and I happen to like my name."

The door to the shop opened then.

Rylea's eyebrows shot upwards.

She may already have a girlfriend, but…well…when Tamsin was right, Tamsin was right.

The two women who walked into The Bean were stunning.

The shorter one had thick, long hair the colour of milk chocolate, but with gold highlights added. She was wearing a blue dress which fit her slim figure perfectly and showed off shapely legs that were encased in black tights with a striking geometric pattern, and which made traitorous thoughts briefly flit through Rylea's mind. Stylish legwear on women was a weakness of hers, and she wondered if she could get Darcie to add more to her wardrobe because she would definitely make it worth her while.

The taller woman was just as pretty as her companion, but because of her height seemed like a goddess who had deigned to walk among mortals for a little while—perhaps just to taste their coffee. This illusion was helped by the absolute jet blackness of her hair. It suggested that if she was a goddess, she was one you didn't want to fuck with.

The villain-goddess was outfitted in tight skinny jeans which helped to point out to anyone looking that her legs went on forever. Paired with the jeans was a snug-fitting sweater in burgundy, which had a V-neck that was cut deep enough to flash a bit of cleavage.

Rylea thought she looked familiar. She was pretty enough—and tall enough—to be a model. Or maybe an actress. Whichever it was, Rylea felt she had seen her before.

Though both women were dressed comfortably and casually, Rylea was amazed that just by glancing at them, one could tell that they were not Cornish women. They had more of a confident, stylish presence to them, the kind which the women even in Truro or Newquay didn't have.

"Told you," Tamsin whispered.

"Hi!" the shorter woman said, as she and her friend approached Tamsin. "We meet again!"

Rylea noticed Tamsin blushing.

"Well," Tamsin began, "when you mentioned coffee, I decided that sounded so good, I wanted some myself."

"Then why haven't you ordered anything?" Rylea couldn't help asking.

This ought to be good, she considered. Her friend *never* drank coffee. She was strictly a tea girl. Coffee, after all, was something Americans drank.

Tamsin turned her head to look at her.

"I was getting to it," she said, her eyes flashing. "One...erm...coffee, please."

"Would you like the light, medium or dark roast, ma'am?" Rylea asked. "Or would you like to try one of our delicious lattes?"

Tamsin looked like she wanted to kill her.

"Erm...medium?" she answered, a bit of a growl in her voice. "And I would like to buy these ladies their drinks as well," she added, turning to the Americans.

"That is so sweet!" the tall one said, smiling a very *non-villain-goddess* smile. "But you don't have to do that."

"I insist!" Tamsin said. "You're newcomers to our village—"

"Which is so super pretty, by the way," the tall one said.

"Thank you," Tamsin replied. "Anyway, as newcomers, you're entitled to one free coffee."

Rylea really wanted to burst out laughing. Wasn't it only *yesterday* that Tamsin was prepared to call the defence minister on these two women because they were obviously the vanguard of an American lesbian attack? And now she was buying them coffee?

The Americans graciously accepted Tamsin's offer and approached the counter.

"What can I get you, ladies?" Rylea asked with a smile.

"A caramel latte for me, please," the tall one said.

"And I would like your dark roast, please," the shorter one said, "but with four shots of espresso added."

Rylea blinked.

"*Four* shots?" she asked.

"Yes, please," the woman said. "And if you can make it really hot too, I'd appreciate it."

Four shots!

Did the woman plan on *swimming* back to America? In one day?

***

"Christ, Darce," Rylea whispered. "I want to be penetrated. Do you have anything?"

It was that night, and she and Darcie were in Darcie's bed.

The pizza-making dinner with Cleo had been a success—at least Rylea thought so. She had let Cleo take the lead and teach her everything she needed to know about how to apply the sauce to the refrigerated dough bought from Asda in Newquay; how to sprinkle on the right amount of shredded mozzarella; and how to apply the slices of pepperoni evenly over the top.

"So that you get a taste of pepperoni in every bite," Cleo had informed her.

Rylea had had fun and was amazed at how seriously Cleo took the task. If the little astronaut decided a life in space wasn't for her after all, perhaps she could become the little chef.

Following dinner, they had all watched TV together. Cleo had wanted to put on one of the documentaries about outer space she had apparently watched countless times, but Darcie asked her to choose something else this time, and that was how they ended up streaming episodes of *Star Trek: The Next Generation.*

Cleo was in bed by nine o'clock, perfectly aware this time that Rylea was staying the night.

Darcie had invited her to do so before Rylea arrived for dinner, telling her that Cleo thought it was a good idea.

Now, they were in bed, and Rylea wondered why they had even bothered changing into their pyjamas, because as soon as they both laid down they weren't able to keep their hands off each other, and the pyjamas were removed hastily.

Darcie's head was between her legs, licking her pussy languidly, each lick starting at her opening and finishing at her clit, which would then be circled a few times, making Rylea groan softly as the pleasure beneath her mound accumulated.

But tonight was one of those nights when just being eaten out wasn't going to be enough. If she were home, playing with herself, she'd already have her dildo out, using her left hand to fuck it in and out of her pussy while the fingers of her right hand rubbed her clit furiously.

Darcie planted a kiss on her wetness and got up.

"Wait right there," she said.

Rylea watched her gloriously nude figure step over to the desk in the corner of the bedroom. Opening a drawer, Darcie removed something that was too small for Rylea to make out. Her girlfriend then walked to the wardrobe, opened the door, and reached up to the top shelf.

Confused, Rylea propped herself up on her elbows, wondering what the desk had to do with the wardrobe.

Darcie came back to the bed, this time carrying a metal box, which she placed on the mattress and then unlocked with a key.

"You keep your toys locked up?" Rylea asked, determining that the key was what Darcie retrieved from the desk.

Darcie looked at her.

"I have a child in the house, Rylea," she said matter-of-factly. She shrugged. "Maybe it's silly, but it makes me feel a little more responsible to make sure she doesn't accidentally come across these."

Rylea blew her kiss.

"It's not silly at all," she said.

Darcie looked down at the contents of the box, and then back up at Rylea. An impish grin was on her lips.

"I think…" she began, "…that this is what you're craving tonight."

In her right hand, she held up a glass dildo with a round base and whose length was punctuated by several smooth beads.

"Yeah, that will work!" Rylea said softly.

"Do you need lube?" Darcie asked.

"Trust me, I'm fine," Rylea answered. "Just fuck me with that, please."

"I love an eager woman," Darcie replied, closing the box and immediately coming to lay back down beside her girlfriend.

Rylea opened her legs wide. Darcie reached over Rylea's left thigh, the dildo in hand, and allowed Rylea to help guide it to her opening.

"Oh, fuuuuuuuuuuuuuuuuck!" Rylea exclaimed, trying to stay as quiet as possible once the toy's tip penetrated her and Darcie began properly pushing it in. "Oh my god, it's so fucking hard!"

It had been so long since she'd had a nice piece of glass inside her.

Who was it again, she wondered?

Lily.

That's right. Lily was the one with the glass dildo. And after Lily, Rylea always meant to buy herself one, but never got around to it.

There was nothing like being penetrated by the unyielding hardness of one of these toys, and Darcie's was no joke.

Jesus, is it that long?

The rigid shaft was still pushing inside her, deeper and deeper, her vagina shaping itself around its beads.

Finally, it stopped.

"So fucking hard!" she repeated. "God, fuck me with it, baby!" she pleaded. "Fuck me with it!"

"Anything you say," Darcie told her, and then started doing just that.

She started slowly, evidently wanting to make sure Rylea was truly primed and girded for it.

"Faster, baby," Rylea whispered after a few moments, and then all she could utter was, "*Mmmph!...Mmmph!...Mmmph!...*" as Darcie gave her what she wanted.

Rylea reached down between her legs and began rubbing her clit with her middle and ring fingers. She knew she wasn't going to last long. In fact, she started worrying about how to stay quiet once the orgasm hit, because she had no doubt it was going to be a big one.

"*Mmmph!...*Kiss me… *Mmmph!...*when I come!" she managed to mutter. "Oh fuck!....Darce!... *Mmmph!...*Oh fuck, kiss me!"

Darcie's lips covered her own the exact same instant her entire vagina exploded in pleasure. She stopped rubbing her clit and instead grabbed the hand Darcie was using to fuck her with, and slammed the glass dildo deep inside herself, holding it there, covering Darcie's hand with her own.

"NnnnnnnnnnnnnnnnnnnnnnngghMmmmmmmmmmmmmmmm mmmmmph!" she screamed into Darcie's mouth as her pussy came on the unrelenting hardness filling it, her rapidly contracting walls squeezing down on it over and over again as if trying to make it yield in the slightest bit.

"NnnnnnnnnnnnnnnnnnnnnnngghMmmmmmmmmmmmmmmm mmmmmph!"

Chapter 33

When Rylea stilled, Darcie broke their kiss.

By now, Rylea was reduced to low whimpers and gasping breaths, and looking down at her, Darcie felt the satisfaction of a woman who had just taken good care of another woman sexually.

"Stay with me," she whispered. She needed to come also, and she expected Rylea to make it happen.

She began pulling the glass dildo out from inside her girlfriend. Her clit spasmed hard as she saw how absolutely covered it was with Rylea's essence, and then her clit spasmed even harder when upon removing it completely, Rylea's pussy squirted a spray of come that landed on the sheets.

"Oh, my baby," Darcie said softly. "Oh, you came so hard, didn't you?"

"Yes!" Rylea squealed, almost childlike.

Darcie didn't waste any time.

With the dildo out of Rylea, she rolled over completely onto her back, spread her legs, and slid the hard toy into her own pussy.

"Fucking hell!" she gasped. The dual lubrication of her own vagina's wetness and Rylea's come covering the dildo meant the toy slid in so easily, and it shocked her at how quickly and deeply she was suddenly filled.

"Get on top of me," she urged. "Fucking lick me! Give me your pussy!"

Rylea obeyed instantly, covering Darcie's form with her head between Darcie's legs, and her pussy above Darcie's face.

Darcie immediately grabbed Rylea's ass and brought her face to Rylea's swollen sex, amazed at how much there was to clean up. It was as if Rylea was still coming, and Darcie just worked her mouth on her folds and her opening, happily drinking it all up.

Meanwhile, her clit was attacked by Rylea's tongue.

"*Nnngh!*" Darcie grunted as she continued using her lips to grab at Rylea's sex, occasionally poking her tongue inside the flooded vagina at her disposal. "*Nnngh! Oh fuck…!*"

She came undone quickly, trembling beneath Rylea, using Rylea's pussy against her mouth to keep her screams from escaping the confines of the bedroom. She felt every inch of the hard glass stuffing her vagina while her passage clutched at it repeatedly. Then, her mind went blank while she lost herself in the throes of the intense pleasure.

When it was over, she stretched her head away from Rylea's vulva, gasping for air. By now, her face, from her nose to her chin, was wet with Rylea's juices, and after a few moments she licked her lips, wanting to taste more.

She grunted when her girlfriend took the dildo out of her. In another moment, Rylea was off of her, collapsing on the mattress beside her, with her head down by Darcie's feet.

Both women stayed that way for a while, breathing hard or letting out tiny moans when sneaky latent jolts of delight leftover from their climaxes would strike.

Twenty minutes later, they were both cleaned up, with the dildo washed and put away.

In bed, with the lights off and the sheets and duvet pulled up over them, Darcie stroked Rylea's hair, using the little available light in the room from the moonglow shining through the curtains to stare into Rylea's eyes.

"You have no idea how happy I am that you're here," she whispered.

Rylea smiled.

"You have no idea how happy I am to be here," she replied.

They snuggled closer and were both asleep in moments.

***

Two weeks later, Darcie's period hit. Informing Rylea of this via a shop-to-shop text, her girlfriend asked if she would rather be alone tonight. A forgivable question. This would be their first period as a couple, and Darcie knew Rylea was only asking what the parameters and expectations were.

So, Darcie sent her the parameters and expectations.

No, I don't want to be alone! I want my girlfriend to take care of me!

Rylea's response came back quickly.

*LOL! No problem. How about a change of plan? I cook you
dinner at your house, we stay in and watch Killing Eve?*

Reading the message, Darcie smiled. Rylea had read her
mind again.

Over the past couple of weeks, as their relationship
deepened, Darcie had been amazed at how she and Rylea just
seemed to always be on the same wavelength with things like this.

It was Friday, and Cleo was going to be picked up from
school by Irene and then spend the weekend with her grandparents
(and Winnie). The original plan was for a date night in Newquay,
and then stay over at Rylea's until Sunday.

Jeannette would have suggested they still go on their date to
Newquay. After all, if in a lesbian relationship, things like dates are
constantly cancelled because one partner has her period, then pretty
soon you're left with two women who never leave the house. *That's*
the kind of thinking Jeannette would have employed.

But Rylea just seemed to naturally understand—from
minimal information—that what Darcie would like more than
anything else would be to stay at home—*her* home—and have her
girlfriend love on her.

Perfect! □ Darcie sent back.
This prompted her phone to ring.
"Hey you," Rylea said.
"Hey you," Darcie replied.
"Look out your window," Rylea instructed.
Doing so, Darcie saw her girlfriend standing in her shop's
doorway.
She sighed.
Crossing the store, she stood in her shop's doorway.
"This is taking twenty-first century technology too far,"
Darcie said, knowing Rylea could see the smirk on her face. "You're
ten yards away."
"Too far to walk," Rylea told her. "I figure it seems we're on
pretty solid ground, relationship-wise, and so I can start making *less*
effort."
Darcie laughed.
"So why did you call?"

"Stuffed shells for dinner tonight?" Rylea asked. "With garlic bread?"

"Mm, sounds perfect!" Darcie told her.

"I'll need to pop into town for some bits then," Rylea said. "Did you want to come along?"

Darcie made a face.

"Do you mind if I don't?" she asked. "Sorry, it's just that I'd rather head home and soak in the tub for a bit before you come by." She was already feeling yucky.

"Say no more," Rylea told her. "Grocery delivery is part of my service. I'll even buy some wine unless you're too much of a snob to trust a peasant like me with that choice."

Darcie cocked an eyebrow.

"Careful," she said. "Just because I'm on my period doesn't mean I won't give you another spanking. Oh, hello Mrs. Chenoweth! Lovely afternoon, isn't it?"

Darcie blushed scarlet as the pensioner walked by.

"Why didn't you warn me?" she hissed, seeing Rylea laughing across the street. She actually couldn't stop herself from chuckling as well.

"I thought you saw her!" Rylea said in her own defence.

Rolling her eyes, Darcie said, "I think I might give you that spanking after all."

***

Darcie closed Shelf Life an hour earlier than normal. She didn't give a damn if the fabled American Tour Group her father always warned her about stopped by while the shop was closed. Her cramps were shite today, and she wanted to get home. Sending a text message to Rylea informing her of her scheme, she made sure the shop was in good order for tomorrow, and then left.

Ten minutes later, upon entering her house, she decided she deserved a glass of wine before going upstairs to get in the tub. Definitely a white. She only drank white wines while on her period, not needing any more of the colour red in her life during the four or five days her prize for not being pregnant lasted.

"Bugger!" she exclaimed, pulling a bottle of pinot grigio from the refrigerator. "I need to tell Rylea not to buy a red!"

She had just pulled her phone out of her handbag when there was a knock on the door.

Typing as she walked back to the front of the house, she had just sent the message flying through the ether when she opened the door.

She gasped, her eyes going wide.

What is she doing here?

"I come in peace!" her visitor stated, holding up her hands to show she was unarmed.

"Erm…" Darcie uttered but couldn't think of anything else to follow that up with.

"I'm sorry for just dropping in on you like this, really I am!" her unexpected guest said. "But if we could talk for just five minutes?"

Despite her shock, Darcie determined that she was intensely curious.

"Of course," she said. "Please come in."

The surrealness of welcoming this particular visitor into her home was then immediately usurped by the even more surreal sensation of standing aside and watching Katelynn Jefferson pass through her front door.

"Again, sorry," Katelynn said.

Darcie thought Katelynn seemed a little haggard, as if she hadn't been sleeping well lately.

Crossing her arms, and not leading Katelynn any further into the house, Darcie asked, "What can I do for you?"

"I'm sorry," Katelynn began, "but do you mind if we sit?"

Darcie nodded and gestured Katelynn to walk ahead of her, in the direction of the living room. The two women sat on the sofa, but at opposite ends.

"People are going to start thinking you're British with all the apologising you do," Darcie said.

Katelynn nodded.

"Tell me about it," she said. "Last night, a waiter apologised for giving me the check in a restaurant."

"Yeah, that sounds like us," Darcie had to admit. "So, how did you find out where I live?"

Now, Katelynn rolled her eyes.

"Are you kidding me?" she asked, her voice tinged with a bit of sarcasm. "When I got into town, I pulled my car over and asked the first person on the sidewalk where I could find someone named Darcie, and she gave me precise directions to your place!"

She frowned then and looked off to the side.

"It was weird, though," she continued.

"Weird how?" Darcie asked.

"The old lady also said something about you being on your period and then something else about spankings."

Darcie had to pinch the bridge of her nose at that.

"Sorry," she said. "Please ignore her. She's one of the village eccentrics. So, anyway…"

"I didn't know!" Katelynn blurted out. "I didn't know about you when I met Jeannette. She said *nothing* about being in a relationship with someone in England."

Anger flared inside Darcie, and she could feel her face becoming flushed with it.

This jibed with the commotion she and Rylea had heard as they exited the wedding that day, and with what Rylea had told her on the way home—that she suspected Katelynn of not knowing anything about Darcie.

How could Jeannette do that? After all they had meant to each other? After all the plans they had made for their future?

What was also upsetting her, was the fact that Jeannette had often travelled for business while they were together. So how many times, during business trips, had Jeannette cheated on her? And with how many different women, until finally settling on one she wanted to marry?

Just then, a tingling started in the back of her mind. It was as if something was telling her that she was missing a salient fact. A fact that she *should* have seen much sooner, but which she had been too distraught to recognise until now.

It took her a moment, but she finally managed to pull it forward and see this fact for what it was: an ugly, monstrous truth.

"When did you meet Jeannette?" she slowly asked.

Katelynn swallowed. She looked at Darcie with eyes which were warning her that what she was about to say was not going to make her feel better.

"Last summer," she said. "When she was in New York for business."

Darcie couldn't help gasping. In fact, she started feeling lightheaded.

She had always assumed that Jeannette had met Katelynn this past January, when she flew back to the States to visit her ailing father.

"I know," Katelynn whispered. "She was doing it to both of us."

"But she *lived* here!" Darcie exclaimed. "In Tremont! *This* was her home!"

"I know!" Katelynn said. "But again, she never told me about you! I was perfectly fine being someone she saw every couple of months or so, whenever she was on a business trip. But even then…I wouldn't have ever gotten involved with her if I knew I was helping her cheat on you! I'll be someone's fling or one-night-stand, fine. But I won't be the other woman! But she made me believe that wasn't the case.

"Then, two trips ago, I guess…she told me she loved me."

Darcie felt a stab in her heart, but she was too angry to cry.

"Next thing I know," Katelynn went on, "she's convincing me we belong together and that I need to move to England with her. That was when she was in New York because of her father."

Katelynn looked down at her lap. Her fingers were fidgeting with the strap of her handbag.

Darcie couldn't prevent herself from reaching out and taking Katelynn's hand in her own.

She's not the enemy…

"So what now?" she asked. "Does Jeannette know you're here?"

"Jeannette doesn't know where I am," Katelynn said. Then she gave a dry laugh. "Although, I'm sure all she has to do is ask anybody on the street and they'd tell her."

Darcie couldn't deny that truth.

"We were renting an apartment together in Newquay," Katelynn said, "but I haven't been home since the wedding. Obviously, she's been trying to reach me, but all I've done is answer the phone to tell her our marriage will be annulled as soon as I can legally get it done."

"Wow!" Darcie exclaimed. She hadn't known what to expect on that score, but she was surprised, nonetheless.

"I can't stay married to her, Darcie!" Katelynn insisted. "Not after what I found out. How am I supposed to trust her again? Hell, she has another business trip to New York next month! Am I really expected to believe she's going to behave herself?"

Darcie nodded.

"I understand," she said. In her opinion, cheating was not a forgivable offence. That kind of betrayal of trust was not something a relationship could come back from. Even if the cheater never did it again, the woman she cheated on would always harbour suspicion every single time they were apart.

Some women could choose to live like that, but Darcie refused to be one of them. If she ever found out Rylea cheated on her, Rylea would be out. End of story. No second chances. Finished. Done.

She was happy to see that apparently Katelynn felt the same way. That she wasn't going to allow herself to be walked over by Jeannette who, quite frankly, probably was not going to change her ways.

"I'm so sorry she did this to you," Darcie stated softly.

"And I'm sorry she did it to you too," Katelynn replied, squeezing Darcie's hand. "But in the end, we're smarter women for it, aren't we?"

"And luckier women too," Darcie said. "We both dodged a huge bullet."

Katelynn shrugged.

"Well, *you* dodged the bullet," she said ruefully. "*I* ended up marrying her, remember?" She shrugged again. "But I guess, long-term…yeah, I did escape something pretty awful."

Darcie then asked, "Will you be going back to America?"

"Actually, no!" Katelynn answered. "I plan on staying here for a while. After all, I've got a portable job, and it's gorgeous here! America can do without me for a bit."

Darcie laughed, making a decision while doing so.

Releasing Katelynn's hand, she picked her phone up from where she had set it on the coffee table when they sat down.

"Number, please," she said, opening the Contacts app.

"Really?" Katelynn asked softly.

Darcie looked at her and was struck by how grateful Katelynn seemed, and also a little scared, as if she was afraid Darcie was playing a trick on her.

"Really," Darcie stated. She then swallowed. "Who says we can't be friends? Besides, now that you've left Jeannette and are staying, you may need help or advice on settling in." She looked heavenward briefly. "Cornish people can be a little…eccentric."

"Like the old lady I met?" Katelynn asked.

"Exactly!" Darcie told her. "I still have no idea what she was talking about regarding my period and spankings but, well, that's Cornwall."

Katelynn provided her phone number. After entering it into her device, Darcie sent her a text.

"Besides," she then said, "I know you're not ready for this yet, but when you are…my girlfriend Rylea and I know where to find the single lesbians in the region."

***

Rylea arrived an hour later, long after Katelynn left.

"Sorry," Rylea said, walking in carrying grocery bags, with her overnight duffle bag slung over one shoulder, "but I nipped home to pack clothes for the weekend. I figure we're going to—"

She stopped talking and sniffed the air, turning her head as if trying to pinpoint the source of what she was smelling.

"Was another woman here?" she asked. "I smell a different perfume."

Darcie laughed and gave her girlfriend a quick kiss.

"Katelynn stopped by," she told Rylea.

"No way!" Rylea's eyes opened very wide.

"I'll tell you all about it while you're cooking," Darcie said, relieving Rylea of her duffle bag and then placing it on the sofa as they walked by, on the way to the kitchen.

Just as they crossed the threshold into that room, Darcie suddenly stopped.

"If you ever cheat on me, you understand there will be no coming back from that, right?" she told Rylea.

Rylea's mouth dropped open.

"I mean it," Darcie went on. "We will be done. No amount of begging, and no amount of gifts will get me back."

Rylea placed the grocery bags on the floor and took hold of Darcie's arms.

"Baby, that is not going to happen," she said, looking directly into Darcie's eyes. "I would never do that to you, okay? Who knows? Maybe we'll only be together for another week, but even if I'm lucky enough to be with you for the next ten years, cheating is not something I will do."

Darcie felt her lip begin to quiver.

Shit!

She wondered if Katelynn's visit had affected her more than she realised.

"I would rather you just tell me that you're unhappy than go fucking another woman," she said, and then sniffed.

"Hey, hey, hey…" Rylea cooed, pulling Darcie to her and enfolding her in her arms. "Shh…I will not cheat on you, okay? And I promise to tell you if I'm unhappy."

"I promise too," Darcie said, her voice slightly muffled by the fabric of Rylea's sweatshirt. "Because if we tell each other, maybe we can fix it."

"Right," Rylea said, stroking Darcie's hair. "And something tells me that we are always going to want to fix whatever is wrong between us, because we're crazy about each other."

Darcie smiled and closed her eyes. She breathed deeply, taking in Rylea's scent, which by this time of the evening was always a mixture of her body lotion, her perfume, and coffee.

She tightened her grip on her girlfriend.

"I am crazy about you, Rylea," she said. "I know it's only been a short time, but I am crazy about you."

"Oh my god," Rylea gasped. "I feel the same. This has been the best few weeks of my life."

Darcie smiled again, lifted her head off Rylea's shoulder and looked at her.

"Kiss me, please, before we ruin this by saying anything stupid," she demanded.

Rylea chuckled.

"Yes, ma'am," she replied.

When their lips touched and their kiss instantly became passionate, Darcie knew she was healed, and that she was kissing the woman she wanted to be with for far, far longer than a week. Far, far longer, even, than ten years.

Epilogue
1 year later

Saturday trivia night.

At the coveted table by the fireplace, The Geezers and the Girls were in a tight battle with The Fisher Kings, and Mr. Trelawny looked as if he was about to murder his arch-rival. According to the most recent scoring check, the two teams were now tied, with only one more question remaining.

Mr. Fisher had countered the addition of Darcie to Mr. Trelawny's squad by adding Katelynn Jefferson to his team.

The American was now living in Tremont, renting a vacant cottage in the southern part of town. She was now a regular at Bean There/Done That, often working on her freelance writing in the coffee shop. In fact, Rylea, Darcie and she had become good friends, which still amazed Rylea considering the circumstances.

However, despite the friendship, somehow Mr. Fisher had gotten to Katelynn first, months ago, convincing her to join *his* trivia team, which proved to be a boon. Katelynn's work as a journalist meant she was devastatingly knowledgeable about current events, as well as topics such as pop culture and world history.

"Right, ladies," Mr. Trelawny began, "courage now! Let's nail this last question. Can't let a team with an American on it defeat us! Courage! Let this be our Dunkirk!"

Mrs. Trelawny crossed her arms and glared at her husband.

"There he goes with bloody Dunkirk again!" she exclaimed impatiently. "Every time he stubs his toe, he mentions bloody Dunkirk!"

Cleo tugged on the sleeve of Rylea's turtleneck. Darcie's parents were out of town this weekend, and so the now eleven-year-old girl was joining them tonight. She had spent most of the time reading an age-appropriate graphic novel based on the *Star Trek* franchise, stopping occasionally to giggle at how silly Mr. Trelawny was

"Dunkirk happened in France," she whispered. "Why is he saying this is Dunkirk?"

Rylea leaned over so she could whisper her answer.

"Because Mr. Trelawny is a little crazy," she said.

Cleo burst into giggles.

On the other side of Cleo, Darcie also leaned closer.

"But we still love him just the same," she whispered, sharing an affectionate look with Rylea, who felt her heart warm.

The quiz master then announced it was time for the final question, and that the category would be Science.

"Dunkirk, Mr. Trelawny," Rylea said, putting on her game face.

"Dunkirk," Darcie repeated.

"Dunkirk," Mrs. Kelly added.

"Don't you three encourage him!" Mrs. Trelawny chided.

"Be quiet, you old buzzard!" Mr. Trelawny said. "At least they're showing the proper *esprit de corps.*"

After a moment, all eyes at their table, including Cleo's, turned to the nearest TV which was now displaying the final question…

On which planet is one day longer than one year?

Unlike most of the other questions of the night, this one wasn't multiple choice. Each team had to provide the correct answer without the advantage of having options to choose from.

"Bugger!" Mr. Trelawny said.

"Bugger!" his wife muttered.

"Bugger!" Mrs. Kelly said.

"Bugger!" Darcie added.

"Damn!" Rylea contributed, just to be different.

"Venus," Cleo said, her eyes once more back on the graphic novel.

Five sets of eyes turned to her.

"Think, girl," Mr. Trelawny said earnestly, "are you sure?"

Cleo looked up at him and nodded.

"Mm-hm," she hummed. "Venus rotates so slowly that it takes 243 Earth days to make up one day there. But it goes completely around the Sun in only 225 days. So, one day on Venus is longer than one year."

"Sounds pretty convincing to me," Rylea said, looking at Cleo with a proud smile.

Mr. Trelawny looked over at Mr. Fisher's table.

"Those idiots don't know the answer!" he exulted quietly.

Rylea had to admit that based on the puzzled looks on their faces, as well as their body language, the members of The Fisher Kings had no clue what the answer was and would, at most, be making a guess.

She shared another look with Darcie, who smiled at her.

"We've got a very smart girl," Rylea said.

"Yes, we do," Darcie replied. "Are you okay?" she then asked. "You seem a little pale."

Damn! Am I being obvious?

"I'm fine," she stated. "Just nervous that Cleo has gotten the answer wrong, and we'll end up losing."

"Hey!" Cleo said, looking crossly at her.

It was a few minutes later, after the quiz master had collected all the answer slips and added up the points, when the name *Venus* appeared on the TV as the correct response.

"Good show!" Mr. Trelawny exulted, extending his hand across the table for Cleo, who shook it, giggling.

Both Rylea and Darcie then squeezed Cleo between them in simultaneous side-hugs.

"Way to go!" Rylea told her.

"Told you!" Cleo said, smiling.

"I never doubted you," Rylea confessed. She then leaned closer so she could whisper to Cleo without Darcie hearing. "I'm just nervous about…the thing."

"Oh!" Cleo said, giggling again.

"What are you two conspiring about?" Darcie asked.

"Nothing!" Rylea said.

"Nothing!" Cleo confirmed, but of course, an eleven-year-old holding onto a secret looked like an eleven-year-old holding onto a secret, which meant Darcie wasn't fooled for a second.

"It's something…" she said slowly, but before she could continue her interrogation, Mr. Trelawny hooted.

"Oh, get a load of Pete Fisher," he said, turning in his chair and glaring at his rival. "He looks like he finally took a good look in the mirror and saw how ugly he is!" He then shouted, "Hey, come over to play for us, Miss America! Feel what it's like to be on a winning team!"

Katelynn, along with the rest of the pub, laughed.

"For the time being," the quiz master called out after the laughter died down, "this puts The Geezers and the Girls in first place."

Mr. Trelawny shared a look with the rest of his team.

"For the time being?" he asked. He then turned towards the quiz master. "What do you bloody mean for the time being? That was the last question!"

The quiz master held up a placating hand.

"There is, in fact, a bonus question tonight," he said.

"*Bonus question?*" Mr. Trelawny squawked. "There's never any bloody bonus question!"

"Ha-ha!" Pete Fisher yelled from across the room. "We'll see who's the losing team now, you old sod!"

Darcie looked at Rylea.

"This is new," she said, a perplexed furrow in her brow.

Rylea shrugged.

"Must be trying to make it more interesting," she said.

Between them, Cleo giggled.

"Okay, ladies," Mr. Trelawny began…

"We know!" his wife said.

"*Dunkirk!*" all of the women at the table said at once.

"And tonight's bonus question is…" the quiz master announced theatrically, raising his right arm in a superb gesture of showmanship.

All eyes in the pub became fixated on the TV screens.

Darcie Spencer, will you make me the happiest woman on earth and marry me?

It took a moment, but then surprised gasps began filling the pub, followed by shouts of delight and even applause.

Rylea had never felt her heart beating so fast in her life. She was beginning to worry the organ would give out before Darcie gave her an answer.

Speaking of…

Rylea watched Darcie's face very carefully. If the stakes weren't so high, she would have burst out laughing. Darcie was frowning, and her lips were moving as she stared at the TV, as if she was reading the words on the screen to herself.

Finally, though, Darcie turned to stare wide-eyed at Rylea.

For Rylea, it was as if everything suddenly stopped, but wasn't that how it was supposed to be?

Wasn't time supposed to stand still as you gazed into the eyes of the woman you loved?

Wasn't the rest of the world meant to disappear as that spiritual connection was made over the space separating you?

Rylea, smirking, pointed downwards, at Cleo.

Darcie looked at her niece, and then let out a startled scream.

In Cleo's hands was the small black box bearing the pear-shaped diamond ring Rylea had purchased last week.

Before she had bought the ring, Rylea had found some time alone with Cleo and spoke to her about her plans, and then asked the child if she would approve of her aunt marrying her.

They had all been living together now for six months, and it had been the happiest six months in Rylea's entire life. She didn't need another six months to know Darcie and Cleo were her future.

In any case, Cleo had told her—in a rather adult manner, Rylea had thought—that she definitely approved of Rylea marrying her aunt. And then together, they cooked up this scheme.

As soon as the quiz master had directed everyone's attention to the "bonus question"—Darcie's attention included—Rylea had slipped Cleo the ring box from out of her handbag.

"Oh my god, I bloody love you!" Darcie squealed. *"Yes! Yes Yes Yes!"*

Relief flooded through Rylea as the crowd in the pub burst into cheers and applause.

Apparently Darcie could no longer contain herself. She leaned over, grabbed the sides of Rylea's face, and kissed her deeply.

This meant that Cleo was stuck between them, giggling but wriggling to get free. Rylea thought that was perfect. After all, it was going to be the three of them forever from now on.

When their kiss ended, Rylea, with tears streaming down her face, turned to Mr. Trelawny.

"Well," she said, "looks like we got the bonus question right too."

THE END